BOOK 1:

THE SAPPHIRE PRISM CAVE

✳ ✳ ✳

A JOURNEY THROUGH
THE SPACE VORTEX

PETER M. LESCHNER

DEDICATION

I dedicate this book to Katherine and Michael, the two most incredible children in the world - make that the universe - and to my wife, Talia, whose love brought us together and made everything else possible.

10/22/2012

Connect with Peter M. Leschner re *The Sapphire Prism Cave* at:

http://on.fb.me/O4SLhC

Also by Peter M. Leschner:

<u>*Startling Connections*</u>
[An adult thriller]

ACKNOWLEDGEMENTS

Thanks to Katherine, Talia, Patti, Nikki, Richard and Kristin for all your help, feedback and suggestions.

1

AT PLAY

With a single leap, James landed on the balcony adjoining the room in which Princess Julia was being held captive. His light saber drawn, he pressed it menacingly against Robert's throat.

"Let her go! Release the Princess! RELEASE HER NOW!" snarled James. Robert froze for a second and then, with a single movement drew his own light saber.

"Let's duel!" James shouted as he cartwheeled away from Robert and sprung to his feet, cutting the air with his light saber like a true Jedi Master.

Robert and James dueled for the better part of a quarter of an hour, neither boy quite getting the advantage over the other.

"James," deadpanned Julia, "with the time this is taking, I'd be dead by now."

"Come on, stay in character," James replied. "Act like a *real* Princess." With that he lunged at Robert and knocked the light saber from his hand.

"Hah, hah. I won! Let's play again," shouted James bursting with enthusiasm and twirling the light saber in his hand.

Robert sighed and pleaded, "Let's do something else. How many times can we play *Star Wars*?"

"Alright. Come downstairs. There are always video games we can play."

"Hey James, what about me?" cried Julia. "Can I join in?"

"You need more practice Julia. You never know what you're doing on these games. Come on Robert, let's go."

Julia shook her head. James could be so annoying. *Well, aren't all brothers?* she thought to herself. But that was James - always running a mile a minute. Annoying, charming and charismatic, but he was, after all, her only brother and, truth be told, she loved him. In fact, though she was loath to admit it, at times she was crazy about him.

Although twins, Julia took on the role of the "wiser, older sister." Technically, she was older, having been born 35 minutes before James. Both siblings had straight, shiny golden blonde hair and blue eyes. Dimples dotted their cheeks. Hints of freckles were sprinkled beneath their eyes and over their noses. Laughter came easily to them and with genuine enthusiasm. Julia was more thoughtful and calculating. James, well, he lived for the moment. His mind caught up with his fast moving body eventually - although sometimes a little too late.

Julia shrugged off her brother's temporary rejection and headed for her room filled with posters of her favorite singers and animals, horses and dogs. She put on the headphones to her iPod and got lost in her music.

The Wyatts lived in a spacious two-story colonial situated at the end of a cul de sac, in Norpine, New Jersey, a picturesque town in the northeast corner of the state. James' and Julia's bedrooms, their parents' master bedroom and a guest room were on the second floor. The master bedroom and guest room each had small balconies facing the back yard and woods beyond. A large staircase led from the front door entryway to the second floor.

On the first floor was a formal dining room adjacent to a bright kitchen with a skylight and a cozy living room.

Downstairs in the living room, James jumped up and down and moved vigorously in front of a large flat-screen television as he played his latest video game, "Space Intruders", with Robert. His movements controlled a figure on the screen as he artfully tried to avoid the space aliens trying to capture him. When it was Robert's turn, he tried his best but the aliens got the better of him.

"Jump and fire now. NOW! Or they'll capture you!" warned James. And sure enough they did. Game over. Defeat wrote itself all over Robert's face.

Jenifer Wyatt, James and Julia's mother, looked in on the two boys and alerted them. "Remember we have to go in five minutes. Robert's got to be home by six o'clock. Please start getting ready."

Jenifer was a kind and caring mom with a strong spiritual core. She had left her career as an interior designer after James and Julia were born to focus on raising them and never looked back. She enjoyed her family, cooking, gardening, horseback riding and yoga. Jenifer stood about 5'7" tall. She was slim and well toned. She had long blonde hair and soft green eyes.

"Come on, Robert. We have time for just one more game. You can do this!" prodded James.

"All right. All right," replied Robert. "Put the game in practice mode for a minute. Then I'll try again."

After giving Robert a short practice run, James started a new game. He went first again and deftly evaded and defeated the aliens. With the confidence gained from his practice run, Robert was finally able to evade and destroy three aliens, but the fourth one got him. Just as this happened Jenifer popped in again.

"Come on boys. Please get into the car. We have to go. Robert's mom will be annoyed if he's late. Come on."

"Just a minute, Mom. I need something from my room."

"James. NOW. We have to go!" commanded Jenifer.

But it was too late. James had already bounded up the stairs and banged open the door to his room. James' room was filled with posters of his favorite musicians and space heroes. It was also cluttered with space charts of planets comprising the solar system, a large telescope, Lego Star War models and all kinds of action figures. Just after putting on his coat, he grabbed two of his favorites, Yoda and Obi-Wan Kenobi, and headed downstairs as Jenifer waited impatiently.

"Julia do you want to come? We're going to drop Robert off at home. Then, we are coming right back."

"Mom, wait one second. Just finishing up a FaceTime chat with Isabel."

"Julia, we'll be in the car. Please hurry."

Robert, James and Jenifer all headed to the car. Julia wrapped up her call and headed down. Finally, fifteen minutes later than planned, everyone was in the blue Lexus SUV and ready to go.

"What are you guys doing for winter break this year?" inquired Robert.

"You won't believe this but we're heading to Disneyland for the first time," replied James with a smile on his face.

"Disneyland or Disneyworld?" asked Robert. "I've been to Disneyworld but not Disneyland."

"Disneyland. You know, the one in California."

"Awesome. I've never been to California."

"Me neither. We leave next Saturday. Our cousins, June and Kevin are supposed to meet us there with their parents Uncle Harry and Aunt Susan, my mom's sister. I can't wait."

"Sounds incredible. I wish I could go but we'll probably just be staying around here."

"I want to go on the 'It's a Small World' ride," chimed in Julia, "and see the castle where the Princess lives."

"Are you serious?" interrupted James rolling his eyes and then glaring at his sister. "That stuff is for babies! I want to go on the new 'Space Mountain Extreme', 'Star Wars' and 'Pirates of the Caribbean' rides."

"Guys, guys. We'll do our best to get to everything," interrupted their mother diplomatically. She saw a fight coming on and wanted to quell it before it escalated. A few minutes later, Robert's house appeared on the left and Jenifer turned into the driveway. Robert and James exchanged a quick goodbye and Robert jumped out, turning around to yell a quick 'thank you' to Jenifer before running inside.

Jenifer pulled away from Robert's house and headed home. James and Julia fell unusually silent for a moment as they gazed out the window to admire a full moon and numerous stars emerging in the clear evening sky. Suddenly, the heavens lit up with multiple fast moving streaks of beautiful celestial light. One giant trail tore through the night sky directly overhead and suddenly burst apart creating a large fireball flare.

"Hey Mom, James!" cried out Julia. "What are those incredible lights in the sky? What's going on?"

"It looks like a meteor shower!" shouted James. "This is so awesome!" he continued excitedly scanning the sky.

"It really is a spectacular sight," agreed Jenifer.

"Wow, look at the that big one. It seems so close. It almost looks like it's on course to crash in the woods near the mountain behind our house," James observed. "Mostly meteors burn up when they pass through the Earth's atmosphere, but if they're big enough and don't fully disintegrate, they can create a crater when they hit," he added.

The meteor shower continued for the duration of the trip back home. The colorful, mysterious streaks of light in the night sky mesmerized and enchanted James and Julia.

"We'll have to tell dad about this," James added excitedly. "I've never seen anything like it around here before. Only in movies or on TV."

"Yes, it's truly amazing. Almost magical," added Julia softly.

By the time their father returned from work, the meteor shower had ended. Fortunately he was able to share in the excitement created by the extraordinary event based on his family's enthusiastic description of the incredible light show which nature had provided.

2

VACATION

Two weeks prior to leaving for Disneyland, Julia pulled out a suitcase and started packing and organizing it. Julia was neat, meticulous and always wanted to be prepared. Not only was she sure to pack her iPod Touch but she also made sure she had a full set of her favorite fashionable clothes and some stuffed animals for company. As the departure date grew closer, she surveyed her suitcase more frequently to make sure that she had everything she would need for the journey.

Thursday night, two days before they were going to leave, James, Julia, their father, George, and Jenifer all sat around the dinner table enjoying a fine home-cooked meal. George had graduated from MIT and subsequently went on to become an aerospace engineer. George and Jenifer met in Boston while in college and fell in love on their first date. Three years after graduation they were married and five years after that they had the twins. George was a striking figure who stood 6'1" tall and had straight, sandy brown hair and deep blue eyes. He had played soccer in high school and was on the swim team in college. George also enjoyed bicycling, tennis and an occasional round of golf. He was a devoted father who, despite his busy work schedule, always tried to make time for his children.

George looked around the table and, while stuffing a large piece of steak into his mouth, casually inquired, "So, are we all ready for our big trip to California and Disneyland?"

"I am!" puffed Julia. "My suitcase is just about packed and ready to go! What time do we leave on Saturday?"

"About 5:30 a.m. And you, James, how are things going?" inquired George.

"I haven't started yet," James stammered, trying to deflect his father's question. He followed up brightly, "But I promise I'll start tonight. Didn't Mom pack for me?" James hedged.

"James, Mom will help you but you have to take responsibility for getting things going. Look at what your sister has already done."

"James, I'll help you," offered Julia.

"Okay Julia. Thanks. I love you."

Wow that James can be a real charmer when he wants to be thought Julia. Jenifer was heartened by such moments. Though they sometimes fought like cats and dogs, James and Julia were actually very close and loved each other dearly.

"Remember, the limo comes at 5:30 Saturday morning and we're on our way. We're staying at the Disneyland Hotel for four nights. We will meet June and Kevin with their parents at the hotel."

Julia and James celebrated simultaneously, raising their hands in a high five exclaiming "Awesome!" in harmony. *Well*, reflected George, *one way or another James will get ready, either alone or with the help of his mother and sister.*

✳ ✳ ✳

The radio alarm clock pierced the early morning darkness with a loud shrill tone followed by a rendition of the now dated song

"Best of Both Worlds" blasting from the speakers. Julia could not believe it was actually time to get up. She pulled the covers over her head to try to make the noise go away. Then suddenly she bolted upright and remembered-*Disneyland! Limo*! She jumped out of bed and barged into James' room.

"Come on, wake up! Wake up, James!" Julia repeated.

"Ugh, leave me alone," moaned James.

"Limo. Plane. Disneyland. Come on. Did you forget? We have to get ready. The limo will be here soon!"

"Five more minutes," pleaded James.

"We're going to miss our flight. I won't let you ruin our vacation! I just won't!" insisted Julia.

"ALL RIGHT!" thundered James now very annoyed but fully awake.

James finally tumbled out of bed and started dressing. He could hear his parents in the master bedroom speaking, as they got ready. As James gradually became more alert, he started getting excited. He could hardly wait for the adventure to begin. After hearing so much about it, he was finally going to Disneyland!

Julia, equally excited about the trip to come, quickly put on the outfit she had carefully set out the night before. James rummaged through his drawers and pulled out a few items of clothing that surprisingly, matched.

After a slow start, James and Julia were finally ready. They headed downstairs toward the front door where the suitcases had been stashed. Glancing at the clock, Julia called upstairs.

"Mom and Dad, come on, it's 5:15. The limo will be here any second! Let's go!"

"Hold your horses, Mom and I will be down in a moment. Why don't you and James grab some cereal while you wait?"

"Okay. But let's go!"

A few minutes later the doorbell rang and the limo driver was at the door. He smiled and introduced himself as Steve. One by one he carried the suitcases and bags and loaded them into the waiting car. George and Jenifer gave the house one last once over making sure all lights and appliances were off. They had left their dog, Misty, with a neighbor the night before.

George was the last one out. He locked the door and stepped into the dark early morning chill. Everyone entered the waiting limo, which then proceeded to the airport. As they headed to New York's La Guardia Airport, the sun began to rise. The grand adventure was about to begin.

Three hours into the flight, James got restless. He fidgeted in his seat and started to annoy his sister, who was sitting next to him in the window seat. His mom and dad sat across the aisle.

"Stop, James! Don't pull my hair! Mom, how much longer? James is *really* starting to annoy me!"

"James! Knock it off. Come on. Time for a bathroom break," said George from across the aisle. He got up and grabbed James for a walk through the cabin to the bathroom.

When they got back to their seats, George sprung for a movie. Peace and quiet was certainly worth the $10.00 price of admission. Thankfully, James settled down for the rest of the flight absorbed in the latest *Star Wars* movie.

After about five hours in the air, the plane finally descended into LAX airport. After disembarking, the Wyatts rented a car and made their way to the Disneyland Hotel in Anaheim. When they arrived, James and Julia were enchanted to see a giant replica of Mickey Mouse carved from a bush standing outside the hotel to greet them. The family checked in and went to their room to quickly unpack. With the preliminaries out of the way, they were ready to explore.

George pulled out his iPhone and called Uncle Harry. He wanted to see if the Silvermans had checked in yet and if they wanted to join them for a stroll down Main Street on the way to the park.

"Hello Harry, it's George. We are all checked in. Where are you guys?"

"We're done too - just sitting down for lunch at the Rainforest Café on Main Street leading to the park. Do you want to join us? We can hold off ordering for a few minutes."

"Perfect, see you at the Rainforest Café in a few."

After lunch, the two families made their way down Main Street to Disneyland. The cousins were very excited to see each other and actually be at Disneyland. Between checking in, lunch, and walking to the main entrance, the early afternoon passed faster than they had expected. The families decided to take in some easy, low key rides the first day and watch the fireworks and the Fantasmic show later in the evening.

After dinner, the families headed toward the lagoon to watch the Disney Fantasmic show. Julia and James were in awe as the colorful 3D holograms danced before their eyes. They stood with June and Kevin pointing at the spectacular holograms perfectly synched to music. After the show, the families stopped at an ice cream parlor before heading back to the hotel. Although the ice cream hit the spot as a late night treat, the travel and day's activities had taken their toll.

"I'm tired," sighed Kevin. Even James, normally a tireless bundle of energy, agreed yawning.

"Yeah, me too, but I can't wait until tomorrow. This place is incredible. So much to see and do," enthused James.

"Me too," chimed in Julia.

The Wyatts and Silvermans clamored aboard the monorail and headed back to the Disneyland Hotel tired, yet filled with anticipation for what tomorrow would bring. Bright stars dotted the dark California sky as George peered out the window of the monorail. For a split second, Disneyland seemed like the sole place on the planet where childhood dreams could come true and reality with its everyday troubles could be forgotten. Pure fun was the order of the day.

3

LOST

James was the first to stir. He cracked open an eyelid and looked at the glowing red lights of a digital clock radio with an iPod dock on the hotel room night table. After a few moments, he remembered where he was and shook off the last semblance of sleepiness.

"Guys, guys, its 8:30! Wake up! We have to get going. We are going to miss everything."

"James, are you nuts? Everyone is still tired. We had a long trip and a long day yesterday! Give us a break!" exclaimed Julia.

"I want to have breakfast and get back to Disneyland!" persisted James jumping up and down on the bed as he spoke.

Julia couldn't stand James' loud voice and bouncing, and in protest, threw a pillow at him half-crying, "Be quiet. We were all sleeping! You are so irritating James! Stop!"

George and Jenifer stirred but did not immediately enter the fray. Finally, George spoke.

"James, your sister's got a point. Take it easy. We will get there, just give us all a few minutes to wake up and get going."

James turned on the television and surfed the channels for some cartoons. He watched for a few minutes while waiting for his family to get up. Once he saw his father head for the shower he knew things would get moving. George quickly showered and dressed and once again called Harry. They made plans to meet at the hotel restaurant for breakfast.

"So, how did everyone sleep last night? Ready for some more action today?" George asked as the two families sat down for breakfast. He then pulled out a map and started planning the day with Harry.

"Why don't we start with 'Pirates of the Caribbean' and then head to 'The Haunted Mansion?'" asked George. "We can stop for some of the smaller rides on the way."

"Sounds like a plan."

"Dad," interrupted James, "I want to go on the new 'Space Mountain Extreme' and the 'Star Wars' rides."

"We have four days left, James. We'll get everything in. I promise," said George.

"Let me see the map," insisted James, grabbing it out of his father's hands impatiently.

"James! How about a 'Dad-please let me take a look at the map?' No grabbing!" barked George.

"Okay. Okay. I'm sorry, Dad. I just want to check out where 'Space Mountain Extreme' is."

Breakfast finally came to an end and once again the families headed back to the park for another packed day. The weather was outstanding- cool, sunny and clear. The families talked as they lined up and waited for the rides. James was smitten with "Pirates" and the "Haunted Mansion" but he continued to push for "Space Mountain Extreme."

As they were walking by some crowds, James spotted a *Star Wars* Jedi training session. He shouted excitedly, "Hey, let's go over there. They have Jedi training and dueling with Darth Vader. I want to go."

"James, the girls aren't interested in that right now. We have to get over to the 'Finding Nemo Submarine Voyage' ride. You'll like that too."

"But Dad! I'll miss it!"

"No you won't. We have to save some of the rides and activities for another day."

Frustrated, James gave in with a pout. As the Wyatts and Silvermans headed toward the submarine ride, James spotted a gift shop. Through the opening he could see that the other side led directly to the Jedi training pavilion that he wanted to explore.

"Could we stop in the gift shop just for a few minutes? Just to look around? Please?" James asked sweetly.

"That might not be a bad idea, George," Jenifer offered. "I want to pick up some post cards and a few gifts for friends."

"All right. Let's take a quick look."

James was elated. He led the way and kept his eye on the exit that led to the Jedi training area. George and Harry talked as they causally looked at some mugs and Jenifer and Susan perused the postcards. James spotted the rest rooms and turned to Julia.

"Julia, I have to go to the bathroom. Tell Mom and Dad."

"Okay, but be quick. We don't have all day."

James darted into the bathroom, finished quickly and headed out a different passageway that brought him closer to the Jedi Training area. He headed to the exit and quickly stepped outside. *Just one minute, no one will know,* he rationalized. James drifted into the crowd angling to get a closer look at the Jedi training session. One by one, little Jedi went to the stage and did battle with Darth Vader, promising never to turn to the "dark side." James was fascinated.

Inside the gift shop, George finished up his conversation with Harry and started rounding everyone up to move on.

"Okay Jenifer. Ready to shove off? Julia, where's your brother?"

"He told me he was going to use the bathroom."

"How long ago?"

"I don't know."

"George, go check on him. He shouldn't have gone in alone," protested Jenifer.

"Julia, why didn't you tell us?"

George came out with a panicked look on his face. "He's not in there. I checked everywhere."

"Are you sure? Maybe he's walking around the gift shop?" Jenifer asked hopefully.

"All right. Everyone look around. He's got to be here somewhere."

Outside the last little Jedi was taking his turn on the stage with Darth Vader. James turned to see how he could get back to the shop, hopefully before anyone noticed he was gone. The crowds of visitors blocked his view. But as he turned to head back, he finally saw the "Space Mountain Extreme" ride in the distance. He knew he should just go back to the store by now but he couldn't resist. He just wanted to get a quick, closer look at "Space Mountain Extreme" and check out how long the lines were. So he followed his heart, leaving reason unprotected to Darth Vader's light saber.

Inside the gift shop, George, Jenifer and the others were starting to get seriously worried as they looked around and called out, "James? James?" Tears welled up in Julia's eyes.

"Mom. He said he was just running in for a minute. It's not my fault," Julia said defensively.

George looked around and finally spotted the Jedi training session as it was ending.

"Ah huh! I bet the little rascal went to check out the Jedi training show. I told him 'no' but he still had to do it! Let me see. I'll be right back."

When George got there the show had just ended and the crowd dispersed. He scanned the area but he could not spot his son. Now he became even more concerned. Fear grabbed at his heart.

James ran his eyes up to the top of "Space Mountain Extreme" and knew he had to be on that ride. He could almost feel it as he saw the spaceships shooting out of the top of the mountain and sliding down so fast it looked like they were out of control. He was smitten, but he knew he should not have wandered off. He could no longer see the store. Now he was scared. He thought of his sister. *Julia. Please help me. I'm at "Space Mountain Extreme."* In his state of panic he didn't know what else to do. He should have approached some Disney employee and asked for help. Unfortunately, the obvious solution had not occurred to him and fear got the better of him. His impish smile vanished and he felt alone. *Julia. Julia. Please help me. I'm at "Space Mountain Extreme,"* he thought again.

George returned to the store, his anxiety rising.

"I can't find him," he exclaimed.

Jenifer approached the store checkout clerk and asked if there was a way to page James. Dark thoughts started rushing through her mind.

"Mom. Mom," Julia cried, pulling on her mother's arm.

"Not now. We have to find your brother."

"But Mom, I know where he is."

"How? What are you talking about?"

"'Space Mountain Extreme,'" she blurted out.

"'Space Mountain Extreme?' What are you talking about? How do you know?"

"He told me!"

"Told you? What do you mean?'

"I heard his voice, in my head. I just know he's there!"

Both families headed for the store exit. George checked his map but quickly saw there was no need for directions since "Space Mountain Extreme" was fully visible from the store's exit. He pointed and said, "There it is! Let's go. Jenifer why don't you and Susan stay here just in case Julia's wrong and he turns up."

"Dad! I know he's there. It's almost as if he was calling to me," Julia protested.

"Let's not waste any more time. Julia, Harry, June and Kevin, come with me. Susan and Jenifer, you stay here. Keep your cell phone on and call me the second you see him. I'll do the same."

James was beginning to freak. He had followed the crowds to "Space Mountain Extreme" but now couldn't seem to find his way back to his family. The ride had seemed like so much fun from afar, but now all he wanted was to find them. Desperation set in. Then he somehow sensed or heard Julia's voice in his head "saying" *James we're coming.*

Julia didn't consciously send James a message. It just sort of sprung into her head as she and the rest headed toward Space Mountain Extreme. The lines to the ride were very, very long. George and Harry looked around scanning the twisting rows of people. Just when George was getting discouraged, he spotted James and shouted.

"There he is! James! James! Over here."

James heard his father's voice in the distance and turned to see his sister, father, Harry, June and Kevin all running towards him. James' smile returned to his face and he too broke into a run.

"James. Thank goodness you're okay," said George. "What the heck do you think you are doing heading off like that on your own? Didn't we discuss this a hundred times? Stay together! No running off!"

"Sorry, Dad. I didn't run off. I just wanted to take a quick look. I was coming right back."

"James, that's it. No excuses. Don't ever do that again!" George thundered but was relieved to be reunited with his son. "All right. We have to let your mother know. Let's all get back to the gift shop and pick up Mom and Aunt Susan."

"James. Thank goodness we found you! I got your message," Julia exclaimed.

"What message?" said James brushing off for a moment the exchange of thoughts he and Julia had shared.

"You know. I'm sure you felt it," protested Julia. "That's how we, or should I say I, found you."

"We'll talk about it later. Come on, I want to enjoy the rest of Disneyland!"

"James. One more time, no wandering off! The next time you will be punished," George warned.

"Okay Dad. I promise," answered James.

James, his father, sister, Harry, and his children rejoined Jenifer and Susan. After another round of hugs and kisses and a good scolding, the families set off to explore the rest of Disneyland.

By evening, the Wyatts and Silvermans were tired and hungry. They stopped at one of the restaurants at the perimeter of a live band stage and dance area. People sat at tables along an upper ring. In the center, visitors tried their hand at dancing, clapping and singing. Whenever the band took a break, there were karaoke contests. James, Julia, June and Kevin sat at a table next to their parents and downed pizza, burgers and soda. Once they were done eating they started paying attention to the music. James bounded down to the dance floor and started demonstrating some incredible break dance moves.

"I didn't realize James could dance like that," marveled Susan.

"Yes. He surprised us with it too. He seems to have picked it up watching videos. He's not taking any formal dance lessons," Jenifer replied.

When the band left the stage for an intermission, Julia and June took the stage to sing a karaoke duet version of "The Climb." Both girls made their parents proud with a moving version of the song. Julia's voice soared with feeling carrying the melody while June chimed in to harmonize. Night crept up onto the stage and a bright moon appeared.

After dinner and the music, the families strolled through Disneyland, stopping at one last store before heading back to their hotel. James wandered through the aisles and spotted a space solar system kit that would allow him to organize and hang the planets orbiting around the sun.

"Dad," he cried. "Can I get this? This is the only thing I'll ask you for the whole trip. Please?"

George went over and looked at the box and description. "Well at least it looks educational. All right, James, but that's it. You're sure that's what you want?"

"Yes Dad. That's it."

"Okay."

In the meantime, June and Julia were crowding around some beautiful rocks. Julia picked up a pink, purple and white one and gasped, "Wow. This rock is amazing. Dad can I get this one and one other? Please!" Jenifer stepped over for a look and agreed, "Yes, it really is lovely."

Another day at Disneyland was coming to a close. As the families headed back to the hotel, Julia mumbled to herself "Wow, that's two days gone. Only two more left. Vacation time always seems to move too fast."

As Julia had observed, the remaining days moved quickly with a seemingly never-ending series of rides, meals and fun. On the third day, James finally got his wish to go on the "Space Mountain Extreme" ride. James, Kevin, Julia, June, Harry and George all lined up and finally after a long wait, took the incredible ride. Jenifer and Susan decided to sit it out. James and Julia were in awe as the mock spaceship rocketed by planets at breakneck speeds and comets swirled by. Enemy spaceships swooped down from nowhere and fired on them. They fired back with laser-like light beams. The ride soared, showcasing a combination of lights, speeding movements and hairpin turns. Before they knew it, the wild ride was over. Not too long thereafter, the Wyatts were back in New Jersey.

4

DISCOVERY

The day after the Wyatts returned from their California vacation, Robert called James and asked if he could come over for a visit after school sometime later that week. He wanted to catch up with James and find out how the vacation had gone. After checking with their moms, they agreed on Thursday after school. When Julia found out that Robert would be coming over Thursday, she promptly made a point of inviting her friend, Vanessa, for the same day. She didn't want to be left out again while Robert and James played.

After school, on Thursday, Robert and James arrived at James' house. Jenifer answered the front door and the boys rushed into the living room with a quick "Hi, Mom," from James. Julia and Vanessa followed shortly thereafter. The girls ran up to Julia's room. Vanessa picked up Julia's iPod, skimmed through the music on it, created a playlist of her favorite songs and played them through the iPod speaker stand Julia had in her room.

In the meantime Robert and James argued about what they should play with.

"Let's play some more video games. We can pick up where we left off with 'Space Invaders Extreme'. Come on, Robert."

"James! Enough with the video games! Let's play outside. It's sunny and a lot warmer than it's been for a long time."

"Okay, Robert," James replied quickly switching gears. "Let's go. I'll grab my coat and tell my mom we'll be outside."

A few minutes later the boys headed toward the backyard. George had built James and Julia a sturdy tree house boasting a brown rope ladder with wooden rungs that could be pulled up into the structure. There were large windows and a roof to shelter them when it rained. At times, it was used as an imaginary fort. James and his friends would pull up the ladder giving them a feeling of being in another world. It became James and Julia's escape over the spring and summer months.

"James, can we go up into the tree house? I love it."

"Sure. Let's go!"

Once they had climbed up they peered out the windows at the beautiful day and surrounding trees.

"Wow. This is so cool. And watch this," said James as he pulled up the ladder. "Now no one can get us!"

"Awesome!"

"So. How was California and Disneyland?"

"It was so cool. I went on the new 'Space Mountain Extreme' ride! It was amazing. The best! I also saw the Jedi training sessions. 'Pirates of the Caribbean' was also unbelievable. Like going through a cave in a ship! I can't wait to go back someday."

"Someone at school told me you got lost for a while at Disneyland. Is that true?"

"Yes," replied James, "but Julia found me," he added casually.

"What happened?" pried Robert.

"It was no big deal. Really. Just sort of got lost in the crowd and drifted away when I saw the 'Space Mountain Extreme' ride for the first time. Julia found me."

"You keep saying Julia found you. What do you mean? How?"

"Our minds sort of connected and she got a message from me."

"Yeah, right. What are you talking about James? Minds don't connect."

"Okay. Just forget about it. They found me, okay?"

Robert and James turned their attention back to the fort. They looked out over James' back yard. It abutted a large wooded area without any houses around except for Mrs. McKenzie's. She lived alone and had a white rail fence surrounding part of her large property. Just beyond her house there were woods and a large mountain with rugged terrain. Boulders were strewn all around the mountainside. The large undeveloped tract and mountain were part of a nature reserve. There were beautiful trails and paths traversing the preserve but they were rarely used.

Robert looked out over the preserve. He pointed toward it and asked, "Hey, James, have you ever gone out there?"

"Sure, I've taken some walks with my Dad and Julia. We sometimes take Misty for walks in the woods when the weather is nice."

"What about the mountain just past Mrs. McKenzie's house? Have you ever climbed that?" asked Robert.

"No. We mostly stay in the woods."

"You know, if you just cut across Mrs. McKenzie's backyard and go over the foot bridge which crosses the creek, its really not too far," pointed out Robert.

"You want to go?" tempted James. "I know, I'll go and tell Mom we'll be taking Misty for a walk."

Misty, a beautiful golden retriever with soft golden hair and a wet, black nose was the Wyatts' dog. They loved her madly and fought over who would feed her and walk her - at least for the first two months after they got her. Now, although James and Julia were often "encouraged" to take care of the dog, Jenifer and George were saddled with many of the responsibilities. James knew his Mom would be grateful if he offered to walk her. The boys scampered down the ladder and ran back to the house.

"Misty, Misty," called James as he walked in. Misty came running to James' side.

"Mom, Mom," yelled James. "Is it alright if we take Misty for a walk in the woods just out back?"

"Okay, James. That would be very nice of you. Remember, just stay close to the house and don't wander off."

"Okay, Mom."

James looked at Robert and gave him a wink. His plan was working perfectly.

"Come on - let's go."

James, Robert and Misty ran outside. Misty pranced on her hind legs and barked in appreciation, her tail wagging like a flag flapping in the wind. After horsing around in the back yard, James started edging towards the woods.

"Come on, Robert," said James. Misty barked and James called her to his side. He picked up a stick and threw it out towards the woods. Misty took off after it. The sun was bright. The air felt cool but not cold. The boys laughed as they ran through the woods playing with the dog and getting closer to Mrs. McKenzie's house.

"Let's get a good look at that mountain," prodded James. "If we cut through Mrs. McKenzie's lawn we'll get there a lot quicker."

"Yes, but Mrs. McKenzie can be a bit nasty. I don't know," protested Robert weakly.

"Come on, she'll never know and we'll save a lot of time. If we take too long my mom will start looking for us."

Mrs. McKenzie was an elderly lady who lived alone on a large, mostly wooded property. Her husband had passed on several years ago. She had long brown hair with a streak of grey. Her face was kind, but it looked tired and pained. Not many people knew that she had lost a child in childbirth when she was younger and had never tried to have children again. After that and the loss of her husband, she remained more secluded. Her sadness was sometimes mistaken for anger. She was a bit abrupt on the outside, but soft and kind beneath the surface. Truth be told she was not a mean or bad person.

James, Robert and Misty headed toward Mrs. McKenzie's house. When they got close, James pointed and whispered, "We'll make a run for the stone bridge over the creek. Once we get over it we'll only be about ten or fifteen minutes from the mountain. When I count to three, make a run for it. One, two, three-let's go!"

With that the boys and Misty bounded forward and ducked under the white rail fence surrounding Mrs. McKenzie's property and headed for the stone bridge. Mrs. McKenzie was in her kitchen and saw them as they ran getting closer to the bridge. She called out at them from a long distance.

"Hey kids. Careful, I don't want you getting hurt on my property."

Robert and James ran as fast as they could, ignoring her warning while giggling nervously. Quickly they approached the bridge and sprinted over it. Misty followed suit, barking as she ran.

Those kids. They don't realize how easily they can get hurt, Mrs. McKenzie reflected. As Mrs. McKenzie watched the boys play, she thought back wistfully at what might have been if only her son had lived.

Robert and James quickly disappeared from view as they ran through some woods toward the mountain. Then they jumped over rocks and ran through some woods up the side of the mountain. There were large boulders, which they had to go around.

"Hey, look at that one," said James pointing to a particularly large boulder sitting in a shallow crater. "It looks like it might be a meteorite. Let's take a closer look."

As the boys approached the giant rock, they noticed that it cast a large shadow. They peered around the rock and they looked at each other in surprise. Dead ahead of them sat the entrance to a large cave.

"Wow, look at that."

"Can you believe this? A cave just minutes from my house. I never even knew this was here," James exclaimed.

Both boys approached the mouth of the cave with caution. Misty sniffed the air. They poked their heads inside and tried to look around.

"So cool. I just can't believe it. We actually found a cave!"

"It's pretty dark in there. Can't see much."

"Should we go inside?"

"I don't know. It could be dangerous. Maybe we shouldn't."

"Oh, come on we have to check it out. We'll be careful. We won't go in too far. Just a little bit."

"Okay, but go slowly. There's not much light in there."

Cautiously, the boys entered the cave with a mixture of fear and excitement. *What adventures lay ahead?* they wondered. The walls were jagged and what light managed to enter from outside bounced off the surfaces in zigzag lines. Misty continued to sniff ahead.

"It's pretty dark. Maybe we should head back," cautioned Robert.

"Just a little further," prodded James.

The boys turned a corner and they could see that the cave opened up and a broader passageway lay ahead. The darkness, however, discouraged further exploration. They could see a faint green and reddish/purple glow in the distance.

"That's about as far as we can go without any light. We'll have to come back with a lantern or a flashlight. Hey, I wonder what that faint green purple/red light is?"

"Can't tell but I think you are right. It's getting late and we have to get back home anyway. My mom will start looking for us. Let's go."

The late afternoon sun was starting to set. The boys realized they had overstayed their visit and exited the cave. They haltingly ran down the mountainside and got back on a trail that would take them home. Misty ran ahead and with a bark called them to hurry along. They debated going through Mrs. McKenzie's property in order to save time but were scared she would be waiting for them. That meant they would have to take the longer route around her house.

"Come on," called James. "We have to hurry. My mom is going to kill us."

With that, the boys scampered into overdrive with Misty leading the way. As they rounded Mrs. McKenzie's house they could hear Jenifer calling "James, Robert, where are you? Come on home. It's getting late."

Out of breath, James shouted as loudly as he could "Coming, Mom. We'll be there in a minute." Within a few minutes they arrived home. Jenifer was annoyed but was glad to see that they were back safely. "All right guys. When I say stay close, I mean close so I can look out and see where you are."

"Sorry, Mom. Misty took off and we had to follow her," James said, stretching the truth.

"Okay," Jenifer answered glancing at her watch. "Time to take Robert home. Let's go."

5

POWERS

That night after dinner, James unpacked the solar system kit his father had purchased at Disneyland and started to assemble it. He pulled everything out of the box and scattered the pieces on the floor. He looked through his astronomy book to make sure he would align the planets in the proper order. *Okay. First is the sun in the center. Mercury is next. Then Venus, Earth, Mars, Jupiter, Saturn, Uranus and Neptune. Further out is the Kuper belt and the Ort cloud.* Once James had arranged the planets in the correct order, he looked for the various metal arms and wires that he would use to create a mock-up of the solar system with the planets surrounding and revolving around the sun. As James passed his hand over the planets he saw that they moved ever so slightly. Surprised, he tried it again. This time he held his hand over Mercury and, sure enough, the toy planet started floating upward. James could not believe his eyes. He was in awe and scared at the same time. He didn't know what was happening.

Just then George walked in. James stopped everything and looked up at his dad. James had heard the front door open when his father had arrived from work, but he was so wrapped up in opening and setting up the solar system model that he didn't run downstairs to greet him, as he normally would have.

"Hey James, how's my little man doing? I see you're already at work on the solar system model we got you at Disneyland."

"Yeah, Dad, it's so amazing. Look at this! I have all the planets lined up. Now I have to make the support so it will look like they are orbiting around the sun. It's going to be so cool!"

"It looks really good. By the way, have you noticed that the sky is super clear tonight? The stars are out. Let's take a look through your telescope."

George grabbed the telescope stationed in James' room and pointed it out the window. "James can you believe that you can see Orion's Belt and The Big Dipper tonight?"

James jumped up and swung the telescope away from his father so he could peer into it.

"Awesome, Dad. I want to be an astronaut or pilot a spaceship someday. I'd love to go up in space. It's so cool. Hey, Dad, can I get a more powerful telescope for my next birthday?"

"James, enjoy what you have. You don't need to get something new every second."

"But, Dad, I mean on my next birthday. I can't wait!"

"James, you just turned eleven. Don't wish your life away. Enjoy what you have today. Your next birthday will come soon enough. Believe me, getting older is overrated, as you'll find out one day."

"Okay, Dad. It's just that I love my telescope and finding out about Space so much!"

"I get it, James. Let's be patient and see what happens when your birthday comes closer. Take a few more minutes to play. Mom told me dinner would be ready in about ten minutes. I am going to wash up. You should too."

James continued playing with his solar system model. He tried one last time passing his hand over a planet. Sure enough the planet slowly rose from the floor to his hand. He didn't understand what was happening or why, but he was excited. James wanted to explore more of what he could do but after a few more minutes Jenifer called upstairs, "Time for dinner. George, James and Julia please come on down." James delayed as long as he could but finally headed downstairs to join his family at the table.

Shortly after dinner, James and Julia bounded upstairs together. As they reached the upstairs landing, James whispered excitedly to Julia, "Come into my room. I have to show and tell you something. Come on!"

"James, I have some homework to finish up."

"Please, Julia, just a couple of minutes. I have some really cool news."

"All right, James, but just a few minutes."

James and Julia entered James' room together and James quickly closed the door. "All right, Julia. You're not going to believe this. You know Robert was here and we took Misty out for a walk."

"Yeah. Okay, so what?"

James' eyes sparkled and he paused dramatically. "Well?" prodded Julia.

"We found a cave!" James whispered loudly shooting up his fist into the air for emphasis.

"A cave? What are you talking about?" Julia asked in disbelief. "There are no caves around here."

"Wrong! Just past Mrs. McKenzie's property if you walk the trails toward the mountain and go about a quarter of the way up, there's this giant boulder. Hidden from view on the other side of the boulder is the entrance to the cave! Can you believe it?"

"James, are you kidding me?" questioned Julia, now getting very interested.

"No, Julia, this is for real!"

"Did you go in? What's in it?"

"We went in a little but it was pretty dark. We have to go back with some flashlights or a lantern."

"James, it could be dangerous. Stay away."

"No, I have to go back. It was awesome! You should see it!"

Julia's curiosity began to pick up. "What did you see? Will you take me?" she begged.

"No way. I'm going back with Robert."

"Fine. I'll tell Mom and Dad. You'll never see that cave again!"

"Wait a minute. Fine, fine I'll take you."

"Promise?"

"I promise."

"When can we go?"

"Maybe next Friday afternoon after school. We'll tell Mom we are walking Misty again. But this time I want to bring the battery powered lantern Dad has stored in the basement and some good flashlights."

"Are you sure we should go?" hesitated Julia.

"Hey, if you don't want to, that's fine with me," answered James.

"No! I want to see it," countered Julia. "Now I have to get back and finish my homework."

"Wait," James said. "I have to show you just one more thing."

"Come on, James, I really have to finish my homework. It's getting late."

"Okay, just look at this," said James pointing to the floor where the model solar system lay.

"So? That's the solar system model you got at Disneyland. What about it? I really need to do my homework. Please, James, can't this wait?"

James looked at his sister and, without saying a word, he passed his hand over the planets. The planets shivered and then rose in unison. Julia's jaw dropped.

"Alright, James. What's the trick? Where are the wires?"

"No wires, Julia. I don't know how, but I am doing it. Look!"

With that, the planets all rose, and started revolving slowly around the sun. Julia watched in silent amazement. "How are you doing that James?" she repeated.

"I don't know, but I am!" answered James again.

Just then their mom called up from downstairs. "Julia, are you finishing your homework? And you, James, are you done? It's getting late."

Julia wanted to stay and find out more but she knew if she lingered her mother would storm upstairs.

"Okay, Mom," Julia called down. Then she turned to James and whispered, "I'm leaving now but tomorrow you have to tell me how you did this and take me to the cave."

James winked, smiled and said a simple, "Okay, until tomorrow,"

Julia's heart was pounding as she entered her room to study. Usually homework came easily to her but tonight she found it hard to concentrate. Her mind raced with thoughts of what James had shown and told her. She could not wait until tomorrow.

6

RETURN TO THE CAVE

James and Julia walked to school together the next day. Julia reminded James about the promise he had made, worried that he might back down. James smiled and tried to allay Julia's concern.

"Don't worry. I made a promise and I'm going to keep it. It's going to be really cool. If we bring some flashlights with us, we'll be able to see even more of the cave."

As they approached the school, a disappointed look suddenly clouded Julia's face. She pouted, "Don't we have rehearsals for the talent show today?"

"Oh yeah, you're right. I forgot that was today. Well, don't worry. There should be enough time left after we get home. It is Friday after all."

"Yes, but if it starts getting dark, Mom will never let us out alone to walk Misty."

"Where there's a will there's a way. We'll do it. If worst comes to worst, we can always see it Saturday morning."

"I know, but now you got me really curious. I don't want to wait until tomorrow!"

"We'll decide when we get home. Let's get to class. See you later."

Julia kept glancing at her Disney watch all morning. Time crawled by as she waited eagerly for the final dismissal bell to ring. Although she was excited about her part in the talent show, which was a song and dance routine, Julia wanted the practice to be over so she could finally see the cave which James had so excitedly told her about.

James enthralled everyone at the practice session with an astonishing gymnastics show. Julia and her friend Stephanie gave an incredible dance performance. Before they knew it, the time had flown by and the hour and a half session had come to an end. James was casually talking with a group of his friends when Julia came up to them and said impatiently, "Come on, James. Let's go! Mom is waiting for us outside. We have to get home."

"Alright. Sorry, guys. I'll see you Monday."

It was a cool clear afternoon and the sun still shone brightly. The days were getting longer but Julia didn't want to take any chances that it would get too late to go to the cave. Sure enough, Jenifer was outside waiting.

"Hi, Mom. Let's get home. I'm so hungry and thirsty. I need a snack. We've been at the talent show practice," said Julia.

"I know. How did it go?"

"Great, Mom."

"And you, James, how did you do?"

"You know James, Mom, he's always incredible. Let's go!" interjected Julia impatiently.

"Yeah, Mom, it went really well," James chimed in modestly.

"When's the actual show?"

"Two weeks from tonight."

James, Julia and Jenifer got home and Jenifer prepared the snack they both wanted. Misty barked a "hello" and jumped in the air to signify that she'd like a walk. James ran upstairs, went into his bedroom and pulled open some of his drawers. After scrounging around, he finally found what he was looking for – a powerful flashlight. He ran to the upstairs pantry and found another one for Julia. He knew that the lantern he wanted to bring was in the basement; he'd pick that up just before they headed out. Julia finished her snack and changed into jeans and sneakers. James ran downstairs with his backpack and threw it by the front door. After some milk and cookies, James and Julia looked at each other. They both wanted to get going but didn't want to make it too obvious to their mother. While their indecision temporarily held them back, they were rescued by the sound of the telephone ringing. Jenifer picked up. It was her sister, Susan.

"Hi, Susan. Yes, things are great here. I know, Disneyland seems like a long, long time ago. What's happening with you and the family?"

This was their chance. James and Julia knew that their mother could spend a long time on the phone with her sister.

"Mom, we're going to take Misty out for a walk. Okay?"

"Wait a minute, Susan," Jenifer muttered into the phone. "What James, what?"

"Misty," he pointed, "Walk, okay?"

"Alright, just don't go running off. I'm sorry, Susan. What were you saying?"

James grabbed Julia and urged, "Let's go now! This is perfect. You know how long Mom can hang on the phone with Aunt Susan."

"I know," Julia agreed. "Let's go."

James ran down the cellar stairs and, after rummaging through some junk, found his father's lantern. It gave off a sustaining bright light, which would make it easier to see inside the cave. Once James had the lantern he came back upstairs and grabbed his backpack. James, Julia and Misty simultaneously burst through the front door to get outside. Then James led the way, with Misty and Julia following.

"Come on, guys. We have to move fast. We have about an hour and a half before it gets dark. We're going to have to cut through Mrs. McKenzie's property. She won't like it but it's the fastest way to get there."

"Are you sure, James? You know how angry she can get."

"Come on, Julia. Don't be a scaredy cat. You'll see. It'll be worth it!"

James, Julia and Misty stayed off Mrs. McKenzie's property as long as they could. It was getting near dinnertime and they knew that her kitchen looked out over the backyard of her large wooded lot. If she was cooking, she would be there. Though he recognized the risk that she might see them, James balanced that with the knowledge that cutting through Mrs. McKenzie's wooded backyard would save them a lot of time in getting to the cave. He alerted Julia and Misty.

"Julia, and you too, Misty, when I start running, just follow me as fast as you can. I think we can make it across the yard without her seeing us, but even if she does, I bet we can get over the bridge before she can stop us. Come on! Follow my lead."

James took a deep breath and began to run, heading straight for the stone bridge, which crossed the stream. Julia and Misty followed him running at top speed. As fate would have it, Mrs. McKenzie was pulling something out of the oven and had her back turned toward the yard. James and Julia, out of breath, saw the little stone bridge and thought they had made it. Suddenly Crystal, Mrs. McKenzie's large black cat, sprung in front of Misty with a hiss. Startled, Misty started barking and frantically chasing Crystal. James quickly tried to prevent the disaster he saw unfolding.

"No, Misty! Over here! Come here!" he yelled.

Though Crystal's ego was bruised, she was otherwise unharmed and scampered up a tree out harm's way. Unfortunately, the barking attracted Mrs. McKenzie's attention and she looked out the window, quickly sizing up the situation. "Darn kids. Just don't realize they could get hurt," she muttered heading for the back door. When she flung it open, she spotted Crystal up in the tree and Misty, Julia and James bounding over the bridge.

"Please listen to me. Next time I catch you, I'll call your parents," she called after them. Then she turned her attention to Crystal.

"Come on down. Everything's alright, that darn dog is gone. Come on down, girl," she coaxed.

James and Julia breathed a sigh of relief as they crossed the bridge. Breathing heavily from their harrowing escape, they paused and rested on the other side of the bridge off of Mrs. McKenzie's property. After a brief pause to re-group and catch his breath, James was ready to move along.

"Come on. Now we have to follow some paths which lead to the mountain and finally the cave."

James did his best to follow the route he had taken with Robert. Just when he thought he might have veered off the correct path, he spotted a fallen tree, which he remembered from his outing with Robert.

"Yes, this is the right way. I remember that tree."

As they neared the mountain, James peered up looking for the boulder that hid the cave's mouth. After a few minutes of unsuccessful scouting he finally saw it and yelled out.

"Hey, Julia! There's the boulder that hides the cave from view. It's about a quarter of the way up the mountain. Do you see it?"

"Yes," confirmed Julia excitedly.

Step by step, the trio followed a rugged path to the huge boulder. After a few minutes of hiking they finally reached it. James hesitated and peered around its' giant bulk.

"Julia, take a look. Here it is!"

Julia joined her brother and peered around the boulder. As he had promised, the entrance to the cave, which had been well hidden by the boulder, lay straight ahead. Together they made their way to the cave's mouth. James pulled off his backpack and handed Julia one of the flashlights he had brought along. He also pulled out the lantern. *The extra light will certainly help,* James thought. Finally, the wait was over. James, Julia and Misty entered the cave together.

The walls of the cave were ruggedly textured. The entrance led down a tunnel, which in turn opened into a larger cavern with a beautiful natural aquamarine colored pool cradled by the cave's floor and some surrounding rocks. The limestone structure from which the cave had been fashioned was beautiful and the flashlights bounced off the walls creating a warm glow in the cavern. The pair eyed the cave's ceiling and saw the stalagmites hanging down from the ceiling. The stalactites grew up from the cave's floor. In places where the two had joined, beautiful pale rose-colored columns were created. A host of columns seemed to surround the pool of water.

"Wow," stammered Julia, "this place is incredible."

"Yeah, it is," agreed James. "Look at these!" he exclaimed pointing to the walls.

"Yeah, it seems like the walls have crystal gems on them. They're glowing. Different colors - pinks, purples, blues, reds and some greens."

"I think they're made of gypsum," stated James authoritatively. "At least that's what Mrs. Binder told us in school. She knows a lot about geology and has been teaching us some of the basics."

Julia's mind drifted as she got lost looking at the stones and crystals. *So many treasures I could add to my rock collection*, she thought. This cave made everything she had seen and bought at Disneyland look like a toy. It was the real thing. The lantern and flashlights drew out the colors in the caves walls. The whole place looked surreal. A reflecting pool of water was in the center. The walls glowed with different colored rocks and crystals. Columns, stalactites and stalagmites were everywhere. The light from the flashlights and lantern shimmered through the gypsum crystals painting the walls in rainbows. James picked up some colored crystals near the pool and shoved them into his pocket. Julia followed suit, picking up some rocks and crystals and putting them into James' backpack.

"Awesome," she said smiling as she turned to James.

"Yeah, well, you know who found it. Yours truly, your one and only brother," James bragged bowing deeply in jest.

"James, enough. Thank you. Thank you. I know you found it. Thank you again, now stop bragging."

James smiled. He knew exactly how to get to his sister and he couldn't resist basking in the glory of the moment. Just as the two were getting comfortable in the cave James glanced at his watch. "Julia, we've got to get out of here. It's almost 5:30! Mom will be furious. We've been gone almost an hour and a half."

"Alright James, just one more moment. Let me just look around and take it all in."

"Okay, but you know Mom. Aren't you supposed to be the responsible one?"

After relishing the last moments of her first visit to the cave, Julia gave in and agreed with her brother. "Okay. You're right. We'd better get going."

They left the large cavern and headed through the tunnel back to the cave's mouth. As they exited, they turned off their flashlights and the lantern and returned them to the backpack.

"James, that was totally incredible! We have to come back soon!"

"Yeah, I told you it was really, really cool. We'll come back soon, but now let's boogie. We have to get out of here."

With that the trio headed down the mountain to the trails and then towards home. They exited the trails near Mrs. McKenzie's yard yearning to save time by cutting through it for the second time. *Dare they risk it again?* James considered silently. They looked longingly at the backyard but unfortunately saw Mrs. McKenzie puttering about. Caution and reason sent them home the longer way around. Luckily their mom was still on the phone with her sister and didn't notice how long they had actually been gone. James and Julia gave silent thanks for small miracles.

7

AMAZING

That night Julia could not fall asleep as she tossed and turned in her bed. Her mind was racing, filled with visions of what she had seen at the cave. She wanted to get back as soon as possible. *What else was there to see or explore? What secrets did its caverns hold?* She thought little of its possible dangers. *It's incredible,* she kept thinking. The thoughts and questions came one after another and wouldn't quit. Unable to sleep, Julia snuck out of bed and lightly tapped on James' bedroom door. When he didn't answer she pulled it open. He didn't move, but Julia could hear his soft, rhythmic breathing as she entered. The house was silent and their parents were sound asleep in the master bedroom. Misty, who was sleeping on the floor next to James' bed, stirred slightly as she entered the room. Julia sat next to James and shook him.

"James, James. Are you really asleep? How can you be after what we've discovered?"

"Huh," James muttered half asleep.

"James, it's me, Julia, I've got to talk to you. Wake up," she whispered.

"Of course, I *was* sleeping, now leave me alone."

"James, I want to go back," stated Julia forcefully.

"Julia, are you crazy? It's the middle of the night, we can't go back now."

"I know that, silly. What I mean is I want to go back there soon! There is so much to see and explore."

"Alright, I get it - you loved it! But for now, leave me alone! I want to get some sleep. We can't do anything now anyway."

"Promise me we'll go back this weekend. The weather is going to be great. We just have to pick our moment when Mom and Dad are distracted and we're not faced with a deadline to get back too soon."

"Alright! Now let's get back to sleep," grumbled James, his voice rising.

Partially satisfied, Julia headed back to bed. She was still too excited to fall asleep right away, but some of her anxiety had diminished since she had at least talked to James about her thoughts. It was one way to get her feelings out. As she lay in bed, a strange thing happened. A "thought" popped into her head. *Don't worry we'll be going back to the cave soon!*

"James?" Julia called out softly, looking around through the darkness. "Is that you?" No one responded. After a few moments, she finally realized that James was not in the room, yet, she "heard" his thought. *Sort of like what happened to us at Disneyland, but clearer and stronger. This is strange ... and incredible at the same time,* thought Julia. *"Sleep well,"* thought Julia tentatively. "Thanks!" came back the thought right into her head. *Wow! James and I are exchanging thought messages again. What's going on? No, this can't be happening. I'm just tired.* Julia tried in vain to understand, but finally her sleepiness got the better of her. Julia's eyes got heavy and fluttered even as she struggled to keep them open. She yawned several times and turned on her side. Tomorrow she would try to figure it all out. Sleep finally came to Julia, confirmed by her gentle rhythmic breathing.

8

DELAYS

At about 8:30 the next morning, George knocked on Julia's and then James' bedroom door. "Come on, sleepyheads. I made a fresh batch of pancakes for breakfast. You shouldn't sleep the day away! Come on down for breakfast," he urged.

James and Julia had been sleeping pretty soundly, but as they slowly returned to consciousness they realized it was indeed getting late and high time to get up. Besides, they were both eager to figure out a way to return to the cave and explore it further. After their wakeup call finally sunk in, they tumbled out of bed and headed downstairs. As promised, breakfast was waiting. James inhaled the pungent smell of fresh coffee, which George had made for himself and Jenifer, sizzling bacon and sausage as he came down the stairs. A stack of pancakes five inches high sat in the center of the table with real Vermont maple syrup on the side. James and Julia, now fully awake, sat at the table and held up their blue leaf patterned plates with eager anticipation, waiting for them to be filled with the breakfast fare.

After breakfast, George and Jenifer informed Julia and James that they would all be going to the mall for some shopping and errands but they might stop at a playground on the way home if there was enough time. They also casually mentioned that they would be having dinner with the Sattlers, friends who lived across town and Claire would be babysitting that night. Julia looked a little saddened by the news, but James took it in stride. In fact, Claire, a sweet 17 year-old, with long red hair was his favorite sitter and he was happy that she would be watching them.

The day passed quickly as the family hit the Sunnyvale Mall and started shopping. Julia and her mom first went to Old Navy to look for a T-shirt and some jeans. James insisted on dragging his father to the Lego store for the umpteenth time to search out the latest creations being offered. He was always looking to add to his collection of artfully made Lego spaceships, space creatures, villains and heroes. Finally, after a few hours of shopping, the family got together for lunch at the Cheesecake Factory. James and Julia sat next to each other laughing and kidding around, while their parents looked on and smiled.

"Boy, they are getting bigger. Time seems to go so fast. You turn around and another year goes by," Jenifer lamented.

"I know. Unfortunately the cliché that 'time flies' is really true. It seems like only yesterday that we were buying their cribs and setting up their rooms getting ready to bring them home from the hospital."

"The beauty is that although they sometimes fight, they really love each other and are actually good friends."

"There's nothing quite like youth - innocence and promise, living for the moment with a long unknown future yet to be discovered. It's an age when dreams are still attainable," added George.

Jenifer and George turned their attention to James as he wrapped a napkin over his hand. He waived his other hand over it and the napkin slowly started to rise.

George looked over and started to laugh. "Good one, James. I know how that's done."

"Really, Dad? Let's see you do it," snapped James.

"You've got a spoon under the napkin so it looks like its rising, right?"

With that James grabbed the napkin and pulled it off his lower hand.

"No, Dad, I don't have a spoon under the napkin. Let's see you do it," James challenged again.

"Wow, that is pretty impressive. I always thought the trick was to use a spoon. I don't know any other way. What's the trick?"

"No trick, Dad. Powers," said James feeling a little feisty.

"Okay, James, enough fooling around," Julia interjected while glaring at him. "Dad, I think we are ready to go," declared Julia, giving James an elbow in his side. James shot back an understanding look.

George glanced at his watch and noted it was indeed getting late. He and Jenifer had to get back in time to get ready for their dinner with the Sattlers.

"Okay, let's get the check and get going," said George.

The Wyatts gathered their belongings, paid the check, and went to their car to head home. On their way, they unexpectedly hit a traffic jam and came to a slow crawl on the highway. George craned his neck to see what had happened.

"At this pace, we're not going to make it on time," he worried.

Julia also looked out the window. The sun was still out but, as the delay grew longer and longer, she worried that it would get too late to return to the cave.

"I'm going to call the Sattlers and give them a heads up. I hope the restaurant will honor the reservation even if we are late."

"Yes and please call Claire. She should come about an hour later than we told her," added Jenifer. George put the car in drive and moved forward a bit. As they inched forward, out of nowhere James blurted out, "A red car hit a bus."

"How do you know that, James? We can't see that far ahead," Jenifer protested.

"I don't know how, Mom, but I know."

Jenifer looked over at George with a mystified look. He was preoccupied with the traffic and hadn't fully picked up on what James had said. The line of cars continued to sit. Up ahead, a tow truck, police cars and an ambulance finally arrived at the scene of the accident. The police and tow truck managed to clear two lanes and traffic finally began to move again. George was able to speed up and finally reached the scene of the accident. Jeniffer's jaw dropped as she saw that a red Ford Fusion had crashed into the rear of a bus.

"James, that's crazy! You were right. How did you know?"

"Dumb luck, Mom," teased Julia.

"What?" asked George absent mindedly as he had not been following the conversation.

"Honey, James seemed to know what had happened before we even got to the accident."

"Wow. That's pretty incredible. We'll have to step on it. The Sattlers are going to be annoyed," George added distractedly.

George tried his best to make up for lost time, but it was getting late. The sun began sinking toward the horizon. Julia knew that if it started getting dark, she and James would never be able to head to the cave.

"James, look out the window," Julia whispered.

"What?"

"It's going to be dark soon. You know Claire will never let us out alone if it's dark."

"Yeah, you're right," agreed James. "It's not looking too good right now."

"We'll have to think of something," protested Julia with a disappointed look on her face.

The Wyatts finally made it home by about 6:45 p.m., over an hour and a half later than they had initially planned. Claire arrived shortly thereafter. George and Jenifer ran into their bedroom and got ready for their dinner outing. James and Julia played with Claire in the living room waiting for their parents to finish getting ready and leave. Julia kept worrying that it would be too late to go back to the cave.

At about 7:00 James and Julia's parents came downstairs ready to leave for dinner.

"We should be back no later than 11:00. Have a great time and be sure to listen to Claire," admonished Jenifer.

"Bye, Mom and Dad. I love you," said Julia.

James looked inquisitively at Julia. Although, they both knew that there was no way that Claire would let them out alone as darkness approached, Julia decided to give it a half-hearted try anyway.

"Claire, can James and I take Misty out for a walk?"

"I have to heat up some dinner for you guys. You can take her out for a few minutes but only right here in the yard. It's almost dark."

Julia glanced at James. She knew it. There was no way they were going to make it to the cave today. Julia and James were both really disappointed, but even they realized it would be too dangerous to go to the cave pressed for time when it was getting dark. They took Misty out but confined her walk to the yard. After about 20 minutes, Claire called them in.

"Dinner's ready. Come on, James and Julia."

James looked at Julia and they both knew they would be inside for the rest of the night. They came in and hungrily chowed down the spaghetti and meat sauce that Claire had heated up for them. Misty joined them, first lapping up some water from her dish and then flopping down onto the kitchen floor. Dinner wrapped up and Julia and James warmed up to Claire. They seemed to momentarily put aside their disappointment that they were not going to get to the cave that night.

"What do you guys want to do after dinner?" asked Claire. "Do you want to watch a movie or play Monopoly?"

"How about playing some Wii Dance?" shouted James excitedly.

"Hey, that's a great idea! Better than just sitting and watching TV. How about you Julia? Do you approve?" Claire queried.

"Yes. Might as well," agreed Julia, concealing her disappointment.

James was in his element and pulled out every dance and gymnastics moves he knew in order to outshine Julia and impress Claire.

"Wow, James! I never knew you were such a good dancer. In fact, you're incredible!" offered Claire with a smile.

James kept dancing and got more and more involved in what he was doing. By the end of the evening, a close observer could detect that as James was taking larger and larger leaps, he could almost suspend himself in midair. When Julia started to see what was happening, she was thrilled and fascinated but wanted to make sure that Claire would not notice.

"James, I think it's getting late. We ought to start heading for bed."

James glared at Julia and said "What's the rush? Mom and Dad won't be here for another couple of hours anyway. I'm having fun."

"Come on. There are some things I wanted to show you upstairs."

Claire looked at her watch and saw it was about 9:30. Jenifer had indicated she wanted the kids in bed no later than 10:00.

"Okay James and Julia. I think you should at least start getting ready for bed. Change into your pajamas and brush your teeth. Then you guys can talk for a bit upstairs, but I think we should get the ball rolling. Your mother's orders!"

It was hard to drag James away from the dancing but finally he followed Julia upstairs. As they got ready for bed, Claire went to look in on them. She dimmed the lights in the hallway and in James and Julia's rooms.

"You guys can talk and play up here for another half hour or so but that's it. Promise me you'll each go into your own rooms and turn off the lights and go to bed. If I hear anything after 10:15 I'll be up here again. Good night Julia. Night James." With that she gave each of them a hug and headed downstairs.

Julia joined James in his room. The lights were dimmed and they were finally alone and able to talk.

Julia started, "Alright, James. We have to talk. What's going on? First, we have this thing where we seem to be able to send mind messages to each other. Then you seem to levitate things, your solar system kit and the napkin. What were you thinking doing that in front of Mom and Dad anyway? We don't want them to know about this stuff or the cave or they'll never let us go there again. Tonight it looked like you could almost fly. What is happening? What 'powers' do we have and where did we get them?"

"I don't really know and I can't fully control them yet, but I can tell you Julia everything seems to have gotten stronger since I went to the cave the second time," commented James.

"Really?" asked Julia, her eyes widening. "When and how can we get back there?"

"I don't know. As I told you before, we just have to wait for the right moment. Hey, Julia, take a look. I have the telescope focused on Mars." James said, his eye up against his telescope. "I love space - it's so cool. Can't wait till I can take real astronomy classes. Maybe I'll be an astronaut or the captain of a space ship someday," dreamed James.

James lowered his telescope and sat down in front of his solar system kit. He raised his hands over it and again the planets slowly drifted upward and then hung in the air. Julia, excited by the possibility said, "Hey, let me try that!" James moved his hands away and the mock solar system fell back to the ground. Julia held her hands over the solar system kit and concentrated. The planets seemed to quiver but did not move upward.

"Julia, just relax. Don't think about it so much. Just hold your hands over the planets. Let's see what happens," James suggested.

Julia tried again, this time acting very nonchalant. Again nothing happened. Julia was frustrated and disappointed and just a tinge jealous. "How come you can do it and I can't?" pouted Julia.

"I'm telling you. Just don't think about it so much," said James. Julia tried to relax. Misty, who had just entered the room, came over and licked Julia's nose. She giggled and petted Misty and stroked her head. Then Misty went over and gave James a big wet lick. Julia took the opportunity to try again. This time the planets slowly rose. Julia screamed with delight.

"James, look at this! I can do it. Look over here."

James smiled broadly, "I told you you could do it. Remember, we are twins. Why would I be able to do it and you wouldn't?"

"The cave. You said after your second visit your 'powers' got stronger. I've only been there once. I have to see if anything happens after our next visit," stated Julia.

The allotted half hour playtime passed very quickly. Before they knew it, Claire had come back upstairs.

"Alright, guys. The half hour is over. Why doesn't Julia head back to her room? Let's call it a night, okay? I want you to be asleep when your parents come home."

"Okay," answered Julia as she headed back to her room. Before she left she rushed over to Misty and then to James giving each of them a hug. "See you tomorrow morning."

"See you Julia. Goodnight."

With that, James jumped into his bed and pulled the covers over his head. Claire flipped out the light on the way out and escorted Julia to her room. Julia yawned and headed to her bed.

"Good night, Julia. Sleep tight. Don't let the bed bugs bite," said Claire as she flipped off Julia's light. Julia turned on her side and pulled the covers over her head much like James had done. As her eyes closed and she started drifting off to sleep a message popped into her head *Good night, Julia. See you tomorrow.* Julia thought back *Night, James. You are the best brother in the world. See you tomorrow. Goodnight.*

Sleep came and took Julia and James to another world.

9

WHAT'S IN A NAME?

S ince it was Sunday, everyone in the Wyatt house slept in. Even Misty was unusually quiet. Finally, at about 9:30 a.m., George glanced at the clock on his dresser and decided it was high time to get up. He threw off the covers and pulled on his old slippers. He headed downstairs to make breakfast, deciding on pancakes and sausages again. On weekdays he stuck to fruit and yogurt, but he figured that on the weekends he could splurge a little. Before he knew it, Misty joined him and snuggled at his leg as he worked. After about ten more minutes in popped James. Always bursting with energy and a sense of adventure, James was a joy to have around.

"Good morning, James. How did you sleep?"

"Great! How was dinner with the Sattlers?"

"Really nice. And how was your night with Claire and your sister?"

"Very good. We had a great time. Played a lot of Wii dance."

"Can you help me set the table? I want everything to be ready when your Mom and Julia come down."

"Sure, Dad." With that, James jumped up on the counter and grabbed the plates from the cabinet and placed them on the dining room table. He went back to the kitchen for glasses, silverware and napkins. In the meantime, George continued cooking away. From the dining room he heard James "whizzing and whirring" as he pretended to push his toy spaceship over the dining room table. Out of sight of his father, he put up his hand and gave the spaceship a shove. He held his hand up and the spaceship seemed to speed forward suspended in midair. Just then George called out. "James, are you focusing on setting the table? Breakfast is almost done. Please finish and run upstairs and get your sister and mother. Thanks." With that the spaceship fell to the floor. James finished setting the table and raced upstairs.

"Julia, Mom, wake up. Breakfast is ready. Dad wants you to come down."

A few minutes later the family assembled together at the dining room table and George brought in the pancakes and sausages he had made. He poured coffee for himself and Jenifer and chocolate milk for James and Julia. The phone rang just as they all finished breakfast. Jenifer answered. It was Grandpa Jake and he sounded distraught.

"Hi, Dad. What's wrong?"

"It's your Mom."

"What's wrong?" Jenifer asked again.

"She's in the hospital. She's pretty bad. She fell last night, hit her head and was knocked unconscious. Then I called an ambulance and we've been at the hospital all night."

"Dad, why didn't you call us sooner?" asked Jenifer anxiously.

"There was nothing you could do. I didn't want to bother you and the family."

"Dad, never do that again. We are always here for you. George and I will be at the hospital in half an hour. Which room?"

"We are in room 505."

"I love you, Dad."

"Love you too," replied Grandpa Jake.

"George, we have to get ready. That was my Dad. My mother is in the hospital. She fell and hit her head. She was knocked unconscious. We have to get right over there."

"Okay. Are we bringing the kids?"

"No, I don't want them to be upset. Let me see if I can get Mary to babysit. I know they like Claire better but she was just here last night. We need to get going right away and Mary lives close by."

Jenifer made some calls and arranged for Mary to come over and babysit. She was a free spirit and a little less responsible than Claire, but Jenifer figured this was an emergency.

Mary arrived and took charge of James and Julia while their parents finished getting ready and headed to the hospital. They had explained to Mary that they were not sure how long they would be, because Jenifer had to see how her mother was doing and wanted to be there for her father. James and Julia were concerned, but Mary kept them occupied to take their minds off their grandmother. Mary let them watch television for a while and then play on the computer. At about 11:30 her cell phone rang with a call from Paul, her boyfriend. A few minutes on the phone turned to ten and then fifteen minutes. Julia looked over at James.

"Let's take Misty for a walk," she suggested.

"Oh yeah, that's a great idea," said James.

Julia went up to James and whispered in his ear, "This is our chance to get back to the cave. You know Mary - when she's on the phone with Paul she's in another world. Get the flashlights and lantern. Meet me at the front door. I'll let Mary know we are going out for a while to walk Misty."

The sun was out and it was a beautiful day. Though worried about her grandmother, Julia could hardly contain her excitement as she thought about getting back to the cave. James bounded upstairs and got his backpack, throwing in the flashlights. He also brought a roll of thin nylon line. He then ran down to the basement and grabbed the lantern, a hammer and a screwdriver. He remembered the rocks and crystals and thought they might come in handy in case he or Julia wanted to add some more specimens to their rock collections.

Mary sat down on the couch still talking to Paul and dreamily looked out the window. James and Julia called Misty to them. Julia poked her head in front of Mary and mouthed, "We are going to take Misty out for a walk." Mary, lost in conversation, mouthed, "Okay." With that blessing James and Julia lost no time and quickly left the house. They didn't want to give Mary too much time to think about what was happening or give her a chance to change her mind.

Misty seemed to know exactly where they were going and this time led the way. James and Julia followed along. Mrs. McKenzie's back yard again proved to be a tempting shortcut. This time they ran across the yard and crossed the stone bridge without incident. As they reached the other side of the bridge off of Mrs. McKenzie's property, James made an observation.

"I guess Mrs. McKenzie must be sleeping in late today or she's at church or something. We didn't even run into her cat. I don't like to keep crossing over her yard but it shortens the travel time so we have more time in the cave."

"I agree," said Julia.

Continuing their now-familiar path, James and Julia made it through the trails, up part of the mountain and to the big boulder. When they finally got to the boulder they held their breath peering around it as if in fear that somehow the cave had vanished or never existed in the first place. Sure enough, and to James and Julia's relief, it was still there. James got out the flashlights and handed one to Julia. Misty stayed close to them as they once again entered the cave.

"You know, James, this place it's magical. I think we should name it."

"What do you want to call it? The Fortress?"

"No. That's too boyish. I was thinking about something like the "Emerald Pool.""

"That doesn't sound like a cave. That sounds like a pond."

"Well, there is a pool of water in the cave."

"I know, but it just doesn't fit." James paused and looked around.

The flashlights and lantern once again created a glow, which made the cave feel warm and inviting. As James moved his flashlight, the beam of light hit the crystals lining some parts of the cave. The crystals split the light creating almost a rainbow effect.

"I've got it, " blurted out James. "The Sapphire Prism Cave."

"A little strange name for a cave."

"I know but think about it. This is not just a big dark boring cave. It comes alive when we bring light in here and it bounces off the crystals."

"You know, James, you're right. I like it!"

"'The Sapphire Prism' - our code name for this cave! Well, we're finally back. Let's not waste any time. We should explore as much as possible. Eventually, Mary will realize that we're gone."

"You're right. What should we do first?"

"Well, we both love the crystals. Let's see if we can find some of the purple and pink ones. I brought a hammer and screwdriver in case we need a little help prying them loose."

"That's a great idea. We picked up a few loose ones last time, but we can get much nicer pieces from the walls."

With that, the two explorers pointed their flashlights at the walls and began hunting. After several minutes Julia let out a yell. "James, come over here. Look at this beautiful purple crystal lodged in the wall. Can you help me get it?"

"Wow, that really is beautiful. Look at the colors. It's mostly purple but there is some pink, red and white swirled in. Let me try with the hammer and screwdriver."

James took out the screwdriver and started banging with the hammer trying to break off the crystal. "Wow this stuff is very hard. I can't seem to break through it."

"Let me try," suggested Julia.

"Come on! I can do it," protested James.

Julia grew impatient and pried the hammer and screwdriver from James' hand. With that, she angled the screwdriver so it was positioned to split the crystal from the cave wall. With three hard strikes, the crystal fell from the wall.

"There James. I told you I could do it!" Julia boasted, proudly picking up the crystal and placing it in the backpack.

"Alright. Good job," James conceded. "Now it's my turn."

James moved his flashlight from spot to spot searching for what he hoped would be a really cool stone or crystal. After a few minutes of searching, his eyes came upon a beautiful sapphire blue rock. Its surface reflected back the light with a deep blue glow. James whooped "Julia, look at that one. The sapphire blue crystal is mine." Julia looked at the crystal with envy. She had to admit, it was amazing, topping even the beautiful one she had just found.

"I have to say James, that one is a real beauty."

"Yes and I found it!" rubbed in James. "Please let me have the hammer and screw driver."

"Remember hit from the back separating it from the cave wall. Don't try to crack through it," counseled Julia.

James followed his sister's advice and after a few firm blows the sapphire crystal fell to the cave floor. James picked it up in awe. He held up the crystal to the flashlight and it seemed to split the beam like a prism held up to the sunlight.

"See Julia. I picked a great name for the cave. "The Sapphire Prism Cave.'"

"I want to try to find one of those crystals too," Julia yearned.

"I don't know," said James. "They seem to be pretty rare. I haven't seen any others."

Julia spent the next few minutes scouring the cave walls. She couldn't find any more of the blue crystals.

"Come on, James. Let's head a little further into the cave and see what we can find. Let's go back to that pool we found last time."

"Okay. Wait one second," said James as he pulled out the nylon line.

"I saw on a TV show that real cave explorers use twine so they don't get lost."

"Good thinking."

"Only problem is I forgot to bring a stake to anchor the line."

"Maybe you can tie it to something. How about this thin column?" suggested Julia.

"Brilliant! That will certainly do."

James tied the end of the nylon line around the column. Then the two made their way through the cave chambers back to the beautiful reflecting pool. When they finally got there, James held up the lantern. The cave glowed and the water looked emerald green. Julia sat down at the edge of the pool and James joined her. Misty sniffed and lapped a few gulps of water. Julia looked into the pool in a semi-trance.

"You know, James, we were excited about the cave, but we should have thought more about Grandma. I'm really worried about her. I hope she's okay."

Julia looked hard into the pool. The water was perfectly still and there were no ripples. She saw her reflection clearly on the surface. As she stared, she suddenly saw her grandmother lying still in a hospital bed.

"James! James! Look at that! I can see Grandma in the water!"

"What? Let me see," he chimed in.

"Look there in the center where the water is perfectly still."

"Yes, you're right - it's her!"

Julia's body quivered with emotion as she reached out and tried to "touch" her grandmother. She stretched out her hand and dipped it into the water, shattering the calm peacefulness of it surface. The waters rippled and the image she and James had seen disappeared. Julia felt the water energize her. She could not believe her eyes.

"We did just see Grandma, didn't we James? I mean, I'm not imagining it, right?"

"We saw her alright."

The water had felt cool and soothing to Julia's touch. Somehow it brought her comfort and confidence.

"We have to visit her, James. When Mom and Dad get back we have to ask them about her and they have to let us visit her soon."

"Okay, you're right. We really should. But right now, we have to head back. You-know-who is going to be looking for us. She's got to be winding up that conversation one of these days."

"James, we have so much more to see and do in the cave. And we have to figure out more about our powers. You do realize we are getting some?" said Julia, repeating the obvious to convince herself that it was in fact true.

James looked right at her, "I know," he smiled slyly.

"Well we've got to talk about them. What can you do?"

"Look at this for starters," James answered. With that he leapt up, arched his back and did a backward flip in midair. "It's awesome!"

Julia looked on in admiration. 'Well, I've got to have some powers too," blustered Julia.

"Yeah I believe you but we've got to head back now. I think we've been gone over an hour and a half. We're going to be in big trouble."

"Yeah, James. I agree - let's head back. What about the nylon twine you brought?"

"Let's leave it. We'll need it next time."

"Yes, you're right. Do we have all the crystals in the backpack?"

"Yes."

Once again, Julia, James and Misty headed out of the cave to return home.

"Julia, this time I'm worried. We got a little carried away. Way too much time."

Misty barked and started chasing a squirrel into the woods. "Come on, girl. We have to get home," called Julia after her.

Misty ran a little further but then heeded Julia's call. By now, James knew the route by heart and he wasted no time leading everyone home. Once they finally made it around Mrs. McKenzie's house they could hear Mary calling them.

"James, Julia, Misty where are you guys? Come home right now! Where did you go?" Mary looked at her watch. She had lost track of time while she had been on the phone with Paul, but now she was genuinely worried. She also felt really guilty. *Why didn't I watch them more closely?* Mary thought to herself. Just when she was thinking of heading back in to call the police, she heard James' voice.

"Hi, Mary. Here we are. Just took Misty out for a walk," James called out as the three emerged from the woods.

"Thank goodness. That was ridiculous. Much too long! Your parents would kill me if they knew."

"Any word from them?" asked Julia trying to deflect Mary's questions.

"Not yet. But come on, guys. Never pull that again on me. Next time I'll have to tell your parents. What if you had gotten hurt?" Mary paused for a moment with a stern look on her face. "All right, come on in for a snack and some milk."

"Can we try to call Mom on her cell phone?" asked James.

"We want to visit Grandma in the hospital soon," added Julia.

"Okay. Let's have that snack and then we'll try to give them a call."

10

CARING

James and Julia quickly entered the house and sat down in the kitchen for some milk and cookies. Once they were done, Julia grabbed the white kitchen phone and called her mother's cell phone.

"Hello, Mom. We haven't heard from you or Dad. We wanted to know what's happening and find out how Grandma's doing?"

"Hi, Julia. We are actually on our way back now. Grandma does not look too good. She was unconscious. Grandpa was pretty down and tired. The visit was pretty sad. We are going back tomorrow night. The doctors couldn't say when or if Grandma will regain consciousness. We can only pray that she will be alright."

"Okay, Mom. James and I want to visit her soon. Maybe tomorrow."

"We'll see. Let's talk about this when we get home."

James and Julia played with Mary waiting for George and Jenifer to arrive. Finally, after about 20 minutes they heard the blue Lexus pull into the driveway. They both ran to the front door to greet their parents. James and Julia gave their mother a big bear hug. They could tell that she needed it. Mary quickly left after receiving Jenifer's thank you and her payment and the family then went to sit in the living room.

Jenifer started off, tears stinging her eyes. "Well, as I told you in the car, things look pretty bad for Grandma. The doctors are not sure if she can pull out of this."

"We want to see her immediately then. Let's go tonight. We need to see her," insisted Julia.

Jenifer grew quiet and looked at George. George looked back and nodded his head.

"We best take them tonight," he counseled quietly.

"Okay. We'll head back at about 5:00. We'll go out to dinner after. I also think they should see her while there's still time. I'll call and tell my father. I'm sure he'll want to see the kids."

"Thanks, Mom. We really want to see her," James said.

The afternoon passed quickly. Julia and James went out biking with George for a while around the neighborhood. Jenifer tried to straighten out the house. At about 4:45, everyone was back and got ready to go. Jenifer brought some home cooked food to give to her father. James and Julia made a get-well card and brought it along.

The family arrived at the hospital and made their way to Room 505. Nobody knew what to expect. The lights were turned down low and Grandpa sat in a chair gazing lovingly at his still unconscious wife. He looked up sadly when he heard the family enter the room. He then got up and hugged Jenifer. He smiled when he saw Julia and James and gave them each a hug and a kiss and he embraced George warmly.

"Thank you all for coming again."

James and Julia went to their grandmother's side. Julia placed her grandmother's hand in her own and gazed at her. After a few moments, she started stroking her grandmother's head.

"Grandma. I just want you to know how much we all love you. We want you to get better."

Grandma Jean's eyes remained closed. Her breathing was steady. Her lips seemed to curl ever so slightly upward into a soft smile. Julia whispered to James, "Look, I think she heard me. She's smiling."

James also held his grandmother's other hand. He said softly, "Yes, we want you to get well. You can't leave us."

Grandma Jean's smile seemed to broaden a bit more.

"Mom, look," Julia said softly. "I think Grandma heard us. She seems to be smiling."

Jenifer came over and looked at her mother. She could see very little change but she appreciated her daughter's attempt to make her feel better.

"Yes, I think I see it as well, sweetheart. Maybe she is smiling." Jenifer walked away discouraged. Julia held her grandmother's hand a while longer. Suddenly, she felt a weak squeeze. She gasped.

"Grandma, are you back? Can you hear me? Mom she squeezed my hand. I'm sure of it. I felt it."

Jenifer came back to her mother's side and looked at her with tears in her eyes. Her mother lay peacefully in the bed without stirring. Jenifer didn't see any change. She appreciated Julia's attempts to be optimistic, but she chalked it up to wishful thinking.

"Okay, Julia, if you think so. I just don't see much change."

The family stayed for about an hour talking and silently praying for Grandma Jean. Finally, they said goodbye to Grandpa Jake.

"Take care of yourself, Dad, and get some sleep," Jenifer counseled.

"I will. Thanks again for coming."

The Wyatt family sadly left the hospital and headed to Antonio's, a small Italian restaurant with great coal oven pizza and other tasty Italian dishes. They all ate well and talked about Grandma. Then they headed home. It was Sunday night and school and work beckoned the next day. Shortly after returning home, James and Julia crawled into bed exhausted after a long day and fell asleep quickly.

11

RECOVERY

The next morning, the Wyatt family woke up early. The sun was shining brightly and the outside air was comfortably cool and dry. A distinct change in the weather could be felt as a refreshing breeze suggested spring was in the air. After breakfast, George headed to work and Jenifer took James and Julia to school. She then went out to run some errands, attend her yoga class and do some shopping. At about 11:30 her cell phone rang just as she was leaving Stop & Shop.

"Hello, Mrs. Wyatt?"

"Yes, it's me. Who is this?"

"Waterlily General Hospital. We have some news about your mother."

Jenifer's heart skipped a beat and she felt queasy.

"Oh no, please don't tell me she's gone!" she pleaded desperately.

"No, Mrs. Wyatt. Quite the contrary, we don't know or understand why, but she's come out of her unconscious state and has even muttered a few words. She asked for you and your father."

"I'll be right over. I'll tell my Dad."

"He already knows and he's on his way."

Just then Jenifer looked at her cell phone and saw her father was trying to reach her.

"Okay. Thank you for the great news," Jenifer finished up. "My Dad is calling. I should take it. As I said, I'll be there as soon as I can."

Jenifer hung up and picked up her father's incoming call.

"Jenifer, you'll never believe this. Your mother has regained consciousness!"

"I know. The hospital just called me! I'll meet you over there as soon as I can."

Jenifer loaded the groceries into her car and headed home to quickly unload them. Then she made a dash for the hospital. She could not believe the news and wanted to see her mother as soon as possible. She knew that Julia and James would also be thrilled. On her way, she called George and told him about the incredible turn of events. No one could quite believe the amazing change.

Jenifer arrived at the hospital first. Her father followed shortly thereafter. Each of them held one of Grandma Jean's hands. Slowly her eyes opened.

"Jenifer. My love. I'm so glad you're here. And you, Jake my wonderful husband."

Tears welled up in Jenifer's eyes as she gazed at her mother. "Mom, we didn't know if you were going to make it."

"I don't know exactly what happened. I seem to remember Julia's voice and her hand in mine. Ever since, I started coming around and feeling better."

Just then Dr. Smith walked in. He looked at the scene unfolding and smiled.

"This is amazing. Just yesterday we frankly had little hope you would come to. It's incredible and we can't medically explain it," he said to Grandma Jean.

"Well, I don't care why, I'm just so happy it's happening," said Jenifer.

Jenifer and her father stayed with Jean the rest of the afternoon. Finally Jenifer glanced at her watch and realized she had to leave to get back home for James and Julia when they got out of school.

"Mom, we'll be back tonight. I'm sure James and Julia will want to see you. They were so worried."

"Okay. I am feeling so much better. I'll see you later."

Jenifer headed home. Her father stayed on with her mother.

Jenifer went to pick James and Julia up from school. After they piled into their mother's car, Jenifer could hardly contain her excitement.

"Guys, I have some incredible news you are not going to believe. I got a call from the hospital this afternoon about Grandma's condition. She has regained consciousness! I went to visit her this afternoon and she is much better. They're not quite sure how or why, but she seems to be recovering very fast."

"Wow, Mom, that's great news! Can we go visit her again tonight?" asked Julia.

"You read my mind. That's exactly what we are going to do."

Jenifer fixed dinner and after George got home the family headed back to the hospital. James and Julia ran to the elevator and pumped the call button impatiently. Once the elevator opened on the fifth floor they ran to their grandmother's room.

"Grandma, you're awake! We were so worried," said Julia.

Grandma Jean smiled. "I am really feeling much better. And I feel even better now that you and James are back to visit."

As the evening wore on, Grandma seemed to gain more strength and alertness.

"I feel so much better. I feel...younger, if that's possible."

Julia gave James a look. She leaned over and whispered, "Do you think it's the cave and crystals?"

"I don't know but we'll talk about it later," James said cutting her off.

The evening moved quickly. The whole mood in Room 505 had changed. James and Julia kidded with their now-recovering grandmother while Grandpa Jake and Jenifer looked on happily.

"Life is so fragile and passes so quickly," reflected Grandpa Jake.

"I know. We can't let a minute of it go to waste."

Dr. Smith stopped in again and took some pulse readings and conducted various other tests.

"One-hundred and eighty degree turn here. I think your mom will be able to leave in one or two days. I am so happy for you. Again, I can't quite explain the rapid turn of events, but the main thing is she looks and feels much better."

"Thank you, doctor. We are thrilled. Thank you for all your help," Jenifer repeated.

After the doctor left Jenifer called to James and Julia.

"It's getting late - we better get going. There's school tomorrow. Say goodnight to your grandmother. She should get some rest too."

"Oh, I'm alright. I feel great. They make me feel that way," protested Grandma Jean spunkily.

James and Julia once again hugged their grandmother and bade her goodnight, thrilled by her amazing recovery.

12

SO, YOU THINK YOU'RE TOUGH?

The next morning, James and Julia struggled mightily to get out of bed and get ready for school on time. George had left very early in the morning to finalize a special project at work. George was an aerospace engineer who worked long and hard hours at his job designing advanced aircraft and spaceships. He was well respected at work and considered a genius at what he did. It was from George that James had developed his deep interest in space and the solar system.

Jenifer shouted upstairs, "Guys we have fifteen minutes to get to school. Come on down and eat breakfast. We have to go. I really don't want you to be late."

After a rushed breakfast, James and Julia tumbled into the car. Their mom took off and dropped them in front of the school. "Have a great day," Jenifer called after them.

James and Julia managed to slide into their classroom seats just minutes before the late bell rang. As the school day wore on, each of their respective teachers took time out to remind everyone that the special talent show was coming up on Friday and that there were only three practice sessions left. James and Julia had both been rehearsing at home in their spare time and they felt pretty confident that they would do well at the show.

When the school day came to a close, all of the students in the talent show headed for the school auditorium. Julia and her friend Stephanie met up in one corner of the auditorium to discuss and further plan their dance routine.

James headed out of his classroom and offered to help his friend Ricky. Ricky was a timid boy who had been born with a birth defect, which resulted in one of his legs being slightly twisted and shorter than the other. This unfortunately caused him to limp and walk slowly. He was gifted with a bright mind and a kind soul, so most kids in his class liked him and tried to help him out. There were also a few, with less heart, who snickered behind his back and made fun of him. They made comments within earshot and sometimes pointed and laughed. Those comments always hurt Ricky deeply when he heard them, but he kept the pain inside and tried his best to ignore them. These boys were clearly in the minority, but they could be annoying and intimidating.

"Hey, Ricky, let me help you with your backpack," James offered.

"Oh, James. Thanks, I'm all right. Please don't bother."

"No trouble. Let me help. I have to practice for the talent show this coming Friday but I can at least get you to the door. My routine doesn't come up until near the end."

"Alright. Thanks."

The two boys headed down the hallway leading from the classroom. Ricky dragged his bad leg and limped along as fast as he could. James slowed down and waited patiently. He had always felt sympathetic toward Ricky's condition and admired him for carrying on as well as he did under the circumstances. The two made small talk as James escorted him to the outside door. Just as they rounded a corner, three of the stronger athletic boys in James' grade, Justin, Clark and Alex made their way up the empty hallway. Seeing Ricky, they looked at each other and a smirk appeared on their faces.

"If it isn't old peg leg," Justin muttered to the others.

"Ricky, how's it going? Don't drag your feet, you'll miss the bus," Clark taunted.

As Ricky and James passed them, Alex stuck out his leg quickly, deliberately causing Ricky to trip and fall. James watched the scene unfold and rage boiled inside him.

"Hey, Alex. Cut it out. What the heck do you think you're doing? You deliberately tripped him! Leave him alone."

Ricky had fallen hard on the concrete floor. Somehow his chin had hit the ground and he bit his lip. Blood flowed from the cut and down his shirt. He tried to get up but the hard fall had stunned him. James threw down the backpack and confronted Alex.

"I said LEAVE HIM ALONE!" thundered James.

Justin, the tallest and strongest of the three, got right into James' face and said nastily "James, you stay out of this. There are three of us, and only one of you. Just stay out of it."

When James was riled up, there was little one could do to hold him down. He was very strong and athletic. He knew that if he tried hard, he could take any one of them alone, but three against one might pose a problem.

"No. That was mean, Alex. You are going to pay for this. I'm going to tell Principal Victoria."

Alex lunged at him and punched James squarely on the chin. "You are not going to tell anyone, you hear?"

"Yeah, you heard him," Justin added.

James exploded. The rage he had tried to contain erupted. He grabbed Alex by his shoulders and pushed him backward, shoving him hard. Alex stumbled and fell. Next, Justin tried to grab James but James cartwheeled away from him. When Justin tried to rush him and grab him around the waist, James leapt high into the air and kicked out his leg like a Kung Fu fighter, belting Justin firmly in the stomach. Justin doubled over gasping for air. Clark made a move like he was going to charge James. James glared at him with angry eyes that looked like they could burn a hole through steel. "Don't even try it," James warned, "or you're next." Clark froze. He could see that James meant business and was frightened by how strong and agile James proved to be. Justin started getting up and James grabbed him by the collar. He felt like he wanted to pound him one last time. He felt a surge of power rush through him. He knew that he was performing way beyond his normal abilities. Suddenly, James came to his senses and dropped Justin to the floor.

"Come on Ricky. Let's go. They won't bother you again. Will you guys?" James glared angrily. They could see that James meant business and felt frightened by his superior power and abilities.

"Thank you, James," Ricky offered as the two walked away. "I'm sorry you had to get in the middle of this."

"Look, those guys were being mean jerks. I just hope they'll lay off you. That was really nasty."

James walked Ricky to the door and said goodbye. Then he headed to the auditorium for the rehearsal.

13

SHOW TIME!

On Wednesday afternoon Jenifer received a call from her father.

"You won't believe this but your Mom is being released from the hospital this afternoon. Her progress has been incredible."

"Wow, Dad, that's great news. We'll stop by tonight for a quick visit."

That afternoon, Jenifer stopped by the school after the second to last rehearsal to pick up James and Julia. She could hardly contain herself. As soon as they got into the car she blurted out, "You won't believe this. Grandma is getting out of the hospital today! I promised Grandpa that we would stop over for a few minutes tonight!"

"That's fantastic Mom!" exclaimed James.

"Mom, if she's well enough can we invite her to the talent show?" asked Julia.

"We'll see. Let's see how she feels when we get there. She may not be up for it."

Once again, after dinner, the Wyatt family headed out to check in on Grandma Jean. When they got there, she was beaming.

"I can't believe it. I feel great. Even my doctor still doesn't understand how I am recovering so quickly."

"Grandma, it's so wonderful to see you back to your old self," enthused Julia. "We have a question. James and I are going to be in the school talent show this Friday. Do you want to go?"

"Why, yes. I'd love to."

"Are you sure you're up to it, Grandma?" asked Julia.

"Of course, I wouldn't miss it for the world. Time waits for no one."

The evening flew by and the Wyatts headed home, elated by Grandma Jean's rapid recovery.

The rest of the school week also went by quickly. Before everyone knew it, it was Friday night. James and Julia got to the school at 6:15 p.m., about 45 minutes before the talent show was going to start. Grandma Jean and Grandpa Jake arrived at about 6:45. Jenifer took a seat next to Grandma Jean and saved a seat for George. He was running a little late at work but promised that he would be there. One by one, the children took the stage and performed to the best of their abilities to an adoring audience consisting of their parents, grandparents and friends. There were dancers, singers, actors and actresses and gymnasts. Although the performers were young, they rose to the occasion and, for the most part, gave commendable performances.

Finally, after about 45 minutes of watching others, it was time for Julia and her partner, Stephanie, to perform. Julia and Stephanie put on an amazing show as they sung and danced to a new hit, "Follow Your Dreams". Julia's voice soared beautifully during her solos and her dancing was incredible. There was something about Julia's performance that really stuck out. She danced and sang better than she ever had. After the two finished, the show director clapped her hands and commented as the two left the stage, "You two were amazing! Great job! Truly magnificent." Julia and her friend Stephanie ran off the stage feeling elated.

Many other children took the stage that night, all trying to do their best. Finally, after waiting for most of the show, it was

James' turn to perform. He was dressed in dark blue jeans and a tee shirt. He wore a black mask over his face. The lights were dimmed and he perched high up on the corner of some scaffolding to begin. When the song "Eye of the Tiger" blasted through the stage speakers, James swooped down from his perch suspended by some ropes, which made it look like he could fly. Then he proceeded to amaze the crowd with an incredible gymnastics and dance show, all choreographed to the music. James was incredibly "on." He leapt high into the air, performing several flips and twists, seemingly suspended in midair as the spotlights followed him. During his floorshow, he performed cartwheels, round offs and spins. James' parents and grandparents looked on in proud admiration of his skills and clapped wildly at every opportunity. The show was clearly spectacular, almost too good to be believed. James felt his natural agility soar with unexplained power and he pushed himself to a level that astounded the entire audience. At the end of his performance, the audience gasped as he took one final leap and performed three somersaults in a row. *How does he do that?* the audience seemed to wonder. At the end of the show the crowd jumped up clapping and yelling "bravo." James took three deep bows and ran off the stage. He knew he had been outstanding.

After the show was over, James and Julia mingled with their friends, talking about how well everything had gone. After about fifteen minutes, Jenifer came over and said, "Come on, Julia and James. We are going to have dinner with Grandma Jean and Grandpa Jake. Say goodnight to your friends. You'll see them Monday. Let's go, guys!"

With that, the Wyatts and Jenifer's parents left the school and headed to Antonio's for dinner.

14

THE LITTLE SEAL

When the Wyatts finally made it home at about 10:00 p.m. everyone was tired. James and Julia headed upstairs and started getting ready for bed. As they climbed the stairs, Julia elbowed James and crowed, "Great show. We both did really well. I think the powers we are developing from the crystals and the cave helped a lot. So when are we going back to the Sapphire Prism Cave?"

"We really need to get back there, but for tonight we can just relax. That was a great show, huh?" James agreed.

Just as the two got into their pajamas and brushed their teeth, a giant thunderclap exploded overhead and rumbled through the house, shaking the windowpanes. Shortly thereafter, a giant lightning flash crackled followed by another loud boom of thunder. Within minutes, thick rain began cascading down from the heavens.

Jenifer had disappeared into the master bedroom bath. As George was putting some things away in the downstairs closet, Julia called to him.

"Dad, that's some thunderstorm. Can you stay with James and me for a while? That lightning and the booms of thunder are pretty loud and scary."

"Alright, I'll be right up. Why don't you go into James' room? I'll tell you a bedtime story. How would that be?"

"Yes, please, Dad, that would be perfect."

George finished up downstairs and headed to James' room. He'd had a long, trying week at the office but he could not resist taking the opportunity to help put his two most favorite children in the universe to bed.

As he reached the top of the stairs, Julia appeared again in her pajamas and nightgown.

"Dad, just one more thing. Can James and I have some hot chocolate to drink while you tell us the story? It'll be so cozy. Please, Dad?"

George was tired and wanted to head to bed soon himself, but he couldn't resist Julia's plea. It would be nice to have some hot chocolate during the storm, he thought, so he shrugged his shoulders and said, "Sure." He headed back downstairs to the kitchen. After about ten minutes he returned with a tray holding three mugs. He pulled a small table from the hall into James' room and placed the tray down on top of it. He told James and Julia to climb onto the bed and handed them each a mug of hot chocolate.

"Be careful, guys. It's hot, don't spill."

"Okay. Thank you, Dad. This is awesome," said Julia.

Just then a lightning bolt crackled and the thunder boomed again. James and Julia drew close to their father and sipped on their hot chocolate.

"Okay Dad, let's hear the story. Which one are you going to tell us tonight?" asked Julia.

"Well, this is a new one. I don't think I've ever told it to you before."

"What's it called?" asked James.

"It's called *The Little Seal.*"

"Awesome Dad," said Julia. "Please, let's start."

THE SAPPHIRE PRISM CAVE

"Okay. Once upon a time, a young girl named Heather lived with her parents in a little coastal village in Alaska. It could be really cold and snowy up there in the winter. Heather had a talent. She learned how to carve ice sculptures and make other ice structures in her backyard. One snowy day, she made a beautiful high tower with a fortress up top. It was almost like a tree house made out of ice. The fortress had a sturdy roof made out of boards she had found in the garage. The walls were made of ice blocks, which Heather had piled up, assembled and sculpted into the tower. Then she made a slide out of ice coming out of one of the windows. The fortress held its shape through the winter since the freezing cold temperatures prevented it from melting.

"One weekend, when the sun was shining, Heather's parents, Sam and Wendy, took her to a rocky coastal cove. They walked along the shore and climbed over some rocks in their path. Sam pointed out how the cove and some rocks in the water provided shelter for this inlet. As they headed back to their car, Heather heard something. Her parents walked on ahead but Heather stopped to listen closely. Again she heard a very faint "barking" sound. She looked among the rocks but couldn't see anything. Then, just as she was about to keep walking, a small face appeared. It was a baby seal! Heather saw the seal and called to her parents.

"Mom, Dad! Come here quickly. I've found a baby seal. It looks like it might be hurt."

"Sam and Wendy picked their way back around the rocks until they reached Heather. Sure enough, when they got there they saw a little baby seal pup. One of its fins was cut and bleeding. The pup stuck out its cute little face and barked, begging for help. Heather pleaded with her parents.

"Mom, Dad can't we help this little seal? Let's bring her home and nurse her back to health. She won't survive if we leave her here alone."

"Wendy looked at Sam. Sam scanned the cove looking for the mother seal, but it was nowhere in sight.

"Please Dad! This seal really needs us," Heather said again.

Sam looked back at Wendy and shrugged. "I don't see the mother anywhere in sight. Heather is probably right. This seal won't survive out here alone. Unless we take care of her, she'll be in for a rough time. Seal pups are pretty heavy though."

"Dad, we have my wagon in the trunk," offered Heather.

"That's a great idea," said Sam. "I'll try to bring it down here. It's going to be tough to maneuver through the rocks."

"We can do it Dad. I know we can."

With a lot of effort and perseverance, Sam finally got the wagon down and loaded the seal pup. The wagon nearly tipped over several times but, with Sam pulling and Heather and her Mom pushing, the family managed to get the little seal into the car and back to their house.

"The seal has to stay in the backyard."

"I am going to build it some steps so it can climb into the fortress and use the slide," promised Heather. "I want to name her. Look at that jagged white spot on her forehead. It reminds me of a snowflake. How about naming her 'Snowflake'?"

"That's a perfect name!" said Wendy.

Little by little, Heather fashioned the fortress into a home for the little seal. A veterinarian was brought in to bandage its wounds. Slowly, Snowflake began to recover. Sam had to constantly bring home a lot of fresh fish to feed her.

One day, as Heather entered the backyard after returning home from school, Snowflake stuck out its shiny black nose from the fortress and looked down the ice slide. When she saw Heather she flopped on her belly and came barreling down landing in the middle of the snow covered yard. Heather shrieked with delight and ran over to her and patted Snowflake on the back.

Over the weeks that followed, Heather and Snowflake frolicked together and became great friends. Heather would sometimes throw a fish in the air and Snowflake would catch it and clap her fins. She barked with approval and sniffed the air for more. As time went on, Snowflake recovered from her injury and she continued to grow. One day Sam and Wendy called Heather to the dinner table. They were quiet at first but then finally Sam spoke.

"Heather, we know how much you love Snowflake and how close you two have become. However, as you can see, she has healed and she is getting bigger. You must know, she can't live with us forever."

"But Dad," protested Heather trying to hold back tears that stung her eyes and then streamed down her face. Sobbing she cried, "It's not fair. We're such good friends and I love her."

"We know Heather. We know. We understand it will be painful, but in your heart you must know it is the only thing we can do. She has to go back to her own home in the cove," Wendy chimed in.

"I won't let you take her away from me!" Heather cried storming out of the kitchen.

"Let her go," said Sam. "She'll realize this is best for Snowflake in a little while. She just needs time."

"I know. You're right but I just hate to see her cry like this," said Wendy.

✳ ✳ ✳

Just then the thunder crashed loudly over the house rattling the walls and windowpanes. James and Julia jumped and drew closer to their Dad. The lightning crackled once again. The rain opened up drenching the roof and the lawn. Drops slid down the windowpanes creating small rivers as the storm bore down.

"Don't stop Dad," pleaded Julia. "We need to find out what happens next!"

"Okay. Where was I? Oh, yes," George recalled.

✳ ✳ ✳

So, Heather was up in her room crying because her parents had just told her that they had to return Snowflake to the cove. After about half an hour, Sam and Wendy went upstairs to try and comfort Heather. She had stopped crying and lay on her bed in a dark room staring at the ceiling. She was quiet as her parents entered.

"I'm sorry," said Heather. "It's just that I will miss her so, so much. We played together every day for the past few weeks. I've grown so attached to her."

"We know you have. But Snowflake needs to go back to her home in the cove. She's better now and she can't stay here with us forever. Let's keep her here until Saturday. Then we'll all go to the cove and say goodbye to her together," offered Wendy.

"All right," agreed Heather holding back tears, "but it will be so hard."

Heather made the best of her remaining days with Snowflake playing with her everyday after school, feeding her fish, watching her glide down the slide on her tummy, listening to her bark and clap her fins in appreciation as Heather threw her some fish to eat. The two could not have been closer. Then, suddenly, Saturday arrived.

Sam had rented a trailer in which to carry Snowflake. He also brought along a special ramp. Sam laid a trail of fish leading from the backyard, up the ramp and right into the trailer. He lured Snowflake from her fortress by holding up a fish and waving it in the air. Snowflake quickly caught on and slid down the slide following the trail of fish. She got to the ramp and ambled up it barking all the way. When she finally entered the trailer, she saw more fish there and merrily jumped in. That was Sam's cue. He quickly slipped away the ramp and closed the trailer door. He called to Wendy and Heather, "She's in the trailer. Come on, let's go."

Sam, Heather and Wendy all climbed into the car and headed back to the cove with Snowflake in tow. Once they got there, Sam backed the trailer up as close as he could to the water. He swung open the trailer doors and attached the ramp. Snowflake quickly slid out. She looked bewildered at first and cocked her head questioningly at Heather. Heather sobbed and tears slid down her cheeks. She stepped close and put her arms around Snowflake's neck and hugged her.

"I'm going to miss you so much, Snowflake."

Snowflake stayed close to Heather and snuggled her, swaying her neck back and forth. She could sense something was about to change. She had grown to love Heather but she sensed that the ocean was her real home. Sam and Wendy put their arms around Heather and held her as she sobbed. Finally, everyone seemed to know it was time. Sam put the ramp back into the trailer and closed it up. Sam, Wendy and Heather stood together and waved a sad goodbye to Snowflake. Snowflake barked and then she turned and headed towards the sea. She arched her back and then extended her flippers several times and quickly pulled herself into the water. She headed outward to the center of the little bay harbored in the cove and then she turned, doing a backstroke. Heather heard her bark and she seemed to wave a flipper.

"I love you Snowflake," Heather called out as she waved goodbye with tears streaming down her cheeks.

※ ※ ※

"Dad," interrupted Julia. "That's so sad! Don't tell me Heather never gets to see Snowflake again."

"Hold on Julia! The story is not over quite yet," objected George.

"Okay. Sorry Dad. It's just sad they had to separate."

The thunder had grown more distant and the rain had slowed to a constant rhythmic drone. James and Julia looked at their father and urged him to continue. George resumed the story.

※ ※ ※

Sam, Heather and Wendy climbed into the car. They were all quiet as they headed home. Sam offered, "Heather, don't be so sad. We can go back to the cove from time to time to visit her."

"It won't be the same, Dad. How do we know if she'll even be there?"

"We can't be sure, but we'll try. I know it's hard sweetheart but it's the only thing we could do."

As the weeks passed by, Heather continued to miss and think of Snowflake. Sometimes she would look longingly at a picture of her, which she had framed and hung on her bedroom wall. Sam kept his promise and would take Heather back to the cove every few weeks. Once they arrived at the cove, Heather would run down to the water's edge hoping to catch a glimpse of Snowflake. Sometimes they would see her and Heather would smile and wave excitedly. Other times, they would arrive and scan the cove but were disappointed because they could not find her. As time wore on, the weeks turned to months and slowly Heather came to accept that Snowflake was indeed better off in the wild.

There was a period of time when Heather and her family didn't see Snowflake at all. Then one year, on Heather's birthday, she begged her father and mother to take her to the cove once again. When they got there, they scanned the bay and sure enough they spotted Snowflake sunning herself on some rocks in the center of the cove's bay. Right by her side was a recently born baby seal. Heather was so happy she waved and turned to her parents in excitement, "Look Snowflake had a baby! That is so awesome." Heather watched for a while and waved. Snowflake barked back. Heather looked on happily and realized that Snowflake now had a family of her own. As the years went on, Heather would visit the cove and try to get a glimpse of Snowflake and her new family."

"The end! And that's the story of *The Little Seal!*" said George turning to Julia and James. "And now it's time for you two to go to bed."

"Dad, is that it?" asked Julia

"Yes, sorry. The storm is almost over and it's getting very late," George said. The thunder rumbled in the far distance. The rain continued, but at a slower, softer pace.

"Julia, into your room. James, please get under the covers. It's late enough. Come on, guys."

"Okay Dad. Thanks for the story," said Julia as she hugged her dad and then her brother goodnight. George tucked James in and then stopped by Julia's room to tuck her in.

"Love you, sleep well," said George giving her a good night kiss.

George turned off the light. He closed Julia's door. Julia turned on her side and pulled the covers over her head. She listened for a few minutes as the rain droplets drummed on the roof. By now the sound had a calming, soothing effect. Julia grew sleepy as she thought about *The Little Seal* story her father had told her and James. Then, from out of nowhere, she thought about The Sapphire Prism. *It's been too long. We have to go back.*

"Don't worry. We will soon."

Julia looked around. There was no one there. She realized that she had received another "mind message" from James. She finally fell asleep content that James had somehow received her thoughts and knowing that they would soon return to the cave.

15

THE EMERALD TUNNEL

Saturday morning finally came around again. Julia stirred but lay in bed for a few moments. Finally she got up and pulled up the blinds. The day was sunny and the bright outdoor light initially stabbed at her eyes. Her lips broadened into a grin as she realized how beautiful it was outside. Julia went into her closet to look for some clothes to wear. As she entered, her eyes fell on a shelf where she had arranged some beautiful green crystals she had taken from the cave. She brought them out of the closet and held a few of them up to the light to get a better look at them. As she did so, they seemed to cast a tall green tunnel of light in her room. She put her hand into the beam to see how the green light would appear on her hand. As she passed her hand into the beam, it seemed to disappear. Julia gasped audibly.

She could not believe her eyes and quickly pulled her hand back. It reappeared. Ever so gently and slowly she placed her hand in the beam of light again. As before, her hand disappeared. Julia was beside herself. She had to tell James and she knew they just had to get back to the cave in order to explore it further. She took some of the green crystals and managed to fashion a small harness around them with some string she found in her desk drawer. Then she hung them by her window. The sunlight poured through them casting a magnificent green tunnel of light in her room. At first, Julia walked around the light tunnel. Then she gingerly tried extending a leg into it. Like her hand, her leg, too, disappeared. She quickly pulled it out. She couldn't wait any longer. She had to tell James. She ran out of her room and across the hall. She barged into James' room, which was still dark with the shades drawn.

"James. Wake up. Wake up. You've got to see this!"

"Julia. What are you doing? I was sleeping. Leave me alone!" James groaned.

"No, come into my room. You won't believe this."

"What?"

"You've got to see it. NOW!" said Julia firmly.

As sleepy and annoyed as James was, he finally pulled off his covers and stood up. "This better be good, Julia. I don't like being woken up for nothing!"

"You tell me after you see it," Julia replied.

The two headed into Julia's room. The sun streamed through the windowpanes. The emerald crystals hung in front of the window and a glorious beam of green light shown into the room.

"This is what you woke me up for? A green beam of light? It looks pretty cool but really, Julia, this could have waited!" said James angrily.

"Well what about this?" taunted Julia sticking her hand into the beam. With that, her hand disappeared. James' jaw dropped. He could not believe his eyes.

"Wait. Do that again. There's got to be some trick."

"No trick," replied Julia and stuck her foot into the beam of light.

James exploded with excitement. "Wait! I want to try it, Julia. That *is* amazing."

In a second, James jumped into the beam and seemingly disappeared. Then in an instant he leapt high into the air and reappeared.

"This is awesome."

James landed back in the green beam of light and looked around. In the distance, he saw the mouth of The Sapphire Prism Cave.

"Julia, Julia, you're not going to believe this. If you walk a bit up the tunnel you come directly to the entrance to the cave. This is like a hologram light tunnel that leads right to the cave!"

"James, let me try," Julia said jumping in.

"Do you realize what this means? We don't have to walk to the cave if we don't want to. We can get to it by going through this light tunnel!"

"Guys?" shouted their dad from downstairs. "What's all the commotion up there? Come on down for breakfast. You can continue playing later."

James and Julia looked at each other and smiled. They knew they had discovered yet another magical aspect about The Sapphire Prism Cave and the crystals.

"I have to check out *my* sapphire crystals," enthused James. "Those things really hold a lot of incredible secrets."

"If we can really get to the cave this way," Julia observed, "we will be able to go there a lot more often and Mom and Dad won't even realize that we're gone. We can just say we're playing in my room and close the door."

"Well, before we do that we have to find out more about what's going on," replied James. "We better head downstairs for breakfast. You know how annoyed Dad gets when we don't get there fast enough."

"You're right. We'd better get going."

James and Julia arrived at the breakfast table together.

"James, can you please get your mother? Everything is ready," exclaimed George.

James bounded up the stairs and brought Jenifer down. The family circled around the table and gulped down pancakes, bacon and English muffins. They made plans for the day together. George and Jenifer mentioned that they would be having dinner with the Sattlers again but this time, Melanie, one of James and Julia's least favorite babysitters, would be taking care of them. Rather than be angry that they were being left out of the dinner plans, James and Julia looked at it as an opportunity to somehow get some further time to explore the cave.

As everyone was finishing up breakfast, George made a proposal.

"Tomorrow is supposed to be a beautiful day also. Why don't we head into New York and go to the Central Park Zoo? We can also invite Grandma Ellen out to dinner with us after the zoo. What do you say?"

"That sounds great, Dad," said Julia.

"Yeah, Dad, great idea. You know how much I love animals."

"Okay. It's set then. I'll give my mom a call and tell her about tomorrow. Today we can go to a playground, do some errands and have a picnic lunch near the Hudson River."

"Great. We have plans for the weekend!" responded Jenifer.

The day, filled with activities, passed quickly and before they knew it the Wyatts arrived back home late in the afternoon.

16

TABLETS

Melanie arrived punctually at 6:00 p.m. She had long brown hair and deep green eyes. She was a bit plump and had a pug nose. Julia rolled her eyes at James as Melanie entered the living room where they were watching television.

"Hey, guys," Melanie said as she plunked down on the couch and popped her gum.

The problem with Melanie was she never actually played with James and Julia. She just stayed with them and watched TV. Accordingly, James and Julia tolerated her but never really warmed up to her like some of their other babysitters.

Their parents came down at about 6:30 and kissed James and Julia goodbye.

"We should be home at about 11:00. They should be in bed by about 10:00. Thank you Melanie. We'll see you later," said Jenifer as she and George left the house.

James and Julia watched some TV. Misty lay on the carpet. Melanie sat on the couch. Above her was a ledge holding some books and a vase of flowers. James looked over at Melanie. She didn't say a word as she sat and watched television. James whispered to Julia, "She's so lame. Watch this."

James concentrated and moved his hand forward. Nothing happened. He tried again. He looked at the vase. It trembled slightly. He concentrated and moved his hand. After a few seconds, the vase tipped over spraying water all over Melanie as it fell next to her on the couch.

"Wow! How did that happen? I didn't touch it," she shrieked as she jumped up off the couch.

"Oh, don't worry, Melanie, we won't tell Mom and Dad that you tipped over the vase. It will be our secret," Julia said winking at James.

James knew he was being a little cruel, but the prankster that he was, he could not resist the urge to experiment with his powers further at Melanie's expense.

Next he looked at Misty. He thought, *bark*, but she was silent. He squinted his eyes and looked at Misty. Then he looked at Melanie. Julia looked on silently and began to understand what was going on. All of a sudden Misty jumped up barking and started chasing her tail. She lunged in Melanie's direction not actually at her but close enough to startle her so that she almost fell off the couch.

"Misty, Misty, calm down girl, everything's all right," assured Julia casting a glare at James.

"Wow, what's gotten into Misty? That was strange," protested Melanie.

James stayed silent but relished the fact that his pranks, driven by his new found powers were actually working. The evening passed by with James, Julia and Melanie watching TV and exchanging small talk. At about 9:15 James said he was heading up to his room to play, leaving Julia to finish the program she was watching.

Once James got to his room, he peered through his telescope at the black sky. First he looked at the moon and then tried to find some planets. Next he lingered over some brightly glittering stars. James was in awe of space. He loved any movie involving space. He also knew that his father worked for a company that created advanced spacecraft but that most of his work was top secret. James wished that he could fly. He continually dreamed of becoming a pilot of some grand spaceship, maybe like Captain Kirk in *Star Trek*, or of an attack spacecraft like Luke in *Star Wars*.

James looked over at the solar system kit he had gotten at Disneyland. He held up his hand and, more effortlessly than in the past, the planets rose and slowly began to revolve around the sun. Although he had accomplished this several times before, he still marveled at his own ability. Then, James remembered the beautiful sapphire crystals, which he had taken from the cave. He scrounged through his drawer and pulled them out. He held them up to the light and looked at them. He put them under the strong beams of his desk lamp, which caused them to glisten beautifully. As he watched the dazzling crystals, he sensed a strange strength and power surging through him. He thought of creating a beautiful sculpture of Lego like pieces. Holograms of building blocks appeared on his desk and he was able to fashion them into small structures. After about half an hour he heard his bedroom door open and Julia came in.

"Hi, James. What are you doing? I told Melanie I wanted to play up here with you for a while and get ready for bed. We have to find out more about my crystals and the light tunnel to the cave. If that really works, it'll be awesome."

"Okay, but look at this Julia, it's so cool," said James, showing Julia the hologram pieces he used to create a structure.

"That's amazing, but what about the cave? Let's check out the light tunnel in my room."

"Okay, okay," agreed James impatiently.

James grabbed his sapphire crystals and followed Julia to her room. Julia flipped on the light and took out her green crystals. Her face suddenly twisted with disappointment.

"How are we going to create the light tunnel? It's dark - there's no sunlight. What are we going to do?" Julia stammered.

"Let's try holding them up in front of your desk lamp," suggested James.

Julia held up the crystals. A very small and faint tunnel did form but it looked different from the one in the afternoon.

"The light doesn't seem strong enough," observed Julia.

James and Julia were clearly disappointed. Suddenly, an idea hit James. Working on instinct rather than reasoned analysis, he told Julia to turn off all the lights in her room.

"James, what are you talking about, turn off the lights. We need light to make the crystals create the light tunnel."

"Less is more. Just do it!" commanded James.

"James, you're not being reasonable," protested Julia.

James couldn't wait any longer and ran around turning off all the lights. He pulled up the window shade, grabbed Julia's crystals and held them up to the bright moonlight. For a few seconds nothing happened. Then in the darkness, an eerie green light began to glow with white wisps of smoke rising from its side. Slowly, a three-dimensional light tunnel formed in the room.

James and Julia stepped back. This light tunnel seemed even brighter and bigger than the one Julia had created in the afternoon.

"How did you do that, James?"

"Not sure, but I think the dark room and the bright moonlight is making this possible," answered James.

James affixed the crystals to the string holster that Julia had created, and finally, the green light tunnel appeared, glistening in the room.

"Better lock the door in case Melanie comes wandering up here. We don't want to have to explain all this to her."

"You're right. Done!" chirped Julia brightly.

"Now for the test," James announced as he jumped and disappeared into the light tunnel.

Once in, James felt like he was right in front of the cave on a glowing green spot. *That must be the connection to the light tunnel,* James concluded.

He entered the mouth of the cave and sure enough, there it was. *Wow! That's awesome!*

James ran back to the green spot and jumped. He popped out of the light tunnel and back into Julia's room.

"It works!" James cried excitedly to Julia. "Come on! You're not going to believe this. Come on!"

James and Julia jumped into the light tunnel together and landed on the green spot in front of the cave.

"Let's go," cried James.

"Hold on. We forgot the flashlights and lanterns."

This stopped James momentarily. *She's right* he thought. *What should we do?*

James entered the cave and Julia followed but she hesitated.

"James, you know it's too dangerous to go in there without any light."

Again, working on instinct, James rubbed his hands together. He looked at the sides of the cave and the rocks. He concentrated very hard. Smoke started pouring from some crevices in the cave. Then suddenly a very bright, clean bluish flame sprung from the walls of the cave illuminating it in a beautiful glow.

James and Julia turned and looked in awe. James ran his hand near the flame. He thought it would be hot, but it was not. It was a cool flame.

"Julia, this flame is not even hot to the touch. Can you believe this? Put your hand near it."

"James, fire is hot."

"Not this one. Give me your hand," coaxed James.

"Okay James, but if you get me burned you're in big trouble!" warned Julia.

Julia tried it and smiled when she realized that James was right. The two entered the cave. As they walked through the cave's tunnels, the flames followed them, popping out to show them the way. James picked up a fallen piece of a stalactite and touched one of the blue flames coming from the walls. It ignited and burned with the cool flame.

"Now this is cool! A torch so we can see even better."

James and Julia went by the reflecting pool they had discovered earlier. Julia looked into the pool. Slowly some images surfaced and disappeared. Julia could see her grandmother and grandfather who looked happy. Next she saw Melanie, still glued to the couch, watching a dating show on TV. Lastly, she saw an image of her parents in a restaurant. Julia wondered if the reflecting pool could conjure up images, people and places of the past and was enthralled to see that it could. Apparently, it reflected images from the past and present. *What about the future?* Julia stared hard into the pool. All she saw was a reflection of her face. She concentrated harder. Still nothing appeared. It seemed that the future was something the pool could not show, or else Julia had not mastered that ability yet.

After some time at the reflecting pool, James coaxed Julia to press on further into the cave. The lighting, afforded by the rock flames, was just right. It provided a dim, mysterious glow, which gave the twins enough light to see, but not so much as to destroy the mystery of the cave. There were still dark corners and spaces and James was glad he had his special torch to use when needed. As they continued their journey through some passages, Julia wandered off into a darkened corner. As she was walking, she nearly tripped when her foot hit something. She looked down to see what had caused her to stumble and saw three, thin tablet-shaped stones.

"James, please bring over the torch. I think I've found something here."

James obliged. Julia scooped up the stone tablets and examined them more closely. They had some intricate etchings at the top and around the sides. The slates looked blank. James brought the torch close to them. He pulled out one of the sapphire crystals he had stashed in his pocket and held it close to the light. It cast a blue beam on the slates. All of a sudden, letters began to emerge on the slates.

"Wow, Julia! Look at that! There's writing on the tablets."

"I see! We have to bring these with us."

"Just looked at my watch. It's almost 10:30. We have to get back. Melanie might actually come looking for us, if she ever gets off the couch, and Mom and Dad will be home soon. We always seem to run out of time."

"I know. You're right. Just remember though, I found the slates and they're mine."

"Yes, but I got the writing to appear with my crystals."

"James, stop. We'll look at them together at home when we get back or tomorrow. Let's go."

James and Julia retraced their steps and exited the cave. Thankfully they saw the green landing spot, stood on it and jumped upward. Sure enough, they exited the light tunnel and were back in Julia's room.

Upon their return they immediately heard banging on Julia's door.

"James and Julia! Open this door now! Your parents will be back soon and you guys can't be up!"

James smiled at Julia. Julia took down her crystals and stored them in her closet together with the newly discovered tablets. James pocketed his sapphire crystals. Once everything in the room looked normal, Julia pulled open the door and Melanie stormed in.

"What have you guys been up to? I've been banging on this door for a good five minutes. Come on!"

"Sorry. James and I were playing. We had some headphones on and we just got carried away and couldn't hear you."

"You must have heard me alright. I've been calling and banging. James go to your room. Both of you get into your pajamas. Your parents will be furious if you two are still up when they get home!"

With that, James and Julia headed for bed. A frustrated Melanie lumbered downstairs and planted herself in front of the television until George and Jenifer returned. After getting paid, Melanie thanked them and left in a huff.

17

ROAMING TIGERS

George woke Julia and James earlier than normal for a Sunday. First, he went into Julia's room.

"Good morning, sweetheart," he said to Julia. "You remember what we're doing today, right?"

"Dad, I forget. It's so early," protested Julia sleepily.

"Yes. Well, you guys asked for it. We have a big day ahead. We're heading to the Central Park Zoo in New York City! Remember?"

"Oh yes, now I do. I love that zoo right in middle of the city. Pretty neat. Is James up?"

"I'm going to wake him up right now," George said walking over to James' room.

"Good morning, James!"

"Hi, Dad. What's going on?"

"Don't you remember? We agreed to head into the city to the Central Park Zoo today."

"Oh, right. That should be fun. I'll get ready."

The Wyatts all got dressed, had breakfast, and left for New York at about 10:30. George wanted to get to the zoo no later than 11:45 so that they would have plenty of time to enjoy the day.

When they arrived in the city, they parked in a garage on the East Side, several blocks from Central Park. As they walked playfully toward the zoo, the city buildings towered above. George pointed out a few significant landmarks along the way.

"Over there is Citicorp Center and further downtown, that tall building is the Empire State building." When they crossed over Park Avenue, George pointed out the MetLife building.

"That building used to be called the Pan Am building, Now it's called the Metlife Building. Its address is 200 Park Avenue."

James and Julia had been to New York City a number of times with their parents. They were simultaneously in awe and intimidated by the large buildings, throngs of people and energy of the big city. With something happening on every street corner, they were both enthralled and curious.

As the family walked by the entrance to an old walk-up apartment building, an elderly lady was sitting on a piece of cardboard on the ground. Her face was grubby and streaked with dirt. Her wisps of greying hair had not been washed in many months. She stared blankly ahead, stealing glancing at the people passing by. A hand written sign, which read simply "Homeless and hungry. Please help," sat next to her. As Julia walked by, the lady held up a cup and thrust it at her pleading, "Please help."

Julia was startled and clung to her mother, who assured her, "It's okay Julia." Jenifer reached into her wallet and pulled out a dollar.

"Julia, give her this."

Julia took the dollar and dropped it into the cup. The beggar's face lit up momentarily with gratitude.

"Thank you so much," she said. "Your daughter is so beautiful, what's her name?" she said turning to Jenifer.

"Julia. What's yours?"

"Nancy. Thank you, Julia. I have a daughter also. She was once young and beautiful like you. I haven't seen her in many years though."

"What are you doing out here on the street?" Julia asked innocently.

"My husband died. I lost my job and I couldn't keep my house. I lost touch with my daughter. I have no choice but to live on the street."

"What about a shelter? Couldn't you go there for help?" asked Jenifer.

"Too dangerous. Even though I have to live out here on the street, I value my freedom."

"Find your daughter. She'll help you," coaxed Julia.

Nancy was silent. She smiled weakly. She wanted to help herself, but she didn't quite know how to start or where to turn. She also wanted to forget an angry falling out she'd had with her daughter.

George and James had walked slightly ahead. When George noticed that Jenifer and Julia had lingered behind, he called after them.

"Come on, Jenifer. We have to get to the zoo."

"Yeah, Mom. I want to get there sometime today," chimed in James.

"Sorry, Nancy. We are heading to the Central Park Zoo and have to go."

Nancy looked at Julia and smiled. "I understand, thank you again. You made my day."

Jenifer and Julia smiled back and moved along to join George and James.

"That lady seemed so nice. I can't believe she lives out here on the street," wondered Julia.

"Some people, unfortunately, don't have much. They struggle just to survive, which is why we should be thankful for all that we have."

"She has to find her daughter, Mom. She can help her. I know she can."

"Maybe you're right, Julia. It would sure help her. She needs all the help she can get."

"That's why you gave her the dollar?" asked Julia.

"She needs a place to live, money, and the love of what family she has left."

"She'll find her daughter. I know she will," Julia said confidently.

All of a sudden Nancy got up and started calling after Jenifer and Julia.

"Hey, wait a minute! Just one minute! I appreciate you helping me out, but look here, I think you made a mistake. This is a hundred dollar bill. I can't take it."

Jenifer checked her purse. "It's not mine. I have all the money I came with. I only gave you a one."

Julia smiled smugly. "Yes, it must be someone else's. We only gave you a one."

"Okay, that is strange. I thought it was a one at first but when I took a second look it had turned into a hundred. Strange. Okay. Thanks and have a great day."

"Find your daughter," Julia repeated and smiled knowingly.

"I'll try," said Nancy.

Yes, you will find her. Julia thought to herself.

Jenifer and Julia waved goodbye to Nancy. The family continued to the Central Park Zoo. As they passed through the iron entrance gates, James and Julia brimmed with anticipation and excitement. James ran toward the seal pool and called the family over.

"Hey, guys, it looks like it's feeding time. Let's take a look at the seals!"

The Wyatt family crowded around the seal pavilion feeding area joining many other visitors as the attendants tossed fish to the barking seals. The onlookers clapped as the seals snagged their food and barked their appreciation.

Julia stood by her father and watched the scene unfold.

"Dad, this reminds me of *The Little Seal* story you told us."

"Yes, I can see how it would," George replied smiling, glad to see that the story had made an impression. James climbed up a rock overlooking the seal feeding area. He reflected on the contrast between the seals and the towering skyscrapers. After the feeding was done, James jumped off the rock with a sweeping leap.

"James, be careful. That's pretty high."

"I got it, Dad. Not a problem," James boasted.

The Wyatts continued through various pavilions, including one for monkeys, a newly-added butterfly walk through exhibit, a new tiger pavilion and one featuring polar bears. At one point, they were behind a family with a very cute baby girl in a carriage. She had a red bow in her hair and smiled happily at everyone. Her big blue eyes were alert and followed everything around her.

"Mom, look at that little baby. Isn't she adorable?" Julia pointed out excitedly.

"Yes, she is," agreed Jenifer smiling.

Suddenly, the Wyatts came across something causing a great commotion. Many of the zoo's patrons were talking excitedly and pointing at a truck. Apparently, the zoo was going to add two young tigers today and people were crowding around the vehicle, which was being used to unload them into their outdoor cage area.

There were three zoo attendants, Mel, Joseph and Sal. Joseph was relatively inexperienced. Mel, the head of the team, drove the truck while the other two handlers jumped out to get ready to open the doors.

Joseph, the youngest opened the bolts to the truck cage but Sal told him to wait. "We have to open the doors to the cage first. Come help me."

Joseph wasn't thinking and ran over to help Sal out. The problem was that Joseph had not bothered to re-bolt the truck doors properly. The tigers could sense the crowd outside and they became nervous. They paced their cage impatiently. Suddenly, one of the tigers lunged at the door of the truck. It ran back and again lunged at it with all its might and the door burst open. The tiger looked around and leapt out of the truck. Sal and Joseph finally saw what was happening. Mel shouted to them. "Grab the tranquilizer dart gun. Tiger on the loose!"

The second tiger wasted no time and shot out of the cage also. The crowd, although quite a distance away, saw what was happening and began to panic. Joseph and Sal fumbled around for a few precious minutes searching for the tranquilizer gun. When they finally found it, they concentrated first on the tiger that had banged open the truck door and initially left the cage. The second tiger, in the meantime, had used its prowess to leap the rocks in the area and started climbing out of the gorge leading to the cage. In no time it managed to get close to the onlookers who started running to get away from it. The Wyatts were caught up in the panic. Mel and Joseph managed to tranquilize the first tiger, but the darts missed the second tiger and now it was out of range.

The second tiger was startled by the continuing reaction of the crowd and it tasted freedom. It continued bounding up the boulders on the hillside. Finally, it gave one last heroic leap and it was on the top of a wall next to the visitor-walking path, which separated the tiger from the onlookers. In doing so, it came face to face with the family with the little baby in the carriage, which Julia had admired. Upon seeing the tiger that close to her baby, the mother froze in fear. The Wyatts were right behind them. James came forward leaping high in the air. He positioned himself between the tiger and the baby. He stared the tiger straight in its eyes. Somehow James mentally "locked" onto its mind and sent a communication to the animal, which froze it in its tracks. James took the lull as an opportunity to speak to the mother. "Move the baby away. Don't run, but move away quickly."

While all this was going on, Mel, Joseph and Sal were running up the embankment, tranquilizer gun in hand, to try to stop and capture the escaped tiger. James held his gaze on the tiger. He mentally "ordered" it to lie down. After about a minute of pacing, it finally obeyed and settled down on the wall. As Mel, Sal and Joseph drew nearer, the tiger became startled. James motioned with his hand for the tiger to continue to lie down. It complied. Julia looked on in wonderment seeking to know how her brother was controlling the beast. Finally, the zoo handlers got close enough and took the opportunity to shoot two tranquilizer darts into the tiger's back. It slumped over and the handlers quickly removed it and put it into its cage. There was a collective sigh of relief all around and a return to normalcy once the beast had been brought under control. Julia noticed that James smiled smugly in satisfaction after the ordeal was over he but deflected any questions from her about his role with a quick, "We'll talk later."

After exhausting the exhibits at the Zoo, James and Julia headed to an adjoining playground. As their parents watched on, James and Julia raced up and down the slide and then jumped on to other activities. James had to show off, just a little. He didn't want anyone to see that he had extraordinary powers, but he wanted to let people know he was really, really good. So as he went down the slide, he managed to do a small flip off the end. Some of the kids and parents watching were impressed. One little boy pointed at James and asked, "How does he do that?" James heard him but just smiled and ran off to try out a cool swing. James and Julia, while playing together trying out all the playground equipment, sometimes shrieked with delight. They were two happy kids, enjoying their youth and the moment.

The sun moved down in the sky as the afternoon wore on. At about 4:30 James ran over to George and said, "Dad, I'm hungry. Can we get something to eat?"

"Okay, James we'll eat, but not here. How about the Chinese restaurant the Sizzling Wok you and Julia love?"

"Yes, Dad, that would be great!"

"Okay. We'll head over at about 5:00. We wanted to eat early anyway since today is Sunday and you and Julia have school tomorrow."

The day came to an end and the family headed to the Sizzling Wok for a great meal to end the day's activities. George called Grandma Ellen to tell her about which restaurant to meet them at. She, however, told George that she had come down with a bad cold and wouldn't be able to make it. James and Julia were disappointed that they wouldn't see their grandmother but quickly accepted the explanation.

When they were seated, James and Julia requested chopsticks, which they had gotten very adept at using. They hungrily wolfed down the wonton soup, fried rice, sesame chicken and other favorite dishes they had ordered. At the end of their meal, they were given the traditional orange pieces and fortune cookies for desert. As they each sucked on a piece of orange, they broke open their fortune cookies.

"James, what does yours say? I love fortune cookies," exclaimed Julia.

"Me too, but you know that they're not real. You go first."

"No, you," countered Julia.

"Now, guys, this is nothing to fight about," chimed in Jenifer.

"Mom, we're not fighting. We're just playing."

George cut in at this point, "Alright, here's mine. 'You have a large project to complete.' Hey, that's pretty accurate," smiled George thinking about all he had to do at work. "What about you honey?" he asked looking at Jenifer.

"'There is no time like the present,'" answered Jenifer. "And what about you two?" she asked looking at James and Julia.

"'Never give up!'" chimed in Julia. "Okay James. Let's hear yours."

"'You will travel far, but, you will return home,'" laughed James. "What does that mean?"

Julia fell silent. For a second, it seemed that she had seen a flash of the future but she could not be sure exactly what it held.

"Alright, we've eaten and we've had our fortunes told. Let's head home. A pretty great day, huh?" asked George smugly.

With that George asked for the check and paid the bill. The Wyatts headed back to their car and then home.

18

WISDOM

Somehow, Julia and James made it through Monday and finally the end of the day school bell rang. James and Julia met as they headed out the front school door.

"Hi, James. Great day we had yesterday at the zoo. How did you do that with the tiger?"

"Don't really know. My mind sort of locked with his and I calmed him down."

"Must be more of the cave's powers at work," Julia surmised.

"It *was* kind of cool," James said modestly.

"James, I have some news," Julia said changing the subject. "Christine told me that she thinks you're cute!"

"Christine Jacobs?"

"Yes."

"What are you saying, Julia?"

"I think she really likes you."

"I don't know. She's pretty, but she's a girl. I don't hang out with girls."

"James, get over it. You know you've always liked her. How come every time she comes over, you somehow come to wherever we are playing and then find some way to show off, doing some kind of gymnastics or dance move."

"What are you talking about? I don't do that!" James said blushing.

"Yes, you do, James. And you know what? I think you really like her but you're too shy to admit it."

"She's okay," downplayed James.

"I know I'm right, James. Come on. Mom said she was picking us up today. We should find her."

"I have a play date with Kevin today at his house," announced James.

"I'm stuck at home alone," Julia complained.

"Can't you get Christine or Mary to come over for a play date?"

"I tried. They're both busy."

James and Julia found their mother waiting outside. She took James to Kevin's house and then headed home with Julia. After a snack, Julia went upstairs to her room.

"I guess I might as well get my homework out of the way," Julia said.

"Good idea. James will be home before you know it and I'll get a jumpstart on dinner."

Julia pulled out her books and started looking over what she had to do for the next day. After about twenty minutes, her mind started drifting. Suddenly, she remembered the tablets she and James had found in The Sapphire Prism Cave.

Julia went to her closet and after a short search, found them.

The tablets had reverted to blank, clean slates. *Do I need James to get that writing to reappear?* Julia wondered.

She put the tablets on her desk. She concentrated hard on them, but nothing happened. Next, she took out one of the green crystals she had brought back with her from the cave and passed it over the tablets. They started to glow a beautiful, emerald green but the writing did not reappear. *What else can I try?* mulled Julia. She hit upon an idea. *James would not like this, but he's not here. I need one of his sapphire crystals.* Julia went to James' room and rummaged through his closet. She could not find the crystals. Next she tried James' dresser drawers. She looked through each drawer and was about to give up when she finally found a small wooden box in one of the back corners of the top drawer in the dresser. Inside, Julia found five of the sapphire crystals. They sparkled and glowed beautifully when Julia held them up to the light. Julia grabbed one and returned to her room. She then held the crystal over the tablets. Within seconds, the sapphire crystal had the desired effect and three-dimensional writing appeared on the tablets. Julia scanned the text. She realized it was a poem of sorts.

In the beginning, you are
In the end, you are what you have made of your stay here
Will anyone take notice or care?
If you are young and unwise, you live in the moment and can't wait until tomorrow and what it may bring
If you are old and have mastered wisdom, you live for today
When you are old, you remember and reflect
When you are young, time has no meaning
Before you understand what time is, you waste it
Once you realize your time is limited, you treasure it like water in the desert
When you are old, the fast passage of time is your enemy
When you are young, you can't wait until tomorrow
When you are sick, it is as if you are old
When you are old but living life, you are still young
When you find love, you have found a treasure
When someone loves you, you are rich
You are born, you learn, you should find a passion for this will be your life's work
If you do not understand
One day you will
Like imagination, this cave holds the key to powers and dreams only you can create

Magic comes from belief in yourself and your abilities
You will at times win and sometimes lose
And you must learn to live with both
Life will offer you great treasures and lessons- some will be happy and amazing; some will be sad and tragic
Like a candle in the wind, life is fragile. It comes with a birth and leaves with death
Nurture and care for love when you find it, for it too is fragile
It is great to be smart, but still better to be wise
Can you find success without losing your inner self?
Can you build and succeed after a failure?
Take the time to listen, learn and experience - it will make you wiser
Some milestones along the way: births, children, birthdays, graduations, learning, spiritual guidance, weddings, funerals

All of a sudden Julia's concentration was interrupted when her mom opened the door to Julia's room.

"Julia, Julia, I've been calling you for a while now from downstairs. Is everything alright? How's your homework coming? I have to run to the supermarket and pick up a few things and then get James. Come on."

"Okay, Mom. Just let me straighten up a few things," Julia said covering the tablets on her desk with a few papers and her homework. "I got a little distracted and still have some homework to finish up."

"Okay, Julia. What happened today? Usually, you are so fast with your homework? Do you need any help?"

"No. Really, Mom, everything's fine. I just got a little sidetracked. I'll finish it after we pick up James."

"Okay, let's go."

Julia was not sure that she understood everything she had read but she was determined to read more and, of course, tell James about it.

19

FOLLOW-UP

George arrived home late from work on Wednesday night. He had been working on a number of top-secret projects and was beginning to feel burnt out. Despite getting home late, he managed to convince the rest of the family to keep him company as he polished off the homemade dinner Jenifer had prepared earlier.

"James and Julia, how would you guys like to come to my office for the day in about two weeks? The firm is putting together a kids' visiting day. They have some tours, special kids' activities and a special lunch planned. James, you can check out the cool giant electron telescope they have. You can really see a lot more of space than on your little home telescope. I can show you my office and tell you a little bit about the projects I am working on. What do you guys say?"

"Sounds great, Dad! Any spaceships? What about school though?" asked James.

"We'll get you a note from my firm to give to your and Julia's teachers, explaining you'll be out and that the day will be a

learning experience. Just make sure you won't be missing anything important at school that day."

"That sounds really great, Dad!" Julia chimed in. "I can't wait."

George finished his dinner and James and Julia headed
upstairs to get ready for bed. He lingered in the kitchen talking to
Jenifer, helping her as she cleared the table.

As James and Julia reached the top of the stairs, Julia whispered to James, "I started reading the tablets we found in the
cave."

"You did?" asked James. "What did they say? I want to read
them! How did you get the writing to appear? Last time you
needed me and my sapphire crystals."

Julia remained silent for a moment. She deflected James'
question by promising, "Don't worry. I'll show them to you. So
far, it's kind of like a poem. You'll have to read it yourself."

"Tonight. I want to see it tonight!" James demanded
impatiently.

"It's late, James and we have school tomorrow. Let's do
this tomorrow or over the weekend when we have more time,"
pleaded Julia.

"Just let me see it for a few minutes. We'll continue over the
weekend."

"Okay," Julia relented.

Julia got into her pajamas and got ready for bed, as did James.
Then she called James to her room and pulled out the tablets.
James had brought one of his sapphire crystals. Sure enough,
when he held it over the tablet the writing appeared again. It
seemed to scroll up and down, much like the writing on an iPad
screen except that the lettering appeared three-dimensional.
James' eyes twinkled as he saw the writing appear. He started
reading, and like Julia, had a little trouble figuring out what the
writing meant. After about five minutes Julia said, "Come on,
James. I kept my promise, but now we have to go to bed. Mom
and Dad might pop in to say goodnight at any moment."

"Just a couple more minutes," James protested.

"Come on, James, we'll have a lot more time for this, another day," replied Julia.

"James, Julia," George called out as he lumbered up the stairs. "Are you guys ready for bed?"

"I told you!" whispered Julia. "Now give the tablets back so I can put them away."

"Okay. Okay," James answered clearly annoyed.

Julia had just managed to stash the tablets back in her closet and James hid the sapphire crystals in his hand when their father opened Julia's door. "Come on, guys. It's getting late. Are you two looking forward to visiting my office?'

"Yes, Dad. We can't wait!" answered Julia.

With that, James headed back to his room. Jenifer soon came up to say good night and make sure everyone was in bed.

As she drifted off to sleep, Julia received a mind message from James. *Those tablets are cool. Can't wait to go to Dad's office.*

20

THE GRAND TOUR

Over the weekend, James and Julia managed to spend a few hours together sifting through the writing on the tablets. Since the tablets scrolled, seemingly endlessly, there was a lot to read and they couldn't do it all in one sitting. James focused on one passage he had found:

Paths are not always marked and clear
Sometimes you must make your own way
Take a chance, but foolish be not
And think before you act, or sorry you will be

"Julia, look at this. There are all kinds of cool things written in these tablets; too much to read in one day though. We'll have to go through it slowly, a bit at a time."

"I know. I told you there was a lot there."

"When are we going to visit Dad's company?" asked James.

"This Thursday. I can't wait!"

"Me neither."

"When are we going back to The Sapphire Prism Cave?" asked Julia.

"Soon, I hope. We need a longer time to explore. Some time when Mom and Dad are busy with other things."

"Yes, you're right, James. We can't keep worrying about being too rushed if we want to do it right and explore the cave carefully."

"We'll find the right moment to go," James assured Julia.

The week seemed to drag as James and Julia waited for the big day. They had never been to their father's office and weren't exactly sure what he did or what to expect. By visiting, they hoped to find out more. Jenifer made arrangements to meet her friend Bridgette for a day of yoga, shopping, lunch at the mall and finally some spa treatment time.

When Thursday finally arrived, George woke Julia and James up extra early. He wanted to get to work with enough time to introduce them to co-workers and give them an overview of his office and the firm. After they finished breakfast, they left the table, hugged their mom and said goodbye. Then they piled into George's BMW and headed for his office.

They drove for about 45 minutes and finally came to a large corporate campus built near a mountain, which was surrounded by a large fence. There was a secure gate where everyone who desired entry was required to sign in and have a fingerprint and eye scan to verify their identity.

"Good morning, Mr. Wyatt. I see you have two visitors today. Welcome."

"Yes, my kids are coming in for the firm's 'Bring Your Children to Work' day. This is Julia and this is James," George pointed out with a smile.

"Okay. Please sign them in and I'll give them identification tags. James and Julia, welcome! Please keep these with you at all times and stay close to the guides you will be assigned. Remember to stay out of any restricted areas marked 'High Security'. Enjoy your day!"

George pulled ahead through the gate.

"Lots of rules and security here, huh Dad?" commented Julia.

"Wow, Dad, this place is awesome!" James interrupted as he craned his neck, looking around.

"Well, as I might have told you, SPACETECK is a cutting edge aviation, spaceship design and manufacturing firm concentrating on space exploration. We do a lot of high-tech work under government contracts and much of what we do is top secret. Today, you will get an overview of our company. You won't be able to see it all, but you will be able to see some pretty neat things. Are you ready?"

"Yes, Dad," answered James and Julia in unison.

"First, I'll show you my office and then I'll bring you to the conference room where all the kids will be meeting."

The SPACETECK corporate offices were built as tiered, white buildings surrounding a beautiful lake. George had a large corner office, with large picture windows affording him a commanding view of the lake and the mountain in the background. He had a spacious black desk and a separate round working table with six chairs surrounding it, where he could spread out and look at plans. He had a leather couch in one corner of the room with a glass coffee table in front of it. It was clear that George was a mover in the company and had been amply rewarded with a big, comfortable office, in which he spent many, many long hours working.

"Wow, Dad! You never told us much about your office. This is really neat," commented Julia.

"I'm glad you like it," George answered with a gleam in his eye.

Julia made herself at home, sliding into her father's leather chair and giving it a good spin. James looked out the window and spotted a large aircraft hanger built into the mountain.

"What's that, Dad?" asked James excitedly.

"That's a highly restricted area, James. It contains prototypes of cutting edge, next generation spacecraft we are working on."

"I want to see them, Dad! Just a quick look, please?"

"That will be up to your guides today. I doubt you'll be able to go into the hanger, but maybe you can see a prototype or two. I'll suggest a quick look, but I'm not sure the company will allow it."

James tried to turn on a high-tech computer on the working desk but was unable to do so, since a fingerprint reader restricted access.

"Alright guys, glad you got to see my office. Now, it's time to head to the conference room and meet the other kids and your guides. The guides will be with you all day and show you around. I'll catch up with you at lunchtime."

George brought James and Julia to a big conference room in the building where the campus cafeteria was located. He introduced them around and finally led them to Linda and Phil, the guides who were assigned to show the children around the SPACETECK campus.

"Hi. I'd like you to meet my children, James and Julia," George said proudly. "You guys listen to what your guides have to say and don't wander off, okay? Have a great day. Now, I have to get back to work."

James and Julia mingled with the other children and introduced themselves. James walked up to Phil to ask him a direct question without mincing words.

"My father told me there are special spacecraft in the hanger built into the mountain. Do we get to go in there and see them? Please, I'd really like to!" James pleaded.

"We'll see, James. That is a highly restricted area," Phil responded.

Linda went to the head of the table in the conference room and asked everyone to take a seat.

"Good morning and thank you for coming. We have a very special day planned for you. Today we want to give you an overview of SPACETECK's corporate campus and laboratories. As you may know from your parents, SPACETECK is a company focused on the exploration of outer space. We look at the skies with our powerful telescopes, we design and manufacture orbiting satellites and advanced spacecraft. Most importantly, we search for and try to communicate with life beyond Earth. We believe there are other life forms on other planets in other galaxies. Much of what we do is very sophisticated and top secret, but we want to introduce you to the basics. Maybe one day you'll design or pilot a spaceship that will take humans to other planets or other galaxies or dimensions.

Today our tour will begin with a look at SPACETECK's optical telescope. It is one of the largest of its kind in the world. The telescope is in that round, silver structure high on the mountain. We'll go there by a special cable car. I think you'll love it."

With that, Linda ushered the 21 children into an electric powered minivan and took them to the cable car base station. They then loaded them into the cable car and took the five-minute ride up the side of the mountain to a very large optical telescope. The cable car moved quietly but swiftly. When it reached the landing platform, the children and their guides got off and took in the spectacular view of the SPACETECK campus, which spread over 400 acres in front of them. After a look at the surroundings, the children were ushered into the building housing the telescope. The astronomers operating the telescope gave an overview introduction of its impressive technical specifications including mirror size and magnification capabilities. Each child was given the opportunity to look through it at stars, constellations and galaxies. They also examined beautiful pictures taken with the telescope, which were shown on flat- screen televisions hung at various locations in the building where the telescope was housed. They were amazed at how the photos revealed the details of swirling galaxies, planets and stars. In his excitement, James managed to push his way to the front of the group.

"Wow, those galaxy swirls are incredible. How far away are they?"

"Many, many light years," answered Andrew, one of the astronomers.

"Will we ever be able to travel to them?" asked James.

"We are working on it, but right now they are out of our reach. One would have to travel many times the speed of light and that is supposed to be impossible."

"Do you think we'll ever find a way to do it?"

"If you can dream it, you can find a way to do it," Andrew answered obliquely. "I should also mention, that, aside from this giant Earth-based telescope, we have a telescope mounted on a spacecraft, much like the Hubble Space Telescope but even more powerful and advanced. It sends us back amazing, incredibly clear pictures from space which are not obscured by the Earth's atmosphere."

Linda gathered the children after the telescope viewing and escorted them to the waiting cable car, which they rode back down to the base station. They then boarded the waiting minibus again and headed to their next stopping point with Linda acting as their tour guide.

"As you can see, the offices are built around this lake in the center of the corporate headquarters. We experiment with pro-totype spacecraft there," she said pointing to a hanger built near the mountain. "But the actual manufacturing of the spacecraft is handled at a separate, top secret SPACETECK facility. I think you are going to really like the next stop we have planned."

James and Julia were sitting together on the minivan. Despite prior instructions to remain seated at all times, James kept jump-ing up to get a better look at things as the tour continued.

"Julia. This is so cool, isn't it? Dad never really told us he worked at such an awesome place," enthused James.

"Yes, I love it. Too bad we aren't allowed to take any pictures though. I brought my iPod Touch."

The minivan finally arrived at a parking lot adjacent to a large building.

"Okay, gang. We made it. Let's get inside and I'll tell you all about it," said Linda.

"Some of you may have had some basic science in school," she continued inside. "As you may know, it has been scientifically impossible to experience weightlessness on Earth because of the pull of gravity, at least until today. You may have heard of special planes that dive in a certain way enabling people to feel weight-less. Well, today we are going to introduce you to a special room where SPACETECK has managed to achieve the impossible. When you go in there, you will be weightless! You will have to put on some padded suits to protect yourself in case you make a movement that's out of control."

Linda asked for a show of hands from those who wanted to be in the first group of five who would go into the weightless room. James' hand shot up quickly and he shouted excitedly "Pick me! I want to try it right away!" Linda and Phil laughed, taken by James' unbridled enthusiasm. Seven other kids raised their hands and Julia also shot up her hand. Phil looked around the room and randomly picked groups of five from among the volunteers.

"James, Bill, Mary, Timothy and Kathleen, you will be in the first group. Julia, Carlos, Katherine, Robert and Heidi, you will be in the second. I'll pick the other two groups later. Each of you will be given a padded astronaut's suit. We'll have a trainer in the room to show you around and fill you in on some safety rules. Aside from the glass window front, the walls of the room are fully padded. Most everything should come naturally to you once you get in the room. Enjoy!"

The first group put on their suits, walked through a special chamber and then into the room. Some of the kids pushed off the floor too hard as they walked in and found themselves catapulted upward, floating in the air. The onlookers, waiting for their turn in the room, watched through the big glass windows in awe as the kids in the weightless room floated in the air and moved around like astronauts they had seen in movies.

James was in his glory. Due to his natural gymnastic abilities coupled with the powers he had acquired from the crystals, he moved around the room with great dexterity. He started performing flips in the air and sailed about in grand fashion, laughing and shouting out from time to time, exclaiming how incredible the experience was. He actually appeared to be flying and Linda and Phil and other onlookers were very impressed. They knew the room enabled people to experience weightlessness, but they realized what James was doing was very advanced and special. They couldn't quite believe his abilities.

"Wow! Your brother is amazing," said Katherine to Julia.

"Yeah, he's pretty cool!"

"How does he do all that stuff?"

"Well, he's always been good at gymnastics and dancing," answered Julia.

"But this is more than that. He almost seems to be flying!" blurted out Katherine excitedly.

Katherine was tall and had long brown hair. Her eyes were a beautiful green. Julia thought to herself, *She's someone I could be friends with.*

All of a sudden, there was a scream for help from the weightlessness room.

"Help!" cried Timothy. "I can't get down! I'm pinned to the ceiling! Help!"

Before anyone else could react, James sailed up to Timothy.

"Don't worry. I'll get you down," promised James calmly. With that he grabbed Timothy around his shoulders and pushed him down. Timothy finally became dislodged and headed toward the floor. James continued to help push him down. When they finally reached the floor, Timothy exclaimed, "Thank you, James. That was a close one. I just panicked and didn't know what to do."

"No problem. Glad I could help you out!"

A supervisor in the room came over and thanked James.

"Thank you, James. It was great you could help Timothy, but next time please let a SPACETECK supervisor or guide render the assistance. We don't want you or Timothy to get hurt."

"Okay, sure thing," answered James somewhat annoyed that he had in effect been reprimanded for helping someone in trouble.

After about ten minutes, the first group left the room and the second group entered. Julia and Katherine continued talking and were fast becoming friends. They found out that they were both interested in dancing.

"Are you taking lessons?" asked Julia.

"Yep. Twice a week," answered Katherine.

"Me too! Wow! Look at us. I've seen weightlessness on television and in movies but never thought I'd be able to actually experience it," commented Julia.

After moving around the room for a while, Katherine said, "Come on, let's try something. How about a weightless dance routine?"

"Sounds cool!"

With that, the two girls went to work improvising a weightless dance routine which left them giggling. Even James, who was watching his sister and her new friend, had to admit the weightless dancing looked impressive.

"Go Julia. Looks pretty cool. You are a great dancer!"

"Thanks James," Julia called back from the other side of the glass.

After the remaining groups had their chance in the room, Linda rounded everyone up.

"Well, believe it or not, it's already time for lunch. We'll head back to the company cafeteria to meet your parents. After that, we'll continue with our tour."

The minivan buzzed with conversations about the weightlessness room.

"James, I want you to meet Katherine," Julia said.

"Great to meet you, Katherine," enthused James. "Does your dad work here?"

"Actually, my mom does. She helps design the latest spaceships."

"Wow! That's cool."

Everyone entered the cafeteria and joined up with their parents. The lunch tables were round and could seat up to eight people. After picking out some food from the ample buffet, James, Julia and George selected a table by a window with a view on the courtyard and the lake.

"So, how's it going?" asked George.

"Awesome, Dad. You never told us how cool this place is. We've already seen the giant telescope and some great pictures from outer space. We also got to try out the weightlessness room! That was the best part. I wonder what other surprises they have planned for us after lunch."

"Phil and Linda are really nice," added Julia. "I also met this really nice girl, Katherine."

"Yes, her mother Natasha sometimes works with me. She is an expert in advanced spacecraft design."

"I wonder what we are going to see after lunch. This company has so many cool things to explore."

"I am not sure," said George, "but you are in good hands with Linda and Phil."

In no time, George, Julia and James had polished off their lunch and it was time for George to get back to work.

"See you guys at the end of the day. Have a great time!"

After lunch, Linda and Phil got the group together, did a head count and piled the kids into the minivan. "Next we go to the design lab. We have some scientists and engineers we want to introduce you to and some films to show you."

This time, Julia and Katherine sat together and talked. James sat behind them half listening to their conversation. From time to time he poked his way into their discussion to add a comment or two. James sat next to a boy named Zachary. It turned out that his father worked with a special division of the company that searched for signs of life on other planets and galaxies. James and Zachary, like Julia and Katherine, quickly became friends. The time flew by and, before they knew it, they had arrived at the design lab.

"This is where our best engineers design the most advanced spacecraft on the planet," advised Linda as the minivan pulled up to the lab. "Let's take a look."

Thomas Watson, the chief engineer, greeted the children and showed them around.

"Our engineers are working on spaceships that can fly at twice the speed of light. That's never been done before, but if we want to explore new galaxies we need to reach those kinds of speeds. Of course, the process and materials we use to achieve these results are secret and highly classified. The best we can do is show you some videos we have."

With that, Thomas led the children to an auditorium, which had tiered seats, a stage and a large video screen. The first set of videos showed the spacecraft being launched into space.

"We strap the spacecraft onto these rocket boosters. They in turn carry the spacecraft into outer space. Once it is beyond the Earth's atmosphere, the spaceship separates from the rocket boosters and the ship's engines kick in. In space, where there is no atmosphere, we are trying to achieve incredible multiple light speed velocities. The next videos you will see show the launch of the spacecraft and its flight in outer space. We hope you enjoy it!"

The children watched in awe and then were given a lengthy tour around the lab. The afternoon wore on and soon it was time for what Linda referred to as the "grand finale."

"Now that you've seen the lab, pictures and videos, it's time to see a prototype of the real thing."

With that, everyone loaded into the minivan to head to yet another destination. James kept his eyes pealed. He had been hoping to go to the high-security hangar all day. Unfortunately for him, that was not to be.

"We are going to the lower hangar. The hangar up the mountain a bit further is high-security and strictly off limits. In the lower hangar, you will be able to see some very advanced prototypes of spacecraft, but not the latest ones, which are still in the testing phase. Those top secret models have not been seen by anyone except the employees of SPACETECK working on them."

When the minivan arrived at the parking lot adjacent to the lower hangar everyone piled out yet again. Zachary and James bounded to the front of the group.

Phil led the way and then the children entered the hangar. They gasped as they saw a structure five times the height of a thirty-foot flagpole containing a rocket launcher and a large spaceship strapped to its side.

While everyone was looking at the spaceship, an electric pickup truck with a tarp cover entered the hangar. Jed, a supervisor on the floor instructed the operator.

"You have to go up to hangar A-1 immediately. They need a part we will give you in a minute. Please deliver it and return here right away. Here's the security authorization slip you'll need."

This all happened within James' earshot. Wheels immediately started spinning in his head. *If I can somehow get on the back of the pickup out of sight, I can head up to the secret hangar and be back soon. No one will even realize I'm gone.*

Uncharacteristically, James fell back from the front of the crowd of kids ogling the spacecraft. As great as this was, James just had to see what was in the top-secret hangar. He hung back and watched the truck pick up the part which needed to be brought up to hanger A-1. There were a number of pillars along the sides of the hangar and James slunk back behind one. The rest of the entourage focused on Phil as he pointed out the rocket booster and spacecraft prototypes.

The operator of the transporter pickup truck loaded the part onto the back and started heading for the exit. As it passed slowly by the pillar James was hiding behind, he took a running leap using all his natural abilities and some he had acquired from the crystals in the cave and landed, squarely but very softly, in the back of the pickup truck. He ducked down and slid under the tarp behind the part. The pickup made its way to a sliding steel garage exit door, which automatically opened as the pickup, approached. The security guard smiled and waved Al, the pickup truck driver, through.

"Delivery to station A-1 and return," barked Al as he left the hanger.

Phil and Linda led the children around the hangar, showing them all the prototypes on hand. Julia and Katherine walked together and admiring the incredible spacecraft. Yet, with all the excitement, the crowd of children seemed a little quieter than usual. Julia was in deep conversation with Katherine. At one point she looked around and noted that something was strange - she didn't hear James' voice. Just as Julia was focusing on that, Katherine exclaimed, "Wow, look at the size of that rocket booster. I can't believe how big it is!"

"I know," responded Julia refocusing on Katherine and the tour.

In the meantime, James was bouncing along in the back of the pickup. He wanted to take a peak in the secret hangar and get back as quickly as possible. He hoped no one would notice he was gone. The ride, however, took longer than he expected. *Come on, go faster,* he thought.

Finally, Al pulled up to the sliding steel door of the high security hangar.

"Hi, Al. Your security clearance authorization slip please. You know the rules. No one gets in or out without special approval each time."

"Yeah. I've got it right here. I've got to get in and deliver the part and return quickly."

"Alright. You're in."

"See you in a few."

The sliding doors opened and Al pulled into the top-secret hangar. It was dark along the sides but brilliant spotlights focused on the super advanced, next generation spacecraft SPACETECK was secretly developing. James poked his head from under the tarp and took in the unfolding scene.

There was a giant cruising spacecraft. It was shaped like two saucers, three flight decks high, connected by a long tube in the middle. It was huge, as big as an entire football field. Three special thruster engines were positioned at the rear-two on each side and one larger one in the center. The engines were far larger than any James had ever seen, each as big as a jumbo jet. Looking around further, his jaw suddenly dropped.

To the left of the cruising spacecraft was what appeared to be a large fighter spacecraft. At the rear, near the engines and laser turrets, there was a special clear dome. Through the small glass-like dome, James spotted something he could hardly believe. He saw glowing red crystals, which looked very similar to the ones he and Julia had found in The Sapphire Prism Cave. *Where did they get them and why were they using them?* James pondered. It also had turrets affixed at various places through which laser beams could be aimed and fired. James felt he had made the right decision. Even though he knew this place was strictly off-limits, getting to see the advanced aircraft was certainly worth the risk, at least to him. In the distance he heard an engineer talking to Al.

"With this last component, the spacecraft, when launched into space for a trial, should be able to reach velocities many times the speed of light. Thank you, Al. We'll send around a truck to help you unload it."

James wanted to get a better look at the spaceships and space fighter craft but he obviously didn't want to be seen. He attempted to accomplish those diametrically opposed goals by getting out of the truck and waiting in the shadows while the piece was unloaded. When Al went with the driver of the unloading truck, James took a good look. He was in awe at the beautiful craft he saw. James wanted to sit in the cockpit of the fighter but he knew that would be foolish to try since he'd get caught for sure. He stepped a little further out of the shadows and craned his neck to get a better look. All of a sudden, screeching alarms sounded and spotlights started combing the cavernous hangar. A voice on a loud speaker announced, "Alert! Alert! Security breach! Guards search the premises. Take all precautions."

Unwittingly, James, by his unauthorized presence, had triggered an ultra sensitive security system in place to protect the hangar and the top-secret spacecraft it harbored. The sirens wailed not only in the hangar but also throughout the SPACETECK corporate campus. Everyone cocked an ear and wondered what was happening. George looked out his window trying to see if he could spot anything. Despite the distant security sirens, Linda and Phil continued their tour with the visiting children.

"While these prototype spacecraft are incredible, SPACETECK has plans and prototypes for even more advanced ships. Unfortunately, they are the ones in Hangar A-1, which, as we told you, is strictly off-limits. We want to let you know that SPACETECK does allow, and in fact encourages, children of employees to do summer high school and college internships here. We need you guys for our future, so, when the time comes and you are old enough, please ask your parents about the programs. We think you will love them and you can get some incredible experience here."

As Linda expounded on some more details of the internship program, Julia looked around the room and again noticed it was too quiet. *Really, where is James?* And then suddenly she got a mind message from James.

Whoa. How am I going to get out of this one?

Julia remained quiet but nervously looked around and thought, *Where are you James?*

Just as Julia was thinking about James, Phil looked right at Julia.

"Julia, do you know where your brother is?"

"Funny, I was just thinking about the same thing. It's far too quiet. Maybe he went to the bathroom?"

"That's a thought, but he shouldn't have wandered off on his own without telling anyone."

"Zachary, you were talking to James. Do you know where he might be?"

"No. I was focusing on the spacecraft and sort of lost track of him."

"Well, this obviously is not good," interrupted Linda. "We have to find him!"

In the meantime, the sirens continued to wail. In the top security hangar the spotlights and security detail converged on James. When they finally got to him, one of the security guards picked up his wireless transmitter.

"You won't believe this. It's just a kid."

"Who are you and what are you doing here? How'd you get in?" asked another mystified security guard.

James was embarrassed and shyly answered.

"I'm James Wyatt, George Wyatt's son. See, here is my ID badge. I am here for the special kid's day."

"We get that, but what the heck are you doing in this hangar and how'd you get in?" repeated the security guard.

"I got sort of lost," hedged James.

"Lost? How could you get lost? Aren't you with a group of kids and guides?"

"Got on the wrong truck I guess!" answered James, twisting the truth.

"Well, you know that you shouldn't be in here at all."

"I know, but it's all so cool!" enthused James for a moment, ignoring the difficult predicament he was in.

With that comment, the security guards relaxed and almost smiled. Keeping a straight face so as not to send the wrong message to James, they radioed the information to their superiors. The sirens and flashing floodlights were turned off. James was brought into the security guards' office and given a stern rebuke for having wandered off and for entering a high-security zone.

"Remember, no more wandering off and don't discuss what you saw with anyone."

"I promise I won't," responded James.

After a few calls to corporate headquarters and the other hangar, one of the security guards, Pablo, was called in and told to take James back to the lower hangar.

There, as the other children were admiring prototypes and completing their tour, Julia blurted out loud to anyone who would listen, "He's okay. He'll be here soon." Phil got off his cell phone call and looked straight at Julia.

"How did you know that? I just got off the phone. They found your brother in the high security hangar and a security guard is bringing him back right now."

All eyes turned to Julia, making her feel quite uncomfortable. As this was happening, Pablo drove an electric transport vehicle through the sliding doors.

"Well, James, we're almost back. Please stay out of any more trouble. You gave everyone quite a scare aside from breaching all the security rules."

"I'm sorry, Pablo. My curiosity just got the better of me," admitted James.

Phil and Linda were angry but relieved to see that James had returned. All the kids crowded around him as he got off the transport.

"James, that was one of the craziest things anyone has ever done at SPACETECK. Aside from violating every security restriction at the company, we were worried sick about you."

"I'm sorry," James lamented. "I love space stuff so much I just wanted to see the latest things SPACETECK is working on."

"James, what did you see?" called out Zachary. "What did it look like?"

"I promised I wouldn't say, but it blows away everything else we've seen!" James blurted out triumphantly.

"Well everyone, the day has just about ended. We will all be returning *together*," Linda emphasized looking directly at James, "to the cafeteria where your parents will meet you. Thank you all for coming. Think about the internship opportunities I mentioned for when you get old enough. We hope you have enjoyed the day."

As everyone filed onto the minibus, Julia went up to James and looked at him with a disgusted look. "Are you crazy, James? When Dad finds out about this, and you can be sure he knows already, you're dead! Why did you have to ruin an otherwise perfect day?"

James hung his head in shame but inside he felt elated. He had gotten to see the latest and coolest things SPACETECK was working on. The other kids looked at James in silent admiration. They wondered how he managed to pull off the stunt and tried to ask him about it. James deflected their questions by reluctantly reminding them that he had been sworn to secrecy. That elusiveness made him seem even cooler in the other children's eyes.

The mini-bus finally pulled up to the parking lot next to the cafeteria and let everyone out. The parents were all waiting to greet their children and take them home. As they climbed off the bus, James and Julia spotted their father. As he stood waiting, he nervously ran his hands through his hair. A pained expression distorted his face. James and Julia knew he was angry.

"Hi Dad," Julia said, "great day. We loved it."

"Yeah, Dad, it was really great!" chimed in James, not mentioning a word about the incident.

"James, sometimes I really just don't know about you. What the heck were you thinking? You were told that hangar was off limits and yet you managed to sneak in and cause a great commotion through out the whole company."

"I guess you know?" James probed quietly.

"Know? Know? How could I not know! Sirens were blaring. Security teams converged on the hangar and, yes, I was called and briefed on everything by the security guards. And you know what else?" George ranted, "The president of the company wants us to stop by his office before we leave. This could cost me my job, James! Really, what is going on? You managed to ruin a perfectly fine day! Come on, I don't want to keep Mr. Silver waiting. Let's go."

George, Julia and James made their way to Mr. Silver's office. His secretary greeted them warmly and told them that Mr. Silver was wrapping up a phone conversation and would be with them shortly.

James and Julia kept silent. George nervously drummed his fingers on the secretary's desk. Finally, after what seemed like an eternity, Sheldon Silver stepped out of his large office and asked them all to come on in. He motioned for them to sit down around his circular working table. Mr. Silver was a mover and shaker with a type-A personality. He was intelligent, boisterous and friendly but he could be difficult and ornery when he wanted to be tough. Mr. Silver had a large telescope in his office. He loved space and he loved running SPACETECK.

James immediately saw the telescope and blurted out, "Cool. Can I take a look?"

"Sure, James," Mr. Silver said, impressed by the boy's incredible enthusiasm.

"James, not now. Mr. Silver wants to talk to us," interjected George.

"George, really it's alright. Let him take a look."

James jumped at the opportunity and after taking a good, long look and asking some questions about its technical capabilities, which Sheldon answered, Mr. Silver again directed everyone to sit down.

"Well, James and Julia. How was your day today? Your father's been a valued and trusted employee at SPACETECK for over twenty years."

"Loved it," Julia answered. "Someday I'd like to participate in the internship program Phil and Linda told us about."

"You heard about that? Good! I hope you'll take advantage of it."

"And you, James. I heard *you* had quite a day."

"Yes, sir," answered James weakly.

"You were told to stay out of high security areas, weren't you, James?"

"Yes," he answered.

"I want to know, just how did you manage to get into our highest security area?"

"I jumped on the back of a pickup truck delivering a part to hangar A-1."

"Wow, that was a gutsy move. Wrong, but gutsy. Why did you do it, James?"

"Well sir, at home my room is covered with posters of space. I love building Lego spacecraft. I have pictures throughout my room of planets, stars and galaxies. I have a telescope in my room also, just like yours. Well, it's not exactly like yours, it's much less powerful, but I love it. To answer your question, I just had to. You don't know how interested I am in this company and space. My enthusiasm got the better of me," admitted James. "I'm sorry I broke the rules and caused such a commotion."

Sheldon continued to be impressed by James' enthusiasm.

"You breached our security. You could have been thrown out right when they found you, but I told them to wait. I wanted to meet you and talk to you. You know what you did was wrong? Totally wrong."

"Yes, sir. I understand that."

"You know, George," Mr. Silver began looking directly at George, "James acted irresponsibly in breaching our security. He broke the rules."

"Yes, Sheldon, I know and he will be punished at home," interjected George swallowing hard.

"But you know, he has real spirit and drive. I love his enthusiasm and his curiosity. I had that when I was a boy. James?" Sheldon paused.

"Yes, Mr. Silver?" responded James.

"Despite your poor judgment today, I want you to consider doing an internship in a few years. If you learn some discipline, I think there may be a place for you here. We need young, smart, enthusiastic workers who love what they do and want to change the world."

"I want to try it one day too!" added Julia.

"Okay, Julia, you would also be welcome. George, so good to meet your kids. Everything is forgiven. Lesson learned, James?"

"Yes, Mr. Silver, and once again I am very sorry."

"Apology accepted. Have a great night."

"Thank you, Mr. Silver."

George got up very relieved at how the meeting had gone. He shook Sheldon's hand and thanked him yet again. With that, the Wyatts left, found George's BMW and headed home.

On the way, George had a few lectures for James, but Mr. Silver's response had put most of his concerns aside. Nevertheless, he was determined to mete out some punishment.

"James, we are going to tell your mom about this and you are going to be grounded!"

"Whatever that means!" huffed James.

"Your mom and I will discuss it," George answered in an annoyed tone.

When they got home, Jenifer was informed about what had happened and James was denied play dates with his friends for a week and was not allowed to use some of his favorite video games and electronics. In all other ways, the day had been a great success and Julia and James told their friends at school all about it. After a few weeks, things returned to normal.

21

VELVET

On a glorious, sunny day in late April, James and Julia were playing in the guest room, which had a balcony facing Mrs. McKenzie's house. In the distance they could make out Mrs. McKenzie puttering about her large, wooded lawn. Aside from her cat, Crystal, they spotted a beautiful, deep red colored Irish setter running beside her on the wooded property.

"James, take a look at this. It seems that Mrs. McKenzie got herself a dog. It's a beautiful Irish Setter!"

"Yeah, you're right. I wonder when and where she got it?"

"I don't know, but maybe Misty can make a new friend."

"Let's go out and take a look."

James and Julia told their mother that they wanted to walk Misty and take a look at Mrs. McKenzie's new dog. Jenifer answered, "Okay. Just stay out in her yard so I can see you from the kitchen window."

James and Julia headed out towards Mrs. McKenzie's backyard. She was walking back towards her house when James and Julia called to her.

"Yes, James and Julia. Nice to see you at a time you're not running through my back yard unannounced."

"We are really sorry about that. We'll go around next time."

"We came to see your new dog. We thought maybe Misty and him could be friends."

"Well," answered Mrs. McKenzie, it's a 'her'. Actually, my sister in Tennessee breeds puppies and she gave me this dog. It's fully grown now. Someone who took her when she was a pup had to give her back to my sister. Then she had to find her a new home, so she thought of me and sent her here."

Misty ran over and the two started sniffing each other in a friendly manner.

"What's her name, Mrs. McKenzie?" James asked politely.

"I named her Velvet. She has such a rich, soft coat of deep red hair."

"Well, Velvet and Misty seem to be getting along just fine."

"Would you two like to come in for some milk and brownies hot out of the oven?"

Julia looked at James and they both answered, "Sure."

After some small talk, brownies and milk, everyone could see that Misty and Velvet had hit it off.

"Well, next time you can cut through the yard, just give me some warning," requested Mrs. McKenzie in a conciliatory tone.

James looked over at Julia and smiled. *Maybe we'll head for the cave after this,* thought James. Velvet was a beautiful dog and Julia was enchanted that she had the opportunity to stroke and play with her. After James and Julia left Mrs. McKenzie's house, they thought of making a run for the cave, but as they exited the house, they heard their mom calling, "James, Julia we have to go out now. Come home."

Julia looked at James and sniffed, "Another lost opportunity."

"Well, we can always use the crystal light beam tunnel one day."

"I know, but I wanted to go back through the woods and up the mountain again."

"We'll try to get there soon," James assured her.

James, Julia and Misty arrived back home and Jenifer asked them, "So, how was Mrs. McKenzie today?"

"Very friendly actually. She asked us in and gave us a snack and let us play with her new Irish Setter, Velvet, who she got from her sister."

"Well, that's good to hear. I always told you she had a good heart."

James and Julia joined their mother and father on some Saturday errands and they all had lunch together. They kept busy for the rest of the weekend and were therefore unable to make it back to The Sapphire Prism Cave.

April slipped into May and the Wyatts could see the end of the school year approaching. One evening after James and Julia had gone to sleep, George and Jenifer lay in their bed reading with the television on in the background.

"What's today?" asked George.

"It's already May 25ᵗʰ"

"Another school year gone by in a flash," commented George to Jenifer.

"I know, its scary how fast the time flies."

"They're still so young but growing up quickly. It seems that their childhood, while not yet gone, is vanishing like the sand draining from one end of an hourglass to the other."

"Yes," lamented Jenifer, "but there's always something new to look forward to with them. A new adventure, a new stage in life."

"Childhood only happens once," observed George.

Jenifer was silent as she drifted off in thought. The television blared about the day's events.

"Always seems to be so much bad, sad news. Things are a lot simpler and happier for kids," George continued.

"Yes. The magical, innocence of childhood," commented Jenifer.

"They never seem to worry about tomorrow. They live for the moment and drink in every second."

"Well, tomorrow is another day. Let's get some sleep."

George clicked off the light in the bedroom. The comfort and solitude of sleep came quickly.

22

PUPPIES

James and Julia were playing in James' room looking through his collection of space posters and at the sapphire crystals he had managed to remove from the cave.

"Julia, it's been too long. We have to go back to The Sapphire Prism Cave soon. I want to see if there is anything else for us to explore. For now, why don't you bring in the tablets and we can read some more of them?"

Julia went to her room and got the tablets. The twins studied the writing, which appeared when James held the sapphire crystals over them.

"What does this mean?" Julia asked James.

Sometimes to find yourself
You must try new things
Sometimes you lose your way, but never your inner self
Then you return to the beginning and understand because you have learned

"How should I know? A lot of this stuff is written in riddles."

"Yeah, I guess we are too young for some of it."

James continued looking through the tablets. Downstairs, the phone rang. Jenifer picked up and listened for a few moments as Mrs. McKenzie spoke on the other end.

"Yes, Mary Ellen. Wow, that's fantastic. I'll tell them. Yes, they can be over there in a few minutes. I think they'll love it."

Jenifer finished up the call and made her way up to James' room. Upon hearing her opening James' door, they quickly hid the sapphire crystals and tablets from view.

"Hi, Mom," Julia said uneasily. "Who was that on the phone?"

"Well, you won't believe it. It was Mrs. McKenzie. She has a surprise for you and James. She wants you both to go over right now."

"Us? Why?" questioned Julia.

"Well, as I said, she has a very nice surprise for you!"

"What? Mom, please tell us."

"Okay. Well, you remember Velvet, don't you?"

"Of course, we saw her about six weeks ago."

"You probably didn't notice then, but Velvet was apparently a few weeks pregnant. She's giving birth to puppies right now!"

"Really, Mom?"

"Yes and Mrs. McKenzie wants you and James to share the experience. It's a real miracle to watch a dog giving birth to puppies. I think you will love it. Only two have been born so far. Irish Setters usually have a litter of five or six."

"Wow, James, let's go! I don't want to miss this!"

"Okay. Let's go."

"Dad and I have to pick up an engagement present. The Sattler's older daughter, Mindy, just got engaged and she will be getting married in a few months. I will call Anita and ask her to stay with you. I'll have her come by and pick you up at Mrs. McKenzie's house in two hours. That should give you plenty of time to watch Velvet giving birth. You can reach us on our cell phones. We should be back in a couple of hours anyway."

"Okay, Mom, thanks," said James.

"I have to bring my iPod touch! I want to take some pictures and video of the puppies being born! James, let's meet downstairs by the front door in five minutes."

"Okay. Can we bring Misty?"

"Usually mothers are very protective of their puppies. I don't think it's a good idea."

"Well, Mom, Misty and Velvet really seemed to like each other. If there's a problem, we'll take Misty outside."

"Okay, but just be careful."

George and Jenifer got ready to leave for their errands. Jenifer called Anita and arranged for her to come by Mrs. McKenzie's house. James and Julia got their things together and headed over with Misty.

James and Julia rang the front doorbell and Mrs. McKenzie answered.

"Hi, James and Julia. Come in. Velvet is in a corner of my kitchen. She's had two puppies so far. I think the third is on its way," she said excitedly. "I think it's best if we leave Misty in the yard."

James and Julia entered the warm kitchen and saw Velvet heavily panting in a cozy corner. She licked the cute little puppies that had been born. Their heads bobbed up and down as they searched for their mother's milk with their eyes still sealed shut. Sunlight poured through the window brightening the scene.

James and Julia looked at the puppies that had been born with glee.

"Soon, you'll see Velvet start to push again. When she gives birth and the puppy is born it will be covered with an amniotic sac. Velvet will break the sac, sever the umbilical cord and lick the newborn puppy to stimulate its breathing on its own," Mrs. McKenzie explained.

Velvet continued to pant heavily. After about 30 minutes she started to push again and, exactly as Mrs. McKenzie had described, the third puppy was born.

"You see, the birth of a baby is a true miracle. The gift of life."

"It's amazing," agreed Julia.

James and Julia watched a fourth and fifth puppy being born. They noticed that the fifth was much smaller than all the others.

"Wow, that last one is so cute, but look how small he is!" exclaimed James.

"Yes, well that one is the runt of litter. They are always very fragile. The bigger pups push the smaller ones out of their way to get to their mother's milk."

Just as Mrs. McKenzie was telling James and Julia this, Misty started barking and jumping outside. It was clear she was getting restless and jealous.

"I think we should go outside and take Misty for a walk. She is getting impatient being alone outside for so long."

"Well, Velvet is probably done giving birth anyway. Perhaps she'll have one more. She needs to rest. I hope you both enjoyed watching Velvet give birth," said Mrs. McKenzie. "It's an experience I remember from my youth. Thank you both for coming. I enjoyed having you and I am glad I could share this with you," exuded Mrs. McKenzie.

"And thank you, Mrs. McKenzie," James and Julia chimed in unison.

James and Julia stepped out into the beautiful sunlight of a glorious day. Misty came running up to them and jumped high in the air. She barked and headed for the stone bridge. James looked at Julia.

"She's leading us back to the cave. Let's go. This is a perfect time. Mom and Dad are out. Anita's supposed to be coming for us in about 45 minutes. We'll have some time to explore."

James, Julia and Misty ran after each other following the now-familiar route to The Sapphire Prism Cave. Shortly after they arrived, the phone rang at Mrs. McKenzie's house. It was Anita, who had gotten her number from Jenifer.

"Hi. This is Anita. I am James and Julia's babysitter. I was supposed to be there shortly but I'm afraid I'm going to be a little late. My car stalled and won't restart. I called and now have to wait for AAA to give me a jump-start. Can you look after them until I make it there?"

"I suppose so but actually they just left my house. Misty was barking and they said they wanted to take her for a walk. I'll see if I can catch them."

Mrs. McKenzie hung up the phone and walked out of the kitchen to her porch. She scoured her backyard but could not see any trace of James, Julia or Misty, who had by now disappeared over the stone bridge and into the woods heading for the mountain. She called out for them but there was no reply. It was a lonely hollow call. The wind rustled the leaves of the trees and in the clear sunny sky, a few clouds appeared. She did not know if they would come back to her house or go directly back to their own home after they were done. Mrs. McKenzie felt uneasy but there was not much she could do. She would have to wait for either James and Julia to return or Anita to show up.

23

THE JOURNEY BEGINS

James, Julia and Misty ran most of the way along the paths, through the woods and up the mountain to the Sapphire Prism Cave hidden behind the large boulder. When they finally arrived at the mouth of the cave, they were out of breath. As they approached it, their hearts beat with the same level of excitement they felt when they first discovered it.

"Well, we finally made it back here through the woods. Our very own cave!" crowed James.

"What do you want to do today, James?" asked Julia.

"I want to see some of the chambers we've already visited. I also want to visit the reflecting pool and search for some more crystals. And there is something new I want to try and find."

"What's that? How do you know what to look for?"

"Well, remember the tablets? One of the things I remember distinctly when I was flipping through its 'pages' was a diagram of a cavern chamber, which seemed to have a light beam shining in from above. Almost like a hole in the cave through which sunlight could shine in."

"Wow! That does sound cool. You never bothered to tell me about it. Well, let's go. Wait, James, we forgot the flashlights and lanterns!"

"Julia, don't you remember? We don't need those anymore. Have you forgotten about the cool flames we can create coming from the cave's walls? Look," he said snapping his fingers as the flames appeared. They seemed to burn from the rock, lighting up the cave and giving it a beautiful, eerie glow with just enough light to show the way, but dark enough to contain its mysteries.

James and Julia entered the cave and took the time to admire all that they encountered. They noted the beautiful stalactites, stalagmites and cave columns; arched ceilings of the caverns that opened up from the corridors that connected the caverns; and the beautiful reflecting pool. At the reflecting pool Julia paused and saw her face. James peered over it as well but his face did not appear reflected in the pure, still water. They pushed further into the cave, finding corridors, tunnels and caverns they had never encountered. James led the way based on instinct and tried to remember the drawings and diagrams he had seen in the tablet.

After following a particularly long tunnel, it finally led into the largest cavern chamber they had ever encountered in their various trips to the cave. The cool, blue light from the flames in the walls lit it up with a calming glow. A beautiful waterfall cascaded down the wall on one side. The peaceful sound of the running water enchanted Julia and James. The columns, stalactites and stalagmites were particularly pronounced. Misty sniffed around but stayed close to the twins. Sure enough, just as shown on the diagrams contained in the tablets, James and Julia looked up and saw a huge hole that led straight through the rocks to the outside through the top of the cave. Beautiful bright light shone into a large, well-like hole in the center of the cavern.

"Wow, this place is awesome. It's the most incredible cavern we've found so far in this amazing cave."

"I know. I am going to try to take some pictures and video," added Julia, pulling out her iPod touch.

As they were taking this all in, James noticed something strange. While the cavern's walls and the walls of the well were covered with huge beautiful crystals, mostly sapphire blue, but some green, purple, pink and red, he noticed that large quantities of the crystals seemed to be shorn off the walls of the cave as if a laser beam had come in and sliced them away.

"Julia, look at this. So many amazing crystals but look over here, it appears that some of them have been sliced away from the walls."

"Let me get a better look. Hmm, you're right, it does look like they have been cut away from the walls."

The dry well hole in the center of the cavern stood directly under the hole at the top of the ceiling. A shaft of bright, white light shone directly into the well, in a way connecting the two. The well opening was large with a surrounding lower rim. James made his way around some rocks and stalagmites to get a better look.

"Look Julia, there's a lower rim. I want to go down there to get a better look at the well and the crystals lining the well wall."

"Forget it, James. That is way too dangerous. There is enough to see right here."

"The rim looks sturdy."

"James! No!"

Before she could get another word out, James took one of his trademark leaps and landed squarely on the lower rim of the well. It was a bit damp. He balanced himself and looked down the well. He could not see too far down and wished that he had a flashlight or lantern. He noted that the crystals were well developed along the upper portion of the well and he wanted to try and pull some loose to bring back home.

"Wow, Julia. You won't believe this. The well is so cool. I can see it goes on and on, but it's hard to see too far down because it's so dark even with the wall firelight. The crystals are really amazing. I've got to get some. There are lots more sapphire colored ones. I'll also try to get some red, pink and purple ones too."

"There are also lots of crystals up here. It's too dangerous, James! We really need to get back. Anita will be worried about us."

"Just give me a minute," James said. "I've got an idea."

With that, James took a large leap upward and landed back on the cave floor. Julia was momentarily relieved. James, however, was not done.

"I just remembered. I can break off a stalactite and use the wall fire to light it. That will give me a better view into the well. Also, I need a small hard rock to help me knock off the crystal pieces I want. It'll only take a minute."

"James, come on, this is really pushing it."

"Not to worry. I'll be fine. This is really a blast," James responded enthusiastically.

James found a perfect stalactite to serve as his torch. Next, he found a sturdy rock on the cave floor. He lit the stalactite torch by holding it up to one of the cool fires on the cave's wall. He handed the torch to Julia. Rock in hand, he jumped back down to the rim of the well.

"Okay, Julia. Please hand me the torch. Don't worry - the flame is cool. It won't burn you."

Julia reluctantly complied.

"Okay, James, this is it. We have to get moving."

"Okay, okay," protested James impatiently as he held the newly fashioned torch over the well.

"Wow, this well is pretty deep. It seems to go on and on. I'm going to drop a pebble down it to see how far it goes."

James tossed a pebble down and waited. He heard nothing.

"Wow, this well is super deep! I haven't heard the pebble land yet."

James stepped forward and held the torch over the well again. He spotted a lot of crystals he wanted to bring back. He used the hard rock he had brought down with him to try and sever the crystals from the rock surface. After some hard banging he looked up at Julia who was standing above on the cave's floor.

"Wow. These are stuck on pretty tightly. Have to keep banging, I guess."

James worked away and finally managed to knock off some crystals. He passed them up to Julia. Then he looked down the well and called out loudly.

"Hello." "*Hello, hello, hello*" his voice echoed from down in the well.

"Julia, did you hear that? An echo!"

"Yes James. Stop fooling around. We need to get back NOW."

"Okay," James yelled down the well laughing. The echo again came back "*Okay, Okay, Okay*".

James was about to turn and leap back up to the cave floor when he spotted a multicolored cluster of crystals. They were a little bit lower on the wall of the well. James couldn't resist and used his rock to try and knock them free. He broke off one beautiful chunk of the crystals and put them next to him. He then went to work on the remainder of the cluster.

"James, you're pushing things too far. Let's go. You have enough crystals for now. We really have to get back."

"One more second, Julia and I'll have the entire cluster I am working on. Believe me, it will be worth it."

With that, James moved a little lower on the rim and blasted the crystals. They broke off and hung by a slender thread.

"I got it loosened. Just have to grab it."

James then reached for the hanging cluster of crystals. Right when he was about to grab them, they broke free. Not wanting to lose what he had worked so hard to obtain, James instinctively lunged for them. Julia watched and could not believe her eyes. James somehow slipped and began to fall down the well.

"No, James! No, James! NO!!"

"Help!" James cried out. "*Help, help, help*" his voice echoed.

The shaft of light shining through the top of the cave brightened. Julia was sure that James was falling down the well never to be seen again.

"James! James!" Julia screamed in horror. "No! No!"

The flames on the sides of the cave flickered and almost went out. James disappeared into the well. Then suddenly there was a strong gust of wind. The light from the cave hole strengthened and bore deep into the well. All of a sudden, Julia saw James coming back out of the well, head down, arms stretched downward, legs pointed up, floating in the air and being pulled upward towards the cave's ceiling hole. The light encapsulated James, covering him with a bright glow as he accelerated upward toward the cave's ceiling hole. He stretched out his arms to Julia. She reached her arms upward to him, as if trying to grab and pull him back down, but they were too far apart to connect. Julia was powerless to prevent James from being pulled towards the light and through the hole at the top of the cave.

"James, come back. James, no!" shrieked Julia in fear and awe.

"Something is pulling me upward. I can't stop it!" shouted James.

Then suddenly James fell silent as he was sucked through the cave ceiling hole. At the last moment, he hit his head on the cave's rocks near the hole and was knocked unconscious.

Julia dropped to her knees on the cave floor and pounded her fists into the dirt as stinging tears poured out of her eyes and down her cheeks. She was distraught and felt very lost and alone. Out of nowhere, she felt a soft tongue licking the tears away. When she looked up, she saw Misty standing over her and sympathetically whimpering with her. Julia put her arms around Misty and held her close. She was so glad Misty was there. Misty and Julia sat together for a few minutes looking at the hole in the cave's ceiling, vainly hoping that somehow James would suddenly appear, that he would tell them it was all a big joke and he was fine. But he did not appear.

Julia closed her eyes and concentrated. She sensed a mind message like the type she had received from James in the past, but it was a blank. Sort of like he was there but nothing was said. This gave her hope. *I can feel James' being, just no message content.* After a good 30 minutes with nothing happening, Julia and

Misty managed to calm themselves down a bit. Julia was grateful that the cool cave wall flames had not extinguished themselves, even though they had fluttered when James disappeared through the cave's ceiling hole.

"Misty, James is gone. We have to get out of here and get back to Mrs. McKenzie's or home. Let's go!"

Misty sensed what was happening and sniffed the ground. Julia hoped she could remember how to exit the cave. Misty seemed to know the way and took charge and led. Julia followed. There were many twists and turns in the tunnels and passages. When they finally made it back to the reflecting pool, Julia was relieved. She took a moment to look into it. She saw her own reflection in the smooth reflecting waters. Suddenly, an image of James lying on his back silently, as if sleeping, hurtling through bright lights with a dark background appeared. Julia gasped and the image flickered and then disappeared. Misty barked as if to call Julia to come along. Julia complied. Finally, they made it to the mouth of The Sapphire Prism Cave. They were both happy to have made it out of the cave safely. Julia noted that somehow, despite all the commotion, she had managed to bring along some of the crystals James knocked off the walls.

"Come on, Misty. We have to get back to Mrs. McKenzie's house and get some help."

Misty barked, seeming to understand exactly what Julia was saying and again led the way. They ran most of the distance. By the time they got to the stone bridge leading to Mrs. McKenzie's property they were tired and winded. They charged to the back porch. Julia rang the bell and pounded on the door leading out from the kitchen.

"Mrs. McKenzie, please, it's Julia! Please hurry! It's urgent!" Julia cried.

After a few seconds of banging, Mrs. McKenzie peered out the window to see who was there and quickly opened the door.

"Julia, Anita's here. We've been worried sick about you and James! Where have you been?" And Mrs. McKenzie looked around and asked, "And just where is James?"

"That's just it - James is gone! We have to get some help to try and find him. He disappeared! You've got to help me!" Julia rambled on between desperate sobs.

"Whoa. Slow down, Julia. We can't follow what you are saying. What happened?"

"James - he's gone!" gasped Julia.

"Child, you have to calm down! We can't help you unless we can understand what happened!"

"We found a beautiful cave up on the mountain. It was James' and my secret hideout. It had so many cool and beautiful things. We used to visit it from time to time to explore it. This time was a disaster. James was reaching for something near a dry well hole in the center of the cave. He slipped and fell. At first, it looked like he would fall all the way to the bottom of the well, but as he was going down, all of a sudden something pulled him up toward the cave's ceiling and finally out of the cave through a hole in the ceiling. There was a glowing light surrounding him. It was amazing but so scary! And now, he's gone! We've got to find him. I need to know he's all right and find out what happened. We need to go now!"

"We have to let your parents know immediately! Anita, can you get them on the phone?"

"Yes, I'll call them right away! They should be coming home soon anyway."

Julia sat at the kitchen table sobbing. Misty sat by her and whimpered sadly. Julia looked around and saw Velvet in the corner with her puppies. The newborns managed to bring a momentary smile to her face. "They're so cute," Julia muttered through her tears.

"Julia, it's going to be alright. James could not have just disappeared. There must be some logical explanation for this. We'll find him!" Mrs. McKenzie said hopefully as she hugged her.

Anita broke in, "The Wyatts are on their way back. We should meet them at home. Let's go, Julia. Come on, Misty."

"Wait!" protested Julia. With that, she went over to Velvet and looked at the puppies. She gently picked up the runt of the litter. Its eyes were closed and its head was wobbly and bobbed from side to side.

"This little one was James' favorite. He told me while we were walking to the mountain. I want to give it a name. James loves space. Can we call it Comet?" Julia hugged the puppy tightly and then placed it back to lie down with Velvet and his brothers and sisters.

"Comet it is," Mrs. McKenzie replied with a weak smile.

Anita, Julia and Misty then headed out the door to return to Julia's house to await George and Jenifer's arrival. Mrs. McKenzie followed them and gave Julia one last hug.

"It's going to be alright. You can come back and see Comet and the other puppies anytime. We'll find out what happened to your brother. We'll find him."

Filled with more hope than confidence, Mrs. McKenzie closed the door pained with worry and lost in thought. As she gazed out the window, she tried to suppress the memory of losing her own son, which this terrible incident had stirred. Yet, somehow she remained optimistic that this situation was different and that one day James would indeed see his family again.

24

THE SEARCH

Julia and Anita were sitting together on the living room couch when George and Jenifer stormed into the house in a panic. Julia rushed over to them and gave them a big hug. Misty followed whimpering.

"What happened? What exactly is going on? Where's James?" Jenifer cried.

"Don't tell me he's run off again after all the warnings he's gotten," George blustered.

"Mom, Dad, it's a lot more serious than that. James is gone," Julia sobbed.

"What do you mean gone? How? Where?" asked George.

"As I told Mrs. McKenzie, James and I found a secret cave, which we named The Sapphire Prism Cave. It's part way up the mountain just beyond the woods behind Mrs. McKenzie's house. We were over there, watching Velvet's puppies being born. We had to leave Misty outside. After awhile she got restless and James and I took her for a walk. We hadn't been to the cave for a while so we went there. We were walking through different parts of the cave when we came to this incredible cavern with a waterfall and a dry well hole in the center. There was also a hole in the cave's ceiling where light shone in.

"I told him not to, but James jumped onto a lower rim surrounding the well. As he was grabbing for something, he slipped and started falling into the well. Then suddenly a bright beam of light appeared and seemed to surround him and pull him upward and out of the cave through the ceiling hole. As he was being pulled upward, he shouted out to me that he couldn't stop it. And then, he was quiet and just disappeared. The last I saw of him, he was pulled out of the cave surrounded by the glowing light and up to the sky."

"Are you sure about this, Julia? Why didn't you ever tell us about the cave before? You two should know better than to play in a dark, scary cave," George scolded.

"It wasn't dark or scary until this happened," protested Julia.

"We have to call the police and my company," said George nervously.

George quickly made a number of calls to the local police department. Within a few hours several search teams were organized and showed up at the Wyatts' house. Julia gave them a full briefing as to what had happened. The police captain was clearly skeptical of Julia's story.

"Julia, I realize you are upset right now, but are you sure you saw your brother being *lifted* through the cave's ceiling?"

"I know it sounds crazy, but that's what I saw."

"Can you take us to the cave? We'll start from there and fan out through the woods."

"Yes, I can take you there."

Julia, her parents, Misty and the search team made their way to the cave. The police brought lanterns and flashlights. With the large crowd, searchlights, cables and equipment, the beautiful Sapphire Prism Cave lost much of its glow and magic. It had seemed so inviting and cozy when James and Julia explored it alone, but with the search team crowd it looked more like a plain rock cave.

"Julia, can you lead us to the chamber cavern where James disappeared?"

"I think so, with Misty's help," answered Julia.

Misty led the way. She sniffed the ground and the cave walls as she retraced the route which she, Julia and James had taken. Finally, they arrived at the cavern and everyone looked up at the ceiling hole. The sound of water from the waterfall had a calming effect. The searchers looked down the dry well hole. They wasted no time and quickly set up a line to lower themselves down into the well.

"We've got to run down all possibilities. We know you said you saw your brother being lifted out of the cave ceiling hole but we have to be sure. Jed and Bruce, you guys should check out the dry well hole."

Jed and Bruce put on harnesses and lowered themselves into the well. They brought radio transmitters and powerful flashlights with them. Strangely, the well widened as they descended. After about 30 minutes of lowering themselves, they shone their flashlights to the bottom of the dry well hole and along its sides. They closely scoured the well hoping to find some evidence regarding James' disappearance as they continued their descent, but found nothing. After about an hour, they returned to the cave's floor surface.

"We tried very hard, but unfortunately found nothing. There's no trace of him ever being down there."

"Let's check the cave ceiling hole."

Using a system of collapsible ladders, the search team assembled a skeletal rig so that they could climb up and reach the ceiling hole. Jed ascended and took a careful look. The hole was nearly circular though its edges were a little rough. He looked out and saw the open sky. Darkness was fast approaching and stars had begun to emerge. Jed was about to give up and head back down when he spotted something. It wasn't much to go on, but he saw some strands of blond hair stuck to a crevice in the back portion of the hole. Using a pair of gloves, he gently pulled them off the rocks and stored them in a plastic bag.

"I don't know if it means anything but I did find some hair caught on the rocks. We'll have to run some lab tests to make certain it's James'. Julia, is there anything else you want to tell us? Any other clues you might be able to give us?"

"No, unfortunately not. I think that's it."

"We'll send our search teams out to the surrounding woods just to check the area and be sure there is no other trace of him."

After the cave had been explored, the Wyatts returned home to await the results of the search team's findings. Three hours passed and finally they heard the doorbell ring. It was Captain O'Leary, the head of the search operation.

"We are sorry. We searched the woods and spoke with your neighbor, Mrs. McKenzie. We found no more signs of James. His disappearance is a true mystery. If he really did disappear through the cave ceiling hole, we are not sure where he went or how he got up there. We sent the hair samples out to confirm it's James' hair. If it happened as your daughter said, we just don't know why or how."

Captain O'Leary and his assistants said goodbye and left. The Wyatts' house felt very empty and quiet without James. Sadness and despair replaced the happy, carefree mood that prevailed before James had disappeared.

"I only hope this is one of James' tricks and he will reappear. But this time, I feel it's different. I'm really worried," said George. "Really, worried," he repeated again softly to himself.

"Me too," sobbed Jenifer sadly.

With that, the family headed for bed and pulled a cover over what had clearly been a heartbreaking, harrowing day.

25

THROUGH THE UNIVERSE

James had been knocked unconscious when he was mysteriously pulled from the cave, but hours later he groggily came to. His head throbbed a bit, but otherwise he seemed to be okay. The bright light continued to engulf him as he soared upward through space on an incredible new journey. The light acted as a transparent shield and protected him on his voyage. He looked around and saw lights, stars, planets and galaxies all whirring by him in a swirl against a dark black sky. James spotted incredible comets as he soared by planets. *So cool!* he marveled. James felt as if he was traveling through space and time as he continued his upward flight, unknowingly being sucked through a giant wormhole space vortex. He felt a combination of fear, excitement and awe. This was indeed his ultimate journey to date! He tried to get a fix on the stars and galaxies he was sailing through but everything was moving much too fast. He could not stop or control his journey so he just absorbed everything he was witnessing. James had no idea where he was heading but the journey was indeed awesome!

26

A LIGHT IN THE DARK

Julia lay in bed, wide-awake before the music alarm went off. When it finally sounded, she hit the snooze button but did not get up. She felt too sad and depressed. After about fifteen minutes, her father stopped by her room to say good morning. He saw her lying in bed staring at the ceiling. He sat down at the edge of her bed and gave her a hug and stroked her head.

"I miss James so much, Dad. I can't move. I can't go to school today. I need some time."

"I know how you feel. It's been devastating for all of us. I'll talk to your mother."

George conferred with Jenifer and they agreed to give Julia a few days to get over the initial trauma of James' disappearance. They did not, however, want her to stay home too long and dwell on the situation. They felt she should return to school as soon as possible so that she would keep busy and be with her friends for support.

Misty lay on the carpet in Julia's room, snuggling and licking Julia from time to time to comfort her. After a few hours, she got up and ambled into James' room and looked around. The room was so quiet and empty. Misty clearly understood what had happened and was every bit as sad as the rest of the family.

Julia and her mother spent the day together talking and reminiscing about fun times they had shared with James. Jenifer made Julia promise never to visit the cave again and Julia reluctantly agreed. George checked in from the office to see how Jenifer and Julia were doing. It was hard to lift the sense of doom they all felt.

Word of James' mysterious disappearance quickly made its way around the neighborhood and through Julia's school. Slowly friends and family started calling in. Jenifer fielded the calls and thanked everyone for their expressions of concern. Julia didn't want to talk. She was not ready to face her friends and answer their questions. Her heart and thoughts were with James. Julia remained so melancholy that her parents thought it best that she remain home for a second day.

George got home late that night. Jenifer and Julia waited for him and they all had dinner together. They sat around the kitchen table feeling lost making small talk. As Jenifer got up to clear the kitchen table she glanced outside.

"Hey, George, Julia, look outside. There are lights everywhere."

Sure enough Julia peered out the kitchen and then the dining room windows. She saw hundreds of small lights flickering in the darkness.

"Wow, they're candles. There are hundreds of people out there holding candles. I see many of our friends from school. They are lighting up the whole yard."

George and Jenifer joined Julia and peered out into the yard. It was a beautiful sight. Suddenly a group of students drew together and then spread out and formed a heart shape. A second group drew together and spelled out "James."

Tears came to Julia's, George's and Jenifer's eyes. No one knew how to find or save James, but everyone knew that the Wyatts needed their love and support at this difficult time. They came by the droves, all holding simple candles throwing off a pure white light. The beautiful gesture did not bring James back, but it showed the Wyatts that hundreds of people loved and cared about them and, of course, James. The family went to the front door. They opened it and blew kisses and waved. Some of the many supporters came up and hugged the family. They thanked everyone for coming and for the beautiful gesture. It was a touching scene that brought them some comfort, if not total healing, for the pain they felt deep in their hearts. After an hour or so the crowd dispersed and the Wyatts headed to bed. They all slept a little more soundly though their ordeal had not ended.

The next day, Julia again pleaded to stay home. It was so unlike her. Julia had done so well at school and had a real love for learning. She generally looked forward to school. Once again, due to the seriousness of the situation, her parents agreed that Julia could stay home.

"Okay, Julia, just one more day. We know how bad you feel but we don't want you to fall behind in your studies. Besides, it will do you good to go to school and see your friends again. Look at how wonderful they were last night. We all need their support at a moment like this."

"Okay, Mom, just one more day. I think by tomorrow I'll be ready."

Julia and her mother spent another sad, quiet day at home. At about 1:00 p.m. the doorbell rang. Jenifer went to the front door to answer. Outside stood Mrs. McKenzie with a large platter of home-baked cookies.

"Hi. I thought you could use these. Cookies. Chocolate chip. I feel just terrible about what has happened. How is Julia doing?"

"Come in, Mary Ellen," coaxed Jenifer. "It so happens that Julia is here and could probably use a visit to cheer her up. Julia, please come to the living room. Mrs. McKenzie baked us some fabulous chocolate chip cookies."

Julia made her way to the living room and joined her mother and Mary Ellen McKenzie.

"Hello, Mrs. McKenzie. Thank you for coming over and for the cookies."

"Why don't we all sit down and I'll bring in some milk. We could use something sweet right now and I'm sure they will be delicious," said Jenifer.

The three sat together for a good hour talking and devouring the cookies and milk. Misty sat on the floor lifting her head from time to time and then dropping it down to the floor again.

"Mrs. McKenzie, I meant to ask, how are Velvet and her puppies doing?" inquired Julia.

"Overall very well but Comet still seems much smaller and weaker than all the others. They push him away whenever he tries to drink some of his mother's milk. You can visit any time you like. They are really cute."

"Well, today is the last day I'm taking off from school. Can I visit them now?"

"If it's alright with your mother it's alright with me," answered Mrs. McKenzie.

"Sure, it's fine. But Julia, you have to come right back home. No wandering off!"

"I'll walk her back," offered Mrs. McKenzie eager to have a visitor.

Mrs. McKenzie and Julia finished their milk and cookies and headed for the door. Jenifer once again thanked Mrs. McKenzie. Misty looked up and barked as if to plead that she wanted to come also.

Julia and Mrs. McKenzie laughed.

"Sure. You can come too, Misty. You just may have to stay outside or in the living room if Velvet is still as protective as she was before," Mrs. McKenzie stated.

Julia, Misty and Mrs. McKenzie arrived at Mrs. McKenzie's house and headed directly for the corner of the kitchen where Velvet and her six puppies lay. It was feeding time and all of the puppies except for Comet were drinking milk from Velvet.

Julia raced over to Velvet's side to look at the puppies. She saw that Comet was very still.

"Mrs. McKenzie. Mrs. McKenzie please come over here quickly. Look at Comet. He's not moving."

"Oh my gosh. Let me see. I thought he looked weak."

Sure enough Comet was quiet. He did not move. Mrs. McKenzie looked at him with tears in her eyes.

"I don't know, Julia. He might have passed away. He's not moving and doesn't appear to be breathing."

"No!" cried Julia. "It can't be. Let see him again."

Julia scooped up the little runt and cupped him in her hands. "Come on, boy. You can't leave us. You can't."

Julia focused her energies on the puppy, much like she had with her grandmother when she was in the hospital. Comet didn't move. Julia held him and wouldn't let go. She closed her eyes. "Come on, Comet. Come on." Still the little pup remained motionless. Julia was about to abandon hope and tears started dripping down her cheeks. She choked up and swallowed hard. Again she closed her eyes and passed her hand over Comet. All of a sudden the little dog stirred. He made a sucking motion with his mouth. Julia pushed two other puppies out of the way and put Comet on his mother so he could find her milk. Sure enough the little creature found his mother's nipple and began to suck hard.

"Look, Mrs. McKenzie! Look! Comet's alive! Comet's alive! Come take a look!"

A smile returned to Mrs. McKenzie's face. She and Julia spent an hour talking.

"I guess I should take you home and back to your mother before she gets worried," Mrs. McKenzie said.

"Okay. Just five more minutes."

"Sure, child. Sure."

Julia stroked Comet and made sure he was eating. Then she called Mrs. McKenzie.

"You know, I can feel it. I can sense it. James is alive. I know it. I don't know where he is but I know he is alive!"

"Bless you, Julia. I pray every day that James is alright and that you will find him."

"We will!" Julia stated firmly.

Julia and Mrs. McKenzie then returned to the Wyatts' house. Julia rejoined her mother, repeating to her the same belief about James that she had expressed to Mrs. McKenzie.

"Mom, I can't tell you where James is but I can tell you that he is well and alive. I feel it! You know how I found him and was right about where he was at Disneyland? I tell you that he is okay. We will see him again. I just know it!"

"I am glad you feel that way, Julia. I can only pray that you are right. Remember, tomorrow it's back to school."

The day ended and dinner was ready for George when he returned from work. Julia went to bed early in order to be rested for school. Her parents stopped by to tuck her in.

"We love you, Julia," Jenifer said.

"I love you and Dad too," Julia responded.

Before drifting off to sleep, Julia once again opened up her heart and let out her thoughts using words that belied her age so that both her parents could hear.

"Until James disappeared, I lived in a kind of bubble where every story had a happy ending and all princesses were rescued. After James disappeared, a part of my childhood innocence ended, but as I told you, I can sense that he is still alive though I cannot see or speak to him. For now, we can't play as we did - running through the fields, laughing and crying. Sharing candy and movies and our childhood. I can no longer read his thoughts-yet I feel he is still with me. There is a part of him that I can sense and I yearn for us to be able to send thoughts again. Although we are physically apart, his spirit and soul still feel so very close. That will never leave me. And somehow, I know as surely as I breathe, that we will see him again. Mark my words. He will return and we will all be reunited."

George and Jenifer looked at each other in wonder digesting Julia's words. They stayed with her until she drifted off to sleep. Julia slept soundly, firmly convinced that she was correct about seeing James again and that he was all right.

27

GALAXY CRUISER

James' journey through space surrounded by the glowing light continued at an incredible speed. Tiny blips of multicolored lights shot by him in a whirl. As he tried to remember how this adventure had begun, he suddenly realized that some parts of his memory had been affected and he couldn't fully remember his life on Earth. James also became restless and curious as to where this amazing journey would lead. Suddenly, far in the distance, he spotted what appeared to be a tiny spaceship. A glowing light trail, which he seemed to be following, led directly to the craft. James' mind wandered. Along with the spinning lights provided by the stars and galaxies he traveled through, he suddenly heard some incredible music that captivated his mind and inspired his imagination. It was as if James' spirit, the universe and life it self were an emotion expressed and captured in music and light. He was free. His mind and spirit soared and sailed throughout the galaxy.

The spaceship that had looked tiny from afar started growing larger and larger the nearer he got. As he pulled closer, he realized that it dwarfed even the enormous spaceship he had seen in the top-secret hangar at SPACETECK's corporate headquarters, though he did not remember that is where he saw it. It was the size of three football fields and was four stories high. Yet, despite its immense proportions, the spaceship was amazingly agile and maneuverable as it sailed weightlessly through space.

James saw that smaller craft left and entered the larger mother ship from a bottom bay and he noted that the path of his flight led directly to that bay. In fact, it seemed as if the giant spacecraft was "reeling" him in in order to swallow him.

James' incredible flight decelerated as he approached the vessel. The music subsided and the whirring lights slowed. He could sense that he was being drawn into the spaceship. The dream he had on Earth of one day boarding or flying a real spaceship was about to become a reality! James went with the flow. The light continued to engulf him. Ultimately, he passed through two giant bay doors, which slid open as he approached. He gently floated through the bay and finally settled, feet first, on a circular pedestal platform, which was quickly sealed with a clear glass cylindrical cover. The glass chamber he was in began to fill with oxygen. The glowing light, which had surrounded James during his incredible journey, subsided. Robot-controlled carts and vehicles crisscrossed the cargo bay. Finally, a forklift-type vehicle came and stuck two metal feet into the bottom of the pedestal on which James stood. He was moved from where he had landed to a large room in the interior of the spacecraft.

James was spellbound as he observed robots and droids moving about the craft. This being outer space, James wondered if he would encounter some alien-looking creatures. Instead, a human-looking figure appeared. He had wavy brown hair and wore glasses. He was thin with piercing green eyes. He looked like he could be a scientist or doctor. He waved to James in a friendly manner through the glass enclosure. He punched a button on a special device. It sent a scan up and down James' body gathering information. The attendant also entered information on an electronic tablet, which looked similar to an advanced generation iPad. The glass vessel lifted and James leapt off the pedestal doing an incredible flip in the air and landed perfectly on his feet on the floor. The man, wearing a scientist's white lab coat, spoke.

"Welcome, traveler," the man said extending his hand.

"Thank you! I've been on the most amazing journey."

"We know, we've tracked you since your travels began on Earth. You have traversed billions and billions of miles through space at speeds many times the speed of light through a giant wormhole space vortex which brought you to our galaxy."

"But what actually brought me here? How did I travel so far and fast?"

"The light glow. It protected you and served as your highway through space."

"But why? Why am I here?"

The man was silent for a moment and then said, "I have to conduct a few more tests on you and then I will bring you to the Captain in the command center. I am sure he will be able to answer all your questions. My name is Verne. Yours?"

"I don't quite remember. I think I hit my head and seem to have some partial memory loss."

"Are you sure you can't remember anything? Does 'James' sound familiar to you?"

"Yes! That's it! That's my name. Thank you for reminding me, Verne. I do remember some things, but they are a little jumbled right now."

Verne further examined James, checking his pulse and his heartbeat. Then he performed some more tests and scans. He noted the bump on James' head where he had hit himself exiting from the cave.

James, taking stock of himself, felt somehow older and wiser. His senses were heightened. He could see, hear and smell better than he ever could. His gymnastic abilities to leap and do somersaults seemed to have increased greatly. His mind, aside from the partial memory loss, was sharp. He felt stronger. It seemed that all of the abilities that the crystals had given him on Earth had somehow intensified. James felt strangely confident, almost supreme.

After Verne had finished his examination of James, he pressed a button on the tablet, which transferred the data he had accumulated to the spaceship's central computer system.

"Let's go. I will now bring you to Captain Jahl, the commander of this vessel known as 'The Galaxy Cruiser.'"

Verne and James boarded a small vehicle that hovered above the floor. It moved forward silently, self-navigating some twists and turns until it reached an elevator bank where it came to a stop. The two got out and Verne led James to a cylindrical, glass elevator, which they entered and headed to the top floor. The elevators opened directly into a large, oval command center surrounded by spacious windows made of a super hard, clear material, which looked like glass but was actually an element a thousand times harder than diamonds. Stars and a distant planet glittered in the distance. The view of space from the command center was awesome.

"Wow. This is so cool! It looks like we are suspended in the middle of space with amazing views of everything!" James exuded.

A team of about 20 crewmembers sat on a large control bridge from which they directed the spacecraft's operations. Captain Jahl, the ship's commander, his navigator, Vlexor, flight operations control operator, Dinitre and Jaselle, his laser beam operator, were at the center of the bridge on an elevated platform. Captain Jahl was very tall, easily standing over six feet, four inches, with jet-black hair down to his shoulders and a strong black beard. His forehead protruded and he had a sharp, angular jaw. He looked tough, weathered and muscular. He did not look up at James and Verne as they approached. His eyes instead were fixed on a screen tracking a spacecraft.

"Vlexor, give me the coordinates of that vessel. It shadows us but stays just outside our firing range," observed Jahl.

"I know, Commander. They are in star sector 71, quadrant 31, 17 degrees 15 minutes."

"Keep the force shields up until it leaves us."

With that last command, Jahl looked up and acknowledged James and Verne.

"Well, look what we have here? Welcome," smiled Jahl, looking directly at James. "What can you tell me about him, Verne?"

"As you know, Commander, we were harvesting some of the crystals from a cave on Earth. James and his sister were in the cave at the time. James became caught in our force beam and was transported through the wormhole space vortex and through many galaxies to our ship. We tracked his ascent through the cave and through space. The beam protected him on his journey. Scans tell us that he hit his head on the way out of the cave and that he has some partial memory loss. His intelligence, strength, and athletic abilities though are truly exceptional for his age. We believe it's in part due to his exposure to the crystals."

"Why am I here and where am I going?" queried James.

"As Verne said, you were brought here because you got caught up in our special beam which was harvesting the crystals. Do you realize that each color crystal has overlapping but different qualities and abilities?"

"Now that you mention it, I do remember there were different color crystals, but I am not sure what qualities each one gave. What do you use the crystals for?"

"That is a secret, at least for now. Let's just say that they give one certain powers and abilities."

Just then there was a large explosion, which shook The Galaxy Cruiser up and down and from side to side.

"Henderson, return fire!" Jahl barked at his laser shotgun commander. "Come on. Fire! You have to work fast. The Sytheon attack ship will disappear."

"Wow! What's going on?" yelled James, excited and fearful at the same time.

"Don't worry. We have the shields up and they'll hold. The Sytheons are testing our defenses."

Henderson lit up the sky as he set off red laser beam blasts trying to hit the Sytheon craft circling The Galaxy Cruiser. Most of the Sytheon attack craft hung back but one ship headed straight for The Galaxy Cruiser. It plowed forward on what seemed like a suicide mission. It accelerated and Henderson wanted to fire as soon as it was in range but Jahl held up his hand signaling for him to wait. Henderson held his fire.

"Now, Commander?" Henderson asked impatiently a few seconds later.

"No. I'll give you the order. I want to blow this craft to smithereens! We'll wait till it's up really close."

Time seemed to be running out.

"Don't worry, we have the shields up in any case."

Finally, at the last possible moment, Jahl dropped his hand and screamed, "Fire!"

There was a laser burst and then a large explosion as the laser beam completely destroyed the Sytheon craft.

"Direct hit!" shouted Henderson. "Spacecraft destroyed."

"Any life forms aboard?"

"No, Commander. It seems to have been a drone craft."

"They are testing our defenses. I feel it. I know it."

"The Sytheon craft all seem to be turning away from us. Their mission, at least for now, seems to be over."

"Keep an eye on them, Henderson. Let's make sure they don't have any surprises up their sleeves."

"Now, Verne. Let's start again. As you were saying, James has indeed traveled a long way."

James stared out the giant clear windows at the twinkling heavens, half-listening as Verne briefed Commander Jahl. Though a bit startled by the Sytheon attacks, James remained amazed and curious about all he had seen on his exciting journey to date.

"Where are we going? How long will we be up in this space ship?" blurted out James.

"We are from the planet Carmesí - 'The Crimson Planet.' It derives its name from the crimson glow the planet emits when viewed through space from a distance. Some particles in Carmesí's atmosphere create this effect. Once we are nearer, we will transport you to the planet's surface by shuttle from The Galaxy Cruiser. It's not visible quite yet, but you will recognize it when you see it. It will come into view in a few hours."

"Wow. I can't wait," exuded James.

"You will meet with the supreme ruler of Carmesí, King Thor. We have briefed him on you and your journey from Earth. He has expressed an interest in speaking with you."

"I look forward to it!" James exclaimed as he continued to survey the spacecraft and the view of space from the command deck.

James, Captain Jahl and Verne continued their conversation. James was fascinated and peppered them with questions. Captain Jahl and Verne did their best to answer as many as they could. They informed James that a shuttlecraft was being readied to take him to Carmesí so he could meet King Thor and that he would be leaving in approximately three hours when the planet came into view. While he was waiting, James continued to explore the spacecraft and learn as much he could about it and the planet he was going to prior to his departure.

28

BACK TO THE MUNDANE

Julia finally returned to school after a few days off. She knew her parents were right to get her to try and get back into the swing of things. She realized that dwelling on James' disappearance would only make her sadder and that she needed her friends and school to get her mind off his disappearance. When she arrived at school, a large number of her classmates saw her and surrounded her.

"Hi, Julia. Welcome back! We missed you!" someone called out.

"Yes, we did. Any news about James?" called out another.

Stephanie ran over and gave her a big hug. A host of other friends followed suit. Julia felt overwhelmed. At first she thought about James and how much she missed him and tears came to her eyes. Then she focused on the warm welcome her friends were giving her. That gave her some comfort and she had a feeling, again, that things would somehow be alright.

When Julia got to her classroom, Ms. Porter was there to give her a hug and a very warm welcome. She also told her that everyone had missed her. At lunch, all of Julia's friends fought to sit next to her.

After lunch, the day moved quickly to conclusion as Julia continued to receive a lot of support and encouragement. Before she knew it, the end of the day bell rang and Julia headed out the door to seek out her mother. Julia soon found her and they walked together over to the car.

"How was your day, Julia?" asked Jenifer tentatively.

"It was alright, Mom. Everyone was really nice. It's just that..." Julia's voice trailed off.

"I know. You miss your brother and you can't get him out of your mind. I can't bear it either."

"Mom, I know he's alright. He has to be!" Julia repeated trying to convince herself as well as her mother.

"Well, let's get home. You can finish up your homework. Dad promised to be home early today."

Julia got home and went to her room. She sat down at her desk to begin her homework. She had a hard time focusing. Misty poked her nose through a crack in her door and wandered in. She turned, wagged her tail and seemed to call Julia to follow her.

"What's up, girl? I know you miss James too. We all do."

Misty barked and Julia got up to follow her. Misty led her to James' room. The first thing Julia saw was James' telescope pointing out toward the heavens. Julia ran over to it and looked longingly out into space. Boy, did she miss James. She looked around the empty room and at James' space posters. She felt like she wanted to smile and cry at the same time. She remembered how she and James used to play and the adventures they had shared, especially discovering The Sapphire Prism Cave. Suddenly she remembered James' sapphire crystals. She found them again in the wooden box in his dresser drawer and decided to bring them into her room for safekeeping. Besides, she reasoned, she needed them to help her read the tablets.

After her short diversion, Julia returned to her room and hid the sapphire crystals. Then she settled in to concentrate on her homework. When she was just about done, she heard the phone ring. Her mom answered and after a few moments called up to Julia.

"Julia, there's a girl named Katherine on the phone. She said she met you that day you visited Dad at the office."

"Oh, yes, she's really nice," Julia answered, as she ran to pick up the upstairs phone.

"Hi, Julia. It's Katherine. I am so sorry to hear the news about your brother."

"Thank you, Katherine. It's been really hard."

"Well I have some news you might be interested in. I overheard my Mom talking about this a few times. It seems that SPACETECK is involved in trying to figure out exactly what happened to your brother. They think there is a possibility he has been transported into outer space!"

"What? Are you serious? But where and how?"

"They don't know, but they are using the telescopes and relying on satellite photos to see if they can discover anything."

"Wow, that's incredible. I hope they can do something. So far the police haven't been able to find out much."

All of a sudden, Julia heard her mother calling.

"Julia, your father just got home. We'll be eating dinner in about five minutes. I just wanted to give you a head's up."

"Okay, Mom," Julia called back.

"Katherine, thank you so much for calling. That was my Mom. She said we're having dinner soon so I have to go, but thank you again for your concern and the information."

"No problem. Maybe we can have a play date one day," said Katherine.

"That would be great. I'll check with my mom and we'll set it up. Bye."

Julia hung up and headed downstairs to greet her father and sit down for dinner.

"Hi, Julia. How was the first day back at school honey?"

"It was tough but at least everyone was really nice."

"That's good. I know it's hard. We all miss James. Even at work everyone was asking me about him."

"Let's sit down," called out Jenifer.

The three all sat around the dinner table and reminisced about James. Finally, Julia asked her dad a question.

"Dad, I just got off of the phone with Katherine. You remember, I met her at SPACETECK the day that James and I visited."

"Yes, I know, and her mother works with me at SPACETECK."

"Well, she told me that she heard her mother talking on the phone and that SPACETECK is helping out looking for James. Is that true?"

"Yes, Julia. It is true but it's also highly confidential. Please don't tell any of your friends yet. We don't really know anything for sure and we don't understand what happened. But we are developing a theory. There is a lot to check out before we can be sure."

"Well, Dad, what's the theory? Please, I have to know. I won't tell anyone. I promise."

"Okay, Julia. We are not sure if this will lead anywhere, but we have a tentative theory. In space there is something called a wormhole space vortex. It's sort of like a giant black hole in space where time and distances can be bent. We are looking into the possibility that James was somehow pulled into space through a wormhole space vortex. We can't be sure that's what happened, but it's our best guess for now. We are checking out all our satellite pictures of Earth, anything to give us a clue. We've found and tracked a bright white beam of light to the cave that you and James were in that evening. It's possible that James was pulled into space through a wormhole vortex by that beam. We don't know how or why. We still have a lot of work to do. It could take years to find out where all the clues lead."

"Years?" gasped Jenifer sadly gazing at George.

"Dad, I want to be involved in the search for James. I'll do anything. I want to volunteer for any summer internship programs or part-time jobs SPACETECK offers. We have to find him."

"Alright, Julia. I'll keep my ears open, but you're still too young for any of those programs."

"Dad, you know I learn quickly. As soon as they let me, I want to be an intern."

"Okay. I'll see what we can do. For now, we have to see what SPACETECK, using all of its resources, can do to help us find James. Mr. Silver has thrown his weight behind this. If its possible to find out what happened and where James is, SPACETECK will do it. We will do it!" George vowed.

29

LEAVING THE CRUISER

James questioned Captain Jahl and Verne and any other crew-members who would listen trying to find out as much as he could about The Galaxy Cruiser.

"How were you able to get a spacecraft this big into space?" James asked incredulously.

"We had to send it into outer space in parts with rocket boosters. Once we had the core, we assembled the rest using the large pre-made sections which had been rocketed into space."

"How many men on board?"

"About five hundred."

"Where do you get your food from?"

"Some of it we grow in dome-covered mini gardens positioned atop The Galaxy Cruiser. They utilize the light sent off by the various stars we travel by."

"Wow, you really have a lot of questions. When you visit with His Majesty, King Thor, he will ask you questions. Please make your answers brief and to the point," Verne laughed.

As they were talking, a reddish glow appeared ahead on the horizon.

"What's that?" asked James.

"That is the glow given off by Carmesí. We are getting extremely close. I expect a visual of the planet very soon."

"Awesome. I'll keep an eye from this deck."

About thirty minutes went by. Finally, the reddish glow grew brighter.

"There it is. Carmesí straight ahead," pointed out Captain Jahl.

"What an incredible sight," exclaimed James.

"Well, James, the time has come. We have to get ready to board the shuttle spacecraft that will take us to the planet's surface," advised Verne.

"I'm ready. Let's go," James proclaimed enthusiastically. "Thank you, Commander Jahl for your hospitality."

A small crew of five, James and Verne met in the room just outside the bay where the shuttlecrafts were kept. Bots made sure that the shuttlecraft was ready for departure and fully stocked with fuel and supplies.

The shuttlecrafts were armed, but not heavily. They had force shields but they were not strong enough to withstand a direct attack by enemy craft shooting their strongest laser blasts. However they did have several important features that could aid them in the event of difficulties. The shuttles were small and highly maneuverable. They were able to turn at extremely sharp angles, very quickly. And they had one more secret weapon - they were able to make themselves invisible, both to the naked eye and to tracking systems. After the preparations were complete, the crew, Verne and James boarded the craft. It slowly pulled out of The Galaxy Cruiser bay and headed for The Crimson Planet.

"The trip should take about five hours," Verne informed James.

James, ever curious, took in the stars and planets of this distant galaxy through a small clear dome on the shuttle's rooftop.

As they made their way to Carmesí, James spotted an asteroid belt and excitedly pointed it out to Verne.

"We have to be careful when we maneuver through these," Verne pointed out.

In the distance, James noted a large spacecraft rapidly approaching.

"Hey, what's that?" he yelled.

The pilot of the shuttle, Stormer, took a look and shouted, "It's a Sytheon attack craft, a Gildonaire! Take evasive actions. Head toward the asteroid belt! Evoke invisibility mode."

With that, the space shuttle craft took a sharp left bank and headed directly into the asteroid belt. It then disappeared from sight.

"I hope that we'll lose them by becoming invisible. Also, the asteroid belt will provide some protection. A large ship is unlikely to risk flying through the belt and getting hit. The shuttle we're in is much smaller and easier to maneuver."

"Captain, they are still coming straight for us!"

"It can't be. We are in invisibility mode so they shouldn't be able to see or track us. Also we're in the belt. They would be crazy to follow us here."

Still the Sytheon craft hurtled toward them at full speed.

Finally, it shot by them, just outside the asteroid belt where the shuttle had taken sanctuary.

"That was close. We must not be their target," observed Captain Stormer.

Sure enough the Gildonaire continued hurtling through space at breakneck speed. It focused on a supply craft heading for The Galaxy Cruiser. With several bursts from The Gildonaire's laser guns, the supply craft exploded in flames. The Gildonaire then took a victory lap around its prey.

Though shocked by the violent explosions resulting from the The Gildonaire's destruction of the supply craft, James, Verne, Captain Stormer and the rest of the crew were relieved to have seemingly escaped its wrath. They continued their trip to Carmesí, eventually leaving the asteroid belt but remaining in stealth mode.

James remained in awe of all he was witnessing and his experience in space, but he grew uncharacteristically quiet as the journey progressed. He looked out into the heavens and at the twinkling stars above and noticed that the craft was fast approaching The Crimson Planet. Despite all the fun and excitement that he was experiencing, there was something missing. He felt a void as he tried to remember his life on Earth. Though he tried his best, he was unable to recall much. He knew he must have a family and friends on Earth, but no matter how hard he tried to remember them, he could not. Frustrated, he remained quiet, lost in thought.

"Hey, James. What happened? You were so talkative before. You've been pretty quiet. What's going on?" asked Verne.

"It's nothing, it's just..."

"What?"

"It's just that I can't remember things about my life on Earth. It feels like something is missing."

"You are here now. Now is what matters. You should look forward to meeting King Thor. He is a wise and compassionate ruler. And just wait until you see Carmesí. You will love it."

"You're right, of course. This is the most exciting thing I've seen or done," answered James, snapping out of his momentary introspective mood.

"Now, James, take a look dead ahead. Carmesí is only 45 minutes away. We'll be getting ready to land shortly."

30

PALACE OF DREAMS

When the Crimson Planet was finally only a few minutes away, the crew of the shuttle prepared for landing. As the craft banked to come in for touchdown, it became clear it would land on a private runway adjacent to a sapphire-colored palace.

"James, you see that large bluish palace on the elevated plateau over looking the capital, City of Pearl? That is where we are heading. Thor has approved our landing on his private airfield adjacent to the palace known as 'The Palace of Dreams.' It is a magnificent structure situated on over five hundred acres of beautifully landscaped grounds with a lake and large flowing fountains throughout."

The Palace of Dreams glistened in the early morning sunlight. Its sapphire blue color contrasted sharply with the reddish glow of The Crimson Planet. Assistants who worked in the palace met the shuttle. James and Verne were whisked away by transport vehicles, which hovered in the air about two feet above the ground. James craned his head to look at the grounds and the city below.

Once at the palace, James was shown to a private bedroom. His quarters were very spacious with a king-size bed centered in the middle. The floors were white marble partially covered by beautiful multicolored rugs. There was also a large balcony, which afforded an incredible view of the city. James bounced on the bed and noted it was comfortably firm. He should have been tired after his long journey, but the adrenalin rush from all the excitement kept him up and alert. He jumped off the bed and ran over to the balcony to take in the view.

While admiring the sights and his new room, he heard a knock at his door. He ran over and opened it. Verne stood there with a slim, handsome boy with long straight black hair and delicate facial features who appeared a few years older than James.

"Hello, James. This is Indra. He works in the palace and has been assigned to show you around and get you acquainted with the palace facilities."

"Hello," said James stretching out his hand towards Indra. "Good to meet you."

"Thank you, James. Good to meet you too."

"I think you'll be fine with Indra. I will leave you now in his hands and meet you back here at 4:00 p.m. Then it will be time for you to meet with His Majesty, King Thor."

"Okay, Verne. Thank you. I'm very much looking forward to my meeting with King Thor."

"If you are ready James, we can begin our tour now," said Indra.

With that, the boys headed downstairs to the ground floor.

"The palace has several wings. The southwest wing overlooking the City of Pearl is where the King resides. It is strictly off-limits to anyone but his family and inner circle of advisors. Over here is the grand ballroom. This is where the King hosts balls, plays and concerts."

Walking further along, Indra pointed out the royal dining hall and a large living room. There were huge flat-screen televisions on the walls and something that looked like a small stage.

"This is a hologram video staging area where videos can be viewed in full 3D," said Indra. "Come on, let's go outside. I want to show you the palace grounds."

Once outside, James admired the beautiful flowers lining all the walkways. There were species and colors he had never seen before. There were purple heart-shaped flowers with pink spots on them. There were also tubular yellow and brown colored flowers and blue ones with a reddish, pink swirl. As they continued walking along the path further into the palace grounds, a flock of pure white, circular disks about the size of a dessert plate flew overhead.

"Hey, Indra, what are they?" James asked excitedly.

"They are Oeras, white saucer-like animals that can fly like a frisbee. If you listen closely you can hear the amazing ethereal music they create when they fly. They have the ability to transform from gaseous, to liquid to solid states. If they fragment they have the ability to regenerate. It's almost as if they are spirits. They usually fly in flocks so you rarely see one alone. They are harmless. They exude a protective force of good."

"Why have they stopped flying forward? Why are they hovering overhead?" asked James.

"They usually congregate over someone or something they sense is worthy. They must sense that about you, James."

"Wow, that's amazing."

"Come on. Let me show you to the stables."

"Stables? You have horses here on Carmesí?"

"No. We have something we call Equiphins."

"What are they?"

"Come on. I'll show you."

James and Indra made their way to the royal stables. Indra opened a large wooden door leading to the indoor stalls where the creatures were kept. As James entered he let out a gasp. The Equiphins were tall and muscled. They had the head and front of a horse with a tail of a dolphin. But the most amazing thing was that they were suspended in the air, almost hovering above the ground.

"Equiphins are amazing creatures. They have the ability to "swim" or fly through the air much like a dolphin on Earth swims through the water. They are an incredible way to get around."

"This one here is called Icarus. He is very high-spirited and fast," said Indra.

"Can I pet him?" asked James. James looked the beast straight in his eyes as he pet the Equiphin's neck and mane. As James did so, Icarus let off a low, satisfied nelly.

"That's it, Icarus. Good to meet you," coaxed James gently as Icarus slowly lifted his head.

Icarus remained calm even as James drew nearer. James held the beast's halter and brought it out of its stall and brushed its mane. Its dolphin-like tail gently swayed in the air. The horse part of the Equiphin was a rich tannish brown. The dolphin tail portion was dark, reddish brown. Its mane was a beautiful, deep shiny black.

Indra took out a bridle, reins and a saddle. Icarus bristled briefly when he saw Indra bringing those items toward him. Again James was able to calm him down.

"You will need training on how to ride him, but today I want you to see how to put on his saddle and reins," explained Indra.

"Okay," said James as he watched Indra put them on.

James continued gazing at Icarus' large brown eyes. He sensed the animal would accept him. Then, with a single leap, James jumped on its back and settled into the saddle.

"Hey," shouted Indra, surprised by James' leap. "You need some training before you can ride an Equiphin. It can be really dangerous if you don't know what you're doing!"

"Really, Indra, I've got this. Don't worry," said James confidently.

James started slowly, spurring Icarus to leave the stable. Then he had Icarus take a few laps at a slow speed around the stable grounds. Indra watched in wonder. He saw that James seemed to have a connection with the animal and had seemingly mastered riding the beast in a few minutes rather than the weeks of training he had initially thought would be necessary.

"James, you should know that an Equiphin can only fly 100 feet or so off the ground maximum. You should never take it higher than that."

James squeezed his knees to hold onto Icarus and experimented with how to make him go left and right, slower and faster and up and down. James correctly assumed that an Equiphin would go faster if he kicked it on with his heels and slower if he pulled back on the reins. What he wasn't sure of was how to coax the beast to fly upward or back down. As he was taking Icarus around the stable grounds they came to a stone fence. Instinctively, James squeezed his knees and gave Icarus a kick with his heels. Sure enough, the animal sped up and sailed ten feet into the air and cleared the fence. Unlike a horse, however, the Equiphin was able to stay suspended in the air and moved forward swinging its tail back and forth. James soon realized that aside from the physical cues, he was able to control Icarus through mind suggestions, much as he had controlled the escaped tiger in the Central Park Zoo.

Indra continued to watch in amazement as James quickly and instinctively mastered the art of riding and controlling an Equiphin. After about 30 minutes, he gave up trying to caution James. Instead, he saddled up his own Equiphin, Tendra, and joined James out in a field.

"Since you seem to have mastered this so quickly, we might as well continue our tour of the palace grounds riding the Equiphins. Come on. Follow me," Indra said and clicked his heals urging his ride onward.

The sun was high in the sky as the two boys playfully continued their tour of the palace grounds. After a 15-minute ride, they came to a beautiful grove of fruit trees. The leaves of the rounded trees were emerald green. Hanging from their boughs were pear-shaped fruits. Some of them were crimson red and others sapphire blue. As the boys entered the grove, James took a deep breath and smelled the air. He detected a pleasant, fruity odor. He dismounted Icarus and walked close to one of the trees studying the fruit more closely.

"Hey, Indra, what's going on? I can actually taste the fruit on this tree but I haven't even eaten it," James excitedly proclaimed.

"That is a feature of these fruits known as Wastraws. You can actually taste them by looking at and smelling them."

"Well, I can tell they will be delicious. Sort of like a combination of watermelon, cantaloupe and various berries, depending on the color of the fruit."

"Right!" answered Indra.

"Can I try one?" asked James.

"Sure."

As James went to grab a fruit, Icarus whinnied.

"I get it. You want one too, huh, Icarus?" James laughed.

Icurus nodded his head. James then pulled four Wastraws off the tree. He handed two to Indra and gave one to Icarus. Everyone dug in. Icarus munched on the fruit, making a sloshy, crunchy sound as he savored the taste and juicy, crispy texture of the wonderfully flavored snack. James was blown away by the taste, which became even more intense when he actually ate the fruit.

After the boys and their rides had finished eating their Wastraws, Indra told James to follow him as he headed toward a lake contained on the palace grounds. Lake Lerna, as the lake was known, was filled with white lily pads. There were small creatures, known on Carmesí as Lilysaurs, that looked almost like miniature dinosaurs, sunning themselves on the lily pads. Indra dug his heels into his Equiphin and coaxed him to rise up and fly at a higher level. He charged the lake and, just when he hit the water's edge, he and Tendra rose higher into the air. James quickly followed, holding on tight to Icarus as he neared the lake. Just as Tendra had done, Icarus sailed up into the air. The Equiphins rose and bobbed up and down as they cruised ten feet above the lake.

"Why go around the lake when you can take a short cut?" hooted Indra as he and James soared forward.

Just when the two were about halfway across the lake, the waters below James churned and suddenly turned white. As

James was about to ask Indra what was happening, Indra cried out, "Watch out, turn up! Fly higher!"

James instinctively looked skyward, dug in his heels and used his mind to command Icarus upward. Just before Icarus reacted, a giant snakelike creature with two shark-like heads propelled its way out of the lake into the air, opening and snapping the jaws of both of its heads while lunging at James and Icarus. Its green and purple scales glistened in the sunlight.

"Wow, what the heck is that?" cried out James.

"A Hydrashark. Very dangerous!" shouted Indra.

"I can see that!" James hollered back. "Icarus, let's get out of here."

James and Icarus soared upward in a near vertical ascent to get out of harm's way.

"Don't worry. The Hydrashark can't fly and it can't live out of water. So as long as we are out of its range, we should be safe," advised Indra.

"That is one scary-looking creature."

"Yes, but as long as you are out of its grasp, you are safe."

"Remind me not to go swimming in this lake," laughed James.

"Come on, James. I want to show you the Timekeeper's Lookout on the hill adjoining the far end of the palace grounds. From the Lookout, you get an incredible view of the palace and the City of Pearl."

Indra and James finished riding across Lake Lerna and headed toward the Timekeeper's Lookout. The Lookout was a flattened landing high on the hill, which overlooked the palace and the City of Pearl beyond it. Incredible multicolored trees, which resembled ice sculptures cast in blends of red, purple, pink, crimson and sapphire, surrounded the landing. A small brook with a waterfall cascaded down the mountain. Its waters ended in a clear reflecting pool, much like the one he and Julia had found in The Sapphire Prism Cave. The boys and their Equiphin finally arrived at the Timekeeper's Lookout and dismounted. James took in the views of the city and palace grounds as Indra pointed out other sites and landmarks.

"And now for the coolest feature here," said Indra. "The reason this is called the Timekeeper's Lookout."

"Why?" asked James.

"You see this reflecting pool?"

"Yes," answered James.

"Well, this pool can act as a mirror reflecting who you are."

"So?" said James confused.

"Well, it can also show you who you were and, lastly, what you may become. It can show you things in the past, as well as glimpses of the future. The legend surrounding the Timekeeper's Lookout is that it serves as a perch, giving you a clear overview of what lays before and around you. It also contains the reflecting pool where you can see where you have been and think of where you should go in the future. Those who master its abilities can actually travel not only to different places but also through time."

"It sounds incredible and also impossible," laughed James.

"Nothing is impossible," replied Indra with a quiet, deliberate confidence. "Remember that, James, nothing."

James grew quiet and reflective as he could see that Indra was quite serious. James tried to absorb all of the amazing things he was observing and learning. He went to the reflecting pool and gazed into it. All he could see at first was the reflection of his face, which somehow looked slightly older and more mature than he last remembered it. James looked out at the City of Pearl and then, back at the reflecting pool. As he gazed into it, he saw what looked like a simplified version of the City of Pearl appear. As he looked on longer, he saw the city change as new buildings and roadways were built. James excitedly cried out.

"Indra, I saw something. It looked like the City of Pearl from many years ago. Then it changed. There were roads built. Buildings constructed. It was incredible."

Indra's mouth dropped. "James. That's amazing. What you saw is one of the first things someone who masters the Timekeeper's Lookouts secrets is able to do. You were able to see back in time and see a bit of how the City of Pearl has changed and developed. Something like that usually takes years of training and concentration, yet you mastered it in minutes."

James grew excited and looked deeper into the reflecting pool. This time he saw scattered images - a dog, a blond-haired girl and a crown. He could not place who or what they were, though they looked familiar. He tried to concentrate harder to determine what he was looking at, but Indra interrupted his concentration.

"James, I am afraid this is all the time we have up here for today. We should get back to the palace. It's about 3:00 and you are to meet with Thor at 4:00. Let's go."

"Okay," said James, his concentration broken, "but I want to come back."

James took one last glance at the reflecting pool and the City of Pearl. Then he and Indra remounted their respective Equiphins and headed back to the palace.

"Race you!" challenged James.

"You really need some more experience," countered Indra.

"Come on. I'm up to it."

"Okay, James, but not too fast."

"I'll be fine," answered James confidently. He dug in his heels and Icarus took off. Throwing caution to the wind, Indra joined in and the two boys raced back over the palace grounds.

"First one who reaches the palace square wins," challenged Indra.

"You're on," replied James.

Remarkably, James and Icarus jumped into the lead. As inexperienced as James was at riding an Equiphin, he was remarkably skilled. Indra tried to keep up, but it was clear it was going to be a one-sided race. James and Icarus arrived at the palace square three full minutes ahead of Indra.

James dismounted and looked around the square. It was beautiful with reddish and white columns surrounding it. A stunning flower garden bordered the edges. The square itself was made of crimson-colored cobblestones laid in a circular design that radiated outward from the center. In the middle of the square was a five-story structure fashioned out of shiny silver metal bars. It looked like a giant three-dimensional tic-tac-toe set with a metal stage suspended in the center. When Indra finally arrived, he saw that James was curiously eyeing the structure.

"Congratulations, James. You win. I really don't know how you are doing this. It usually takes months of practice to master riding an Equiphin."

"Thank you, Indra. What's this?" James asked turning his attention to the interesting metal structure in the square.

"That is a three-dimensional gymnastics frame stage. There will be skilled gymnastic performers here tonight along with a music and light show. They do dives, flips, spins and swings throughout the frame structure. It's pretty incredible. The King will watch from a balcony or terrace. You will probably be invited to watch it."

James eyed the structure. He looked at Indra and smiled. Suddenly, he took a leap and wrapped his hands around a bar. He pulled himself up over the bar with his arms. Then he leaned forward and spun around the bar. He let go and swung to another rung. Before long, James was spinning and flipping through the air, moving from bar to bar with the grace of an acrobat. He climbed to the top of the structure and dove for the ground, grabbing a bar at the last second before catapulting himself upward and spinning in the air. Again Indra was silent and spellbound as James performed an impromptu gymnastics show every bit as good as the one expected that night. Unbeknown to both boys, Thor peered out from a palace window and observed what was happening. Although Thor was a king and the ruler of The Crimson Planet, from what he had seen and learned of his visitor so far, he eagerly anticipated his meeting with James.

31

PREPARATIONS

When James was done with his show on the 3D gymnastics grid, Indra offered to take the Equiphins back to their stable so that James could return to his room and get ready for his meeting with Thor. Although James had come to love Icarus and wanted to take him back to the stable himself, he took Indra up on his offer so that he would have enough time to prepare. He patted Icarus on his forehead and said goodbye.

The room in which James was staying had closets that were well stocked with beautiful, luxurious clothing. Indra told him that he could use anything he found in the room. Remarkably, most of it looked like it would fit James.

James decided to take a steam shower. The walls of the shower were covered with beautiful, shiny stones and rocks. A hot, but relaxing, stream of water and steam was released as James showered and washed himself with a scrub brush. As the water and steam poured over James, he had a few moments to reflect on his incredible journey. Again he had an incredible sense of excitement and exhilaration from all the amazing things he was seeing and experiencing, but he also felt that something was missing. He tried to remember the beginning of his journey but still could not recall much. After fruitlessly meditating about it for several moments, he refocused on his upcoming meeting with Thor.

James left the shower and grabbed a soft, blue towel to dry off with. He looked through the clothes he found in the closet drawers. Finally, he came across a beautiful deep crimson red shirt and matched it with dark blue pants. He also put on a gold sash belt. He found a brush in his bathroom and brushed his hair. He had never met a King before, let alone the ruler of a planet, so he wanted to look his best. As James was putting the finishing touches on getting dressed and ready for the meeting, there was a sharp knock on his door. He opened it and found Verne standing there.

"King Thor is waiting for you. Let's go, James."

32

VIEWS FROM A TREE HOUSE

Julia gazed out her window, trying to concentrate on her homework. James had been gone for over four months but the passage of time had not made things any easier for Julia and her parents. A new school year had begun. Though no one ever came out and said it, people in town began to doubt that James would ever be found. Some harbored darker thoughts. Julia would simply not accept the notion that harm had come to her brother or that she would never see him again. In fact, she redoubled her efforts to find out more about what had happened to him. The search for James became a central focus and purpose in her life.

Julia also studied the tablets she had found in the cave whenever she found the time. She tried to understand their meaning and see if she could glean any useful information that would aid in her search from the writings. One day she came across a passage that interested her.

The waters that reflect your face hold deeper meaning below.
See the past, see the present

Reading the tablets stirred something in Julia, which tempted her back to The Sapphire Prism Cave. Though she had promised her mother that she would not go back on her own, Julia continued to feel drawn to do so. She justified a return to herself on the grounds that she was willing to do everything and anything to find James.

Finally, her desire and curiosity to return to the cave overwhelmed her. She went to her room and set up the green light tunnel, which led directly to the cave, just as she and James had done in the past. She promised herself that she would only go as far as the reflecting pool and decided she would not bring Misty with her. She also decided to bring her iPod touch in case she wanted to take a photo or video of anything she saw. She did bring a strong flashlight as a backup in case she encountered difficulty in making the flames from the walls appear to light her way. She locked the door to her room and turned on her radio, hoping the music would hide her absence. Her mom was on the phone and Misty was sleeping downstairs in the living room. Her father was still at work. Julia knew she would have to move quickly and keep track of her time. She did not want her mother to come looking and not find her in her room.

Once the green light tunnel appeared, Julia jumped in and walked a few feet. There she was, right in front of the cave. She turned on her flashlight just to be on the safe side, but was pleasantly surprised when the cool blue flames appeared to light her way. Julia thought about James as she pressed her way into the cave in search of the reflecting pool. Within minutes she found it and stopped. She gazed into the now-familiar waters with hope and fear. At first all she could see was the reflection of her face. As she gazed a bit longer she gasped. She saw a reenactment of what had happened when she and James had been there together last. The vision reconfirmed her belief that James had been pulled upward through the hole in the cave ceiling. After the scene went blank, she gazed into the waters hoping for signs as to what was happening in the present. Nothing appeared for a while. Suddenly, there were bright stars and flashes of light. The scene showed James bathed in a white light traveling through the heavens. Then it went blank. Julia was frustrated. She had seen scattered fragments of what James had gone through, but nothing concrete.

Finally, after a few minutes, Julia saw what appeared to be a crimson-colored planet. The scene on the planet was confused and quickly faded. Julia glanced at her watch and decided she had to get back to her room. If her mother came up and tried to come through the door, things could get sticky. Julia ran back through the now-familiar caverns of the cave to the entrance. She saw the green tunnel light and jumped out. She was back in her room. Things had gone well. Julia could hear her mother still on the phone. On the other hand, Misty was pawing at her door and let out a bark.

"Julia, Julia, why is Misty barking?" Jenifer called upstairs.

"It's okay, Mom. I've got her," Julia called back just in time.

Julia quickly hid the green crystals she had set up to create the light tunnel, opened her door and let Misty in. Misty looked around with her tail wagging. She could sense something had happened but she could not discover what it was so she just sniffed around and quickly settled down. Julia then buckled down and finished her homework. When she was done, she rose to go downstairs, but Misty got up and led her first to James' room.

Julia looked in and studied the telescope and space posters on James' bedroom wall. She suddenly had a brainstorm.

"Misty, I've got it! James always loved space. I want to set up a space club with some of my friends at school. I want to invite Katherine to join it. She would be perfect. I'll also ask Laurie, Stephanie and a few of my other friends. That way we can learn more about space and keep up the search for what happened to James. What do you think, Misty? I'll ask Mom and Dad. Come on, I'll take you for a walk in the backyard before dinner."

Julia and Misty ran downstairs and stopped into the kitchen. Jenifer was just winding up a second lengthy telephone call.

"Hi, Mom. Homework's done. I'm going to take Misty out for a short walk in the backyard."

"Okay, but remember, no running off. Dad will be home soon and we'll be having dinner together."

"Okay Mom. Come on, Misty."

Julia and Misty ran into the backyard. Julia threw a ball and Misty bounded off to retrieve it. As Julia walked further into the yard, she spotted the tree house she used to climb up into frequently with James. Remembering the fun she used to share with him, Julia grew a little sad and wistful and decided to climb up the ladder to the tree house. After Misty retrieved the ball, she raced to bring it back to Julia. When she saw Julia climbing the ladder she started barking and jumping into the air. Julia pressed upward until she reached the tree house. She looked around and admired the view, gazing at the woods and the mountain in the distance. Misty continued to bark. Julia then remembered a wonderful way that she and James had managed to get Misty into the tree house before.

Their father had built them a large open wooden box and attached it with metal chains to a rope, which could be pulled up to the tree house with a pulley. There was a handle, which could be turned to lift the box up to the tree house and thus bring things up without having to carry them. Misty could just about fit into it. Julia, using a trick she had picked up from James and from her powers obtained from the crystals in The Sapphire Prism Cave, used her thoughts to calm Misty and coax her into the box. Julia would not have ordinarily been able to lift Misty on her own, but through the leveraged pulley and handle system, she was able to pull her up to the tree house with a few quick turns. Misty jumped off the lift and ran over to Julia, playfully trying to lick her on the nose. Julia laughed.

"It's great to have some company up here. Come over here, Misty," said Julia bending down to hug her. Julia gave the play ship steering wheel a good turn and looked around. *If only James were here.* After about 20 minutes of playing with Misty, Julia heard her mother calling.

"Julia, come on in. Your father is home. It's time for dinner."

"Okay, Mom. I'll be right there."

"Come on, Misty. Let me lower you back down."

Misty complied and stepped into the wooden box. Julia lowered her back down to the ground and then climbed down the ladder. Then the two ran inside.

Julia washed up and joined her mother and father at the table.

"Hi, Dad. How are things at SPACETECK? Any news on their search for James?"

"Not much new information has come in since I told you about their theory as to what may have happened."

"How are you doing, Julia?"

"Better, Dad. Actually, I came up with two ideas that I wanted to tell you and Mom about."

"Just a minute, Julia. I'll be at the table in a moment," Jenifer called out.

Once Jenifer had served a dinner of grilled chicken, steamed broccoli and salad, she sat down and joined the conversation.

"So, Julia, what did you have on your mind?"

"I'd like to start a space club. There are about four or five friends I'd like to ask to join first. That way I could increase my knowledge about space while spending time with my friends and I could research more about James' situation. And don't forget Dad, that I'd still like to intern with SPACETECK when I'm old enough."

"That sounds like a splendid idea," her mom replied.

"Yes, Julia, it sounds good to me too," reiterated George.

"Okay. I'll ask my friends. At the beginning I'd like to have the meetings here in James' room. Will that be alright?"

"Sure, as long as you'll be careful."

"I will be, Mom."

"And what's the second thing?" asked her father.

"I heard that this is the first year we are going to be able to vote for and elect class officers."

"So?" asked Jenifer.

"Well, I'd like to run for President of my class!" said Julia.

"Wow! That's great, Julia. Are you sure you're up to all the extra work and responsibility?"

"Yes Dad, I need something to keep my mind off missing James so much."

"Okay then, I think you came up with two very good ideas."

"When does the election campaign begin?"

"In two weeks."

"Well, it should be fun and you'll learn a lot."

Julia looked forward to it. After some more small talk, Julia looked at her mom and dad and asked with tears in her eyes "Do you think we'll ever find James? Will he ever come back home?"

Her parents continued eating slowly without saying much. George tried to reassure Julia.

"You said yourself that you think he's okay. We'll find him. Somehow we'll find him," George blustered.

A tear trickled down Jenifer's cheek and she covered her face with her hands. Misty placed her head on the floor between her paws. The moon shown brightly in the sky as Julia gazed out the dining room window and into space. The Wyatts clearly missed James but were at a loss as to how to find or contact him.

33

THE KING AND THE PRINCESS

James and Verne walked briskly down the corridor leading to the room in which Thor was to meet James.

"Don't be nervous, James. Everything will be fine."

"I'm actually looking very much forward to the meeting. I've never met a king before," James replied enthusiastically.

James and Verne finally reached a sealed, bright red, double door. Verne ran his hand through a security hand scanner located off to the right side. The doors slid open, allowing the two to enter. The room was as long as a basketball court. The ceilings were four times as high as normal ceilings on Earth. There were windows and skylights, which let light in from all directions. There appeared to be no one in the room. James and Verne entered and approached a large table surrounded by wooden seats with armrests.

Just as they were about to sit down, there was a flash and white, odorless smoke formed. A large, circular platform seemed to appear out of nowhere and descended from above, slowly lowering itself to the ground, carrying Thor, his assistants and guards.

Thor was a commanding, muscular figure. He stood six and a half feet tall. He had piercing blue eyes, flowing white hair down to his shoulders and a handsomely chiseled face, worn from life's experiences. He wore gold armbands on both arms and a crimson robe with beautifully interwoven gold patterns and fringes. He was a smart, tough ruler with a kind heart. His crown was pure gold, sporting real sapphires and rubies fitted into the crown points. Thor had an authoritative voice, which carried throughout the room as he spoke.

"Hello, James, welcome to Carmesí!" Thor boomed. "I have been briefed about you and your long, long journey from Earth. I am impressed with your background, physical abilities and intelligence," Thor continued, not mincing words.

"Thank you, Your Majesty, very pleased to meet you," James replied politely. James looked at Thor and at first was at a loss for words. Then James noticed that Thor had some sapphire and red crystals hanging around his neck.

"Where did you get those?" asked James pointing at the crystals.

"The same cave on the planet Earth where we found you."

"Wow! What do they do?"

"You should know. They give one certain powers. You have some yourself, James."

"Your Majesty, one thing I should tell you is that I can't seem to remember certain things. Verne told me that I hit my head on the way out of the cave. As a result, I can't quite remember my life on Earth."

"You are in good hands with us here, James. Think of this as your home. I have made arrangements for you to live here in the palace. You will attend the Starflight Academy. It is our finest leadership and warrior training school reserved for the best and brightest. You will learn about our planet. You will learn how to think. You will learn how to fight. You will learn how to pilot and command the latest spacecraft. You will learn to believe in yourself and you will learn to never give up. You will learn about your strengths and weaknesses and you will learn to lead."

"That all sounds amazing. When can I start?" asked James enthusiastically.

"We will give you a few weeks to settle into your new home here. You've come a long way and there are some things you should learn before you enter the Academy. In addition, I would like you to accomplish three tasks. They are really challenges to demonstrate to me that you are worthy of the trust and benefits we will bestow on you.

First, you must climb and then descend Mount Serpentine, the highest mountain in the vicinity of the City of Pearl, by The Black Ice Toboggan Run. Then you must either capture or kill the Hydrashark which lives in Lake Lerna. And, finally, you must solve the labyrinth and decipher three riddles, which I will ask you. Indra will be available to advise, assist and accompany you on the tasks, but he cannot accomplish them for you. You must rely on your own intellect, abilities and cunning to complete the tasks."

"That second one is some task. Kill the Hydrashark? I saw it, with its two shark heads as I was crossing the lake with my Equiphin, Icarus. That is one scary creature."

"I have confidence in you, James. I know you will succeed. But first you will need a few days to get familiar with your new surroundings. We also have some celebrations planned at the palace."

Just as King Thor was about to continue, one of the most beautiful girls James had ever set his eyes on appeared. She had straight, raven black hair, which flowed to her waist, red cherry lips and emerald green eyes. She stood about five feet tall with a slender, graceful build. She looked as if she was 13 or 14. She entered through a door located at the back of the room. As she made her way towards the elevated stage on which Thor was sitting, she seemed to float. All eyes turned toward the unannounced visitor and Thor stopped talking.

James elbowed Verne, leaned over and whispered excitedly in his ear, "Who *is she*?"

Before Verne could answer, Thor got up and called out "Alisha, my daughter, what brings you here? Can I help you?"

James was silent as he watched the Princess walk over to her father. She gracefully ascended the platform on which Thor had entered the room on. After kissing her father on the cheek, she took a seat next to him. Thor then took the opportunity to make some introductions.

"Alisha, this is James, our new visitor."

"James, as you must have gathered by now, this is my daughter, Princess Alisha."

"Very pleased to meet you, Princess."

"Pleased to meet you as well, James," answered Alisha.

"Alisha, James has joined us from a very, very far away planet, Earth, situated in a distant galaxy. He has traveled many billions of miles through a wormhole space vortex. He possesses extraordinary powers and abilities. I asked him to stay here with us at the palace and attend the Starflight Academy and he has agreed. Haven't you, James?"

"Yes, your Majesty. I have."

"To start things off, I am inviting James to dine with us tonight in the royal dining room and afterwards to join us on the balcony to view some incredible gymnasts performing on the 3D cube in the palace square." Turning to James, King Thor continued, "And I know that you have some extraordinary gymnastic capabilities yourself, James."

James smiled modestly but did not reply immediately. James finally thought of a question.

"Your Majesty, is Alisha your only child?" James asked.

Now it was King Thor's time to grow quiet. He turned his back towards James and Verne and looked out a window. He became lost in thought for a few moments. The room grew sadly quiet. Finally, the King spoke.

"James, there is a bit of history you must know before I answer your question. You remember on your journey here, you first arrived and traveled for a while on The Galaxy Cruiser to get closer to Carmesí. While you were on it, there was a surprise attack by the Sytheons. The Sytheons in fact originated on

Carmesí. They claim that they were being mistreated here so they rose up and killed a great number of our citizens and escaped on three massive spacecraft. They broke away from The Crimson Planet over two thousand years ago and resettled on a planet they named Sytheus and built up a new civilization there. The problem was that as the centuries went by, they started using up their natural resources. They continued to wrongfully blame many of their problems on us. As they ran low on energy sources, supplies and building materials on their planet, they started looting other planets. They also attacked other spacecraft for their supplies. During these attacks, they took hostages to demand delivery of food, money, energy supplies, weapons, and spacecraft, anything they needed. In fact, Carmesí has been a constant target of their attacks and ill will. Generally our space patrol and planetary defenses have been strong enough to keep them at bay.

Unfortunately, there have also been some cunning surprise attacks which have managed to succeed. You see, one time, about seven years ago, we were celebrating the carnival of Zitree, a celebration of nature and peace, in the City of Pearl. My son, Hyacinthus, was twenty-one at the time. He had completed the Spaceflight Academy training months earlier. He was piloting a space patrol space fighter V-12 vessel guarding the airspace above the City of Pearl. Three Sytheon attack space vessels appeared out of nowhere over the city. Our defense patrol spacecraft were quickly sent to head them off and destroy them. Unfortunately, those crafts were diversionary vessels. A fleet of six, high-speed stealth space fighters appeared almost from nowhere. They destroyed the force that led the charge against the three diversionary craft. Although my son fought bravely and brilliantly, he was overwhelmed when three of the attack vessels turned on him. I never got to say goodbye to him. Make no mistake about it, the Sytheons are ruthless and heartless. We must be on constant guard against them."

"I'm sorry to hear about the loss of your son, Your Majesty. He must have been an incredible person and fighter."

"Yes, he was, James. And we miss him so. I see many of his characteristics in you," Thor admitted reflectively.

"I am honored that you would compare me to your own son."

"He would have succeeded me as king here on Carmesí, but now that will never be," Thor reflected wistfully. "Carmesí will need a strong ruler once I am gone."

"Gone? You look very well to me, Your Majesty. I am sure you will reign for many years to come."

"Yes, James, but my best years are behind me. Age creeps up silently behind you, suddenly appearing like a mugger from the shadows with a dagger at your back, asking 'what did you expect?' Time waits for no man."

"I have scientists looking into unraveling two of life's unsolved secrets. The first is finding an unlimited energy supply. The second is immortality. Both are probably pipedreams but our work is ongoing. We get encouraging results from time to time. The crystals in the cave where we found you are very rare. We use them to help power our advanced spaceships. We are also using them in our search for the 'fountain of youth,' the path to immortality. As we discussed, those crystals can also imbue one with certain powers and enhance one's natural abilities."

"That's amazing," responded James. "Do you know what powers they give?"

"Well, James, to a certain extent it depends on the person and the color of the crystals. We have not yet discovered all of the powers they can impart but we know that strength and athletic ability can be enhanced, telepathic powers, intelligence, curing powers, and other powers we are still discovering. James, since you were exposed to many crystals at close range, we will bring you to a special room in the palace where the crystals we have harvested are guarded. That way you will be able to spend some time in their presence so that you will be able to sustain and enhance the powers you have developed so far."

"Thank you, Your Majesty."

"James, you have met me and my daughter. I would like to also introduce you to Devlin, a close assistant. Sometime soon I want to introduce you to my nephew, Constantine, who is not here today. He is already enrolled in the Spaceflight Academy and will be able to help and guide you once you enter.

Remember, we will have dinner together at 7:00 p.m. The gymnastics show begins at 9:00. Tomorrow Indra will introduce you to your tasks in more detail and you will have two weeks to accomplish them. There will be a special ball the following Saturday evening. Shortly thereafter, if all goes as planned, you will be enrolled in the Academy."

"Thank you again, Your Majesty. I am so excited by how much there is to see and learn here. I would like to tell you more about Earth, but when I try to remember details about it and the people I must know, I just can't. I know I must have a father and mother, but I still can't remember them."

"James, perhaps in time you will. For now, let's focus on the present. Until 7:00."

"Yes, see you then. Goodbye Alisha, great to have met you."

"Yes, same here, James," answered Alisha.

Though James sensed that King Thor was a kind man, he felt uncomfortable that the King and Verne did not seem to want to address his loss of memory in more depth.

As James and Verne headed back to James' room, Verne pointed out other parts of the palace and they spent time talking. Before they knew it, it was 7:00 and time to meet the King, his family and assistants for dinner.

34

GYMNASTS

James and Verne entered the enormous dining room to which they had been summoned for supper. There was a large dinner table, centered in the room, which could seat 26 guests. As the doors to the adjacent kitchen opened an incredible scent of delicious, but unidentifiable foods permeated the air. The King, surrounded by his aides, conversed with some visitors. He waved when he saw James but continued talking to his guests. James glanced at King Thor and waved back, but his eyes settled on Alisha, who stood supremely alone in a white flowing dress. Her face was framed by long teardrop earrings cradling sapphire blue and emerald green jewels. Her long, black hair flowed loosely down her back. She wore golden slipper-style shoes with a ruby tip. As befitting a princess, she wore a beautiful crown of gold topped with rubies. As James approached her, he could smell a sweet fragrance wafting through the air. It was lilac-scented perfume, which made her all the more alluring. James felt slightly nervous as he approached her, but he was not shy. He wanted to talk with and get to know her better.

"Princess," James stated simply when he reached Alisha's side, "good to see you again. This palace is a remarkable place."

"Hello again, James" answered the princess smiling and blushing slightly.

"Your home, The Crimson Planet, is also so amazing. I have a lot to learn and explore. I've seen part of the palace grounds but there seems to be so much more. It's a bit overwhelming."

"Well, you'll need a guide," observed Alisha with a sly smile.

"Indra and Verne have tried to show me what they could so far."

"I can show you far more of the palace itself. I know it well," offered Alisha.

"Thank you, that would be great," replied James.

As Alisha and James continued talking, the room began to fill with people. Soon it was time to eat. A waiter entered the room and sounded a loud gong. Thor raised his voice above the din.

"Everyone please sit down. Dinner will be served shortly. James and Alisha, come and sit with me please."

James and Alisha made their way through the guests to Thor, who took his place at the head of the table. Alisha sat to his right and James sat to his left. Verne sat next to James. As everyone took their seats, Thor picked up a glass of ice cold Renoiris, a bubbly, non-alcoholic drink, that resembled champagne but was a rich, blue color and had a clean pear like taste. As he drank a sip from the thin, fluted glass he offered a toast.

"Tonight, we have a magnificent dinner and gymnastics show planned for you. Make yourselves at home. Welcome our musical trio consisting of Cleo, our harpist, Tang, our flutist and Remy, our classical guitar player. Last but not least, I would like to introduce you to a very special guest. James here has come from another galaxy, through a space vortex, traveling billions of miles on an incredible journey from the planet Earth. Please welcome him."

The room filled with curious, polite applause. The trio began to play some beautiful music, unlike any James could recall hearing before. It had a soft, but rhythmic lilt, with melodies, which for a time soared loudly and then lowered to mellow background music, allowing the guests to talk comfortably at dinner.

Waiters carrying covered plates and trays served dinner with great fanfare. Lobster cocktail was followed by a sherbet to cleanse the palate. Next came what looked a bit like steak with string beans and baby potatoes. A salad with red, green and purple lettuces, purple and sapphire colored heirloom tomatoes and cucumber was served with a pungent, sweet vinaigrette dressing. As the guests dined, Thor turned to James.

"I know you've only been here for a short while, but how are you enjoying your stay on Carmesí, James?"

"So far it's been incredible, Your Majesty, I learn something new everyday."

"Tomorrow you will commence the tasks I told you about. Do you think you are up to them?"

"Yes, Your Majesty, but they do sound challenging and pretty dangerous."

"You must rely on your abilities, instinct and wit. I am sure you will succeed. Indra will be with you to advise, assist and guide you, but, as we discussed before, you must actually accomplish each task on your own."

"I understand," said James confidently.

"You are lucky, James. You are young and have your whole life before you. You see, you only get two chances to experience childhood."

"Two?" interrupted James "I thought it was only one."

"The first is when you are actually a child living through that wonderful time- the fun, the laughter, the wonder, the joy, the discoveries, the adventure, innocence, the secrets and the dreams. You don't realize it now, but looking back, it goes so fast and it is gone in a flash. You are left with memories of times long gone by. And then, if you are very lucky, you have another chance to experience it from a different perspective. That is when you have children of your own through whom you can experience it again, with the wisdom, knowledge, perspective and appreciation which you lacked as a child."

"I never thought about it that way," commented James.

"You will understand one day."

Changing the course of the discussion, Thor asked Alisha, "How are you enjoying the meal? I really think it's outstanding. Wait until you taste the dessert. I ordered a special dark chocolate mousse filled with red, blue and green chocolate chunks containing toffee crunch all covered with a coffee syrup and glittering snowflake shaped sugarplums just for you."

"Thank you, Father. You know it's my favorite!"

The dinner and conversation continued until everyone had finished. Again Thor stood up and clinked his glass with a spoon to get his guest's attention.

"Everyone, please follow me to the terrace. As I mentioned, we have an outstanding evening of entertainment planned. I have requested that the finest gymnasts from all over Carmesí assemble here to present this show. Please turn your attention to the palace courtyard below."

The guests then filed outside. Three beautiful full moons of Carmesí lit up the dark night sky. Torches emitting beautiful red, deep blue, orange and yellow flames illuminated the palace courtyard. Ten young gymnasts, five men and five women, filed into the courtyard and stood near the three-dimensional cube. They waved to the King and his guests. James and Alisha sat on either side of Thor at the front of the terrace, which afforded them a spectacular view. The gymnasts warmed up, getting ready to perform. Lively background music with a strong rock beat filled the courtyard replacing the quieter dinner music. The gymnasts soared through the air, performing forward and backward flips, spins and cartwheels. Some juggled fire sticks. Others did flips through a ring of fire. Thor and his guests watched and applauded frequently as the gymnasts displayed their incredible talents. After a while, Thor leaned to James and said, "I saw you earlier, James. You have real talent. You should consider advanced classes when you are at the Starflight Academy. Do you want to go down and perform?"

"No, Your Majesty, but thank you."

"Oh, please, James. Please do!" begged Alisha.

"I really shouldn't," answered James again modestly.

"Why not? I'd really like to see you perform."

James couldn't resist Alisha's plea. He rose and, with a single leap, landed in the palace courtyard. King Thor waved to the gymnastics team and gave James a "thumbs up." The other gymnasts stood to the side. James muttered under his breath "Here goes nothing." With that, he jumped onto the 3D cube and performed a breathtaking ten-minute routine filled with twisting flips, cartwheels, round offs, dives and other advanced gymnastic moves. Thor and the visitors could not believe their eyes. James' natural abilities, bolstered by the powers he received from the crystals at The Sapphire Prism Cave, enabled him to perform with skills far surpassing what would have been normal for a boy of his age on either Earth or Carmesí. When he finally finished and landed straight on his feet in a perfect dismount, the crowd went wild, giving him a standing ovation. He looked up at the terrace and smiled at Alisha.

The gymnasts resumed their show and James rejoined Thor and Alisha.

"Well done!" bellowed Thor to James as he returned to his seat on the terrace.

The evening wrapped up with some fireworks over the courtyard. James and Alisha planned to meet the next morning for the in-depth palace tour, which Alisha had promised James. It was also agreed that after lunch James would meet with Indra and Verne to plan how he would accomplish the tasks. After the show ended, Thor made some small talk and thanked everyone for coming. Then he bid his guests "goodnight" and left the room. Alisha followed waving to James as she exited and called out, "Until tomorrow!"

35

THE PRINCESS LEADS THE WAY

James returned to his room and got ready for bed. After changing into his pajamas and washing up, he turned off the lights and threw himself onto the bed. He was exhausted from the long day's events, but his mind was racing and he couldn't sleep. He put his hands behind his head and gazed out through the window at the sparkling stars and Carmesí's three brightly lit moons. Everything felt like some incredible dream to him. He reflected on his long journey through space, his exploration of the palace of Dreams' grounds with Indra and Icarus, his meeting with King Thor and, of course, Alisha. It was all wondrous and exhilarating to James, yet something continued to gnaw at him. He missed some people and places from before his journey began on Earth, yet he could not remember who they were. He grew frustrated as he tried to recall them, but as before, nothing came to him. He tried to concentrate but his eyes fluttered and he yawned several times. After fighting to stay awake for a while, James finally fell into a deep sleep.

The following morning, James awoke early. He remembered that he was to meet Princess Alisha for a palace tour after breakfast. He was not sure where he supposed to get breakfast, but he got dressed. Just as he was finished, he heard a knock on his door. James opened it and a palace butler wheeled in a cart with a full breakfast.

"Good morning, James. I have your breakfast here - hot cocoa, waffles, bacon and a fresh fruit salad. The Princess will meet you in front of the door to the Crystal Ballroom at 9:00."

"Thank you," said James. "I'm sorry, but I don't know where that is."

"Don't worry, Verne will be by shortly to show you the way."

"Thank you again. I'll wait for him then."

James eagerly polished off the breakfast and waited for Verne, checking his clothes and combing his hair three times. He wanted to look just right for the Princess. Verne arrived at exactly 8:50 and the two walked over to the ballroom. The Princess was already there with two of her assistants.

"Good morning, Princess. So glad to see you again."

"Enjoy your tour of the palace with the Princess. Remember, this afternoon you will be meeting Indra again. He will give you an orientation with respect to your tasks."

"Okay. Thank you, Verne," James answered.

The Princess started with the ballroom, known as the Crystal Ballroom, which James had briefly seen with Indra. Next she took him to the palace kitchen. The kitchen had five chefs who greeted the Princess as she entered. There were eight large ovens, four preparation tables and six stoves. The kitchen was well stocked with all kinds of exotic foods. Delicious smells emanated from the ovens baking breads and cakes.

"Next, James, I want to show you the royal residence area. It is off grounds but I can point it out to you. My father and I live in the southwest wing."

"I should have asked this before, but where is your mother, Alisha?"

"It's a long story James. My mother passed away many years ago. I'd rather not talk about it right now."

"Of course. I am so sorry to hear that."

"And you, James. What about your family?"

"That's something I've been thinking about. You see, as I've told you, I can't remember many things about my life on Earth and my family is one of them. Maybe with time..." James' voice trailed off.

"Well, let's both focus on the palace," suggested Alisha.

"As I said, this is the wing where we live. The palace is built around the courtyard. The back opens up toward the flower gardens, the lake and the palace grounds. The front overlooks the City of Pearl below. On the first floor are the ballrooms and the dining room and kitchen. We have two living rooms in the palace. There is a central one where all the guests who stay at the palace can congregate on the first floor. We also have a smaller one in the royal section of the palace. Come on, I want to show you something special."

James happily followed Alisha, taking everything in. She took him to the ground floor and off to the side of the palace. They stepped through a glass door. Inside was a beautiful, emerald green, heated swimming pool completely enclosed in a huge glass dome the size of half a football stadium.

"Do you swim, James?" asked Alisha playfully.

"Yes, I love it."

"Well, this is the place. I'm a champion swimmer," added Alisha with a smile.

"We'll have to race someday!" challenged James.

"Sure, you've got it. Come on, there's more."

Adjacent to the swimming pool was a large playroom filled with all kinds of arcade and video type games. One big feature was that many of the games were three-dimensional and were controlled by movements of the player. Of course, James was enthralled and jumped in to spontaneously try a few of the games.

"I can tell you've done this before," laughed Alisha as she watched James play a few games with great skill and dexterity.

Next, Alisha showed James a giant "media room" and a bowling alley. The media room was filled with plush chairs. A movie was running in full 3D. In addition, to the three-dimensional visual effects there were smells, water sensations and movements affecting the chairs. The combination of features created a virtual reality. James and Alisha paused a few minutes to look in on a three-dimensional film enhanced with special effects.

Next Alisha took James to the second floor where she stopped in a large room filled with books.

"This is a library. Those dusty, paper volumes are mostly for show. They are antique books. All modern books are written and published on electronic tablets. That way we can store and access millions of books."

"This palace has everything!" James proclaimed.

"Now for a couple more special things I want to show you," said Alisha. Alisha led James down a dark hallway. She came to a stone panel in the wall. Using a special gesture, she put her hand up to the stone panel and pushed. It opened and James poked his head in.

"Secret passages in the palace walls. Great for shortcuts, hiding and making a getaway in times of need," quipped Alisha.

"Amazing."

"Of course, your palm print has to be programed into the security system before they will open. I used to play in these secret passageways with my brother. We used to disappear into them and pop out at unexpected places," said Alisha wistfully.

"Lastly, I want to take to you to the roof. There is a walled-in garden and a small sitting area. It has an incredible view of the City of Pearl."

Alisha led James up a stairway, which ended at a door, which in turn led to the roof. The palace rooftop was a glorious place, open to the skies above with a beautiful sitting area. James and Alisha wandered over and looked out at the City of Pearl. Alisha pointed out a few sites to James.

"Down there is the Fire, Wind and Thunder Stadium. Over there is the Hero's Arch. The city is laid out in concentric circles surrounding a giant park, The Shooting Star Park, at its center. Those floating vehicles are hover taxis, which whisk people around the city. You will see more when you actually visit."

"Can you take me some day?"

"I'll have to talk to my father about that. I'm sure he will make the necessary arrangements."

James and Alisha continued exploring the palace together with Alisha explaining as much as she could. Finally, it was lunchtime. Indra and Verne joined James and Alisha in the royal dining room. After lunch came to an end, James thanked the Princess for her hospitality in showing him around and bid her farewell. It was time for James to be briefed by Indra on the tasks he was to perform.

36

THE SWUN

Indra led the way and took James and Verne into a special room in the basement of the palace. It was filled with testing equipment, special apparatuses and weapons. The special equipment was held in a room sealed like a vault. Beyond that room were armed guards and another vault.

"What's in there, Indra?" asked James, pointing to the guarded vault.

"That is actually a top-secret room. It's where the special crystals harvested from around the universe are kept. Only Thor and those he specially chooses are allowed access. The crystals, as you know, James, contain the key to your special powers. Scientists also believe that they may contain the secret to immortality and to unlimited energy supplies, but they have not yet figured out how to harness them for those purposes just yet."

"James, I have to run some additional tests on you, similar to the ones we ran when you were aboard The Galaxy Cruiser. We want to establish a baseline for your condition and powers here on The Crimson Planet. With our advanced medical scans and testing equipment, it will only take a few minutes."

"Okay, Verne. Let's do it."

Verne hooked up some testing sensors and ran some scans. He fed the results into a computer and, after reviewing the results, picked up his wireless communicator and paged Thor. He stepped away to talk in private.

"Your Majesty. I just ran some tests on James. The results are quite amazing. When he left Earth he was eleven years old yet, now he seems to have developed so that he has the capabilities and intellect of a fourteen-year-old. All of his innate abilities and powers have significantly increased since he arrived on The Crimson Planet. He is much stronger, more intelligent and capable than we thought. It seems that The Crimson Planet itself is enhancing his abilities and powers."

"That is truly amazing. I think we made an incredible choice in bringing him here. Let's get the briefing done. I am anxious for him to commence the tasks so that we can see what he is capable of under very difficult circumstances. His powers will continue to increase and he will have them to rely on. I am hoping he will accomplish the tasks I have laid out as a challenge with flying colors," responded Thor.

Thor and Verne finished up their conversation and Verne returned to James and Indra.

"I have some amazing news, James. As I just explained to Thor, it seems that your strength, intellect and other abilities have increased significantly since you have arrived on Carmesí. Your abilities are also being enhanced by the planet itself. When you left Earth, you were eleven. After a brief time here, you have developed the intellect and capabilities of a fourteen-year-old. Indra, why don't you explain to James what he must accomplish in the first task."

"As Thor told you, the highest mountain in the immediate area is Mount Serpentine. You must climb the mountain and descend via the 'Black Ice Bobsled Run.'"

"That one almost sounds like fun. Especially the bobsled run," quipped James.

"It may sound easy but believe me, James, it's not. First of all, the climb up the mountain is unbelievably steep and rocky. At times you will have to climb sheer rock cliffs in order to continue. As you head up the mountain, the temperature drops. There is always significant snow at the top of the mountain. One more thing you should know about Carmesí, James. While it has very advanced hi-tech spaceships, weaponry and electronics, it also has some very ancient and dangerous animals. On Earth they might be the equivalent of dinosaurs, which still live here to this day. They have been kept out of highly- settled areas like the Palace of Dreams and the City of Pearl, but they still at times roam and are spotted in more desolate areas. Just so you know, Mount Serpentine is one of those areas.

"To aid you in your tasks and help you defend yourself, I have been asked to give you several weapons. The first and most important of which is a combination laser gun and sword called a 'Swun.' The advantage of combining the two is that it lets you shoot laser and electric blasts of energy which can stun or kill, in addition to providing a sword-like laser to fight hand to hand."

"Can I see how it works?" interrupted James.

"Yes, in a few minutes you will be given extensive training in how to use the Swun and in how to operate the special bobsled we will be using," answered Indra.

"You will also have to rely on the powers you have, as they have been enhanced by the crystals. You know some of what they are, but you will discover others as you undertake your tasks," he continued.

Indra and Verne briefed James further and gave him devices, tools and weapons that would aide him in his tasks. James spent the rest of the day and the following day training and learning to use the Swun and the other devices he had been given. At the end of the session, upon special orders from Thor, the highly guarded vault containing the crystals was opened and James was allowed to enter and spend an hour with them. By the time he finished his training, James felt confident and empowered.

37

TAMING MOUNT SERPENTINE

Indra readied and then packed the supplies he and James would need for the climb up Mount Serpentine. Early the next morning he went to retrieve James from his room.

"Good morning, James. Are you ready for an adventure? First we will have breakfast here in the palace. Then we'll pick up Icarus and my Equiphin, Tendra, from the palace stables. We can ride them to Mount Serpentine, but we will have to climb and descend the mountain on our own. It takes two full days with an overnight stay about midway to reach the summit. I have brought the necessary supplies, equipment, weapons and other devices, which were demonstrated and given to you over the past two days. You can carry the Swun in the holster around your hip."

James' Swun had a beautiful white handle. Its case was shiny silver with sapphire, crimson and white stones inlaid along its sides. The Swun itself was a laser, which could be extended to about four feet long. When used in hand to hand combat, it took on the look of a sword fashioned from a laser beam which would enable him to cut through hard objects and defend himself. James could also extend the Swun directly in front of himself and, with a flick of his wrist, shoot laser force beams, which could be directed like a bullet or hurled like explosives. The beams could also be set to stun rather than kill.

"What's that?" asked James, pointing to a silver bobsled-type vehicle which glided across the floor in back of Indra.

"That is a Magnum Bobcat Glider, which we will use to sled down the mountain. There are points where we will hit 100 miles per hour!"

The Magnum Bobcat Glider was shaped like a silver bullet with a rounded nose and a clear, retractable top. It had a rudder in the back with a steering wheel up front, brakes and some sharp running blades that could be lowered from the vehicle when it was cruising on an icy surface. Two gliders could be joined so that they traveled together. The "hover mode," Indra explained, was used to easily move the vehicle along when it was not being used to go down an ice run. In fact, each of them would have one of the gliders attached in a way so that their respective Equiphins could drag them behind them, sort of like a horse pulling a sleigh. All of the supplies would be stored in the gliders until they arrived at Mount Serpentine. After breakfast, Indra and James went to the palace stables, picked up their Equiphins and set out for Mount Serpentine.

Their route took the boys first through a forest, then over plains and then through some elevated, sparser, rockier terrain. Finally, after a five and a half hour journey, they reached the mountain. At its base were a lodge, a camp and a corral like resting area for the Equiphins. The boys would leave the Equiphins in the corral when they climbed the mountain. Indra suggested that they sleep an evening in the lodge and then journey up the mountain the following morning with a guide to show them the way.

At the crack of dawn the next day, James, Indra and their guide, Zelick, headed up the mountain. Glowing orange embers of the early morning sunrise gave way to bright sunlight as morning awakened. Though the day was sunny, the air was crisp and cold and grew more so as the team ascended the mountain. The

first part of the trip was uneventful. After lunch things got trickier. The winds increased and the terrain got much steeper and
rockier. Indra and James became tired and wanted to rest, but
Zelick pushed the boys on.

"Remember, we have to make it at least halfway up the mountain and camp before nightfall. We cannot continue in the darkness - it's too dangerous. Let's go on a bit further before we rest."

The boys pulled their gliders, which were set to hover mode,
behind them. This made it easier than carrying supplies on their
back, but as the path grew trickier, pulling the gliders became
more difficult.

Indra and James looked down from the mountain from time
to time as they climbed higher and higher. They could see the
City of Pearl and the palace grounds far in the distance. Zelick led
the way with James in the middle and Indra bringing up the rear.
Just as the party was walking by a large boulder, they heard a loud
rattle and hissing sound. A giant snake, as long as a fire ladder and
as thick as a small tree trunk, uncurled itself and raised its head
high, while rattling its tail. It was pure white with jagged crimson and black zig zags along it long body and a crimson diamond
shape on its head. It hissed again looking straight at James.

"Don't move," cautioned Zelick. "That is a Snow Cobra. They
are extremely rare. They are the only type of snow snake that
exists. They have a rattle like a rattlesnake and fangs like a venomous cobra. Most snakes can't create any body heat so they are
dormant in the cold. This unique snake thrives in the snow and
moves quickly. It is very deadly."

Keeping his eyes on the snake, James instinctively drew his
Swun in self-defense. The Snow Cobra hissed and rattled its tail
yet again. As it rhythmically moved its head back and forth and
then forward and back, it focused on James' eyes. Suddenly, from
the corner of its eyes, the snake spotted a small animal called a
Rablope, which looked like a combination of a rabbit and antelope, jump out from behind a rock attempting to make a run for
safety. In a split second, the Snow Cobra opened its mouth and

lunged at the Rablope. It sunk its venomous fangs deep into the Rablope, which died almost instantly. Then it tossed its prey upward, unhinged its jaws and violently swallowed it whole. It seemed to James that the Snow Cobra was almost smiling. The snake refocused on James. James was silent but he had his Swun ready. Indra froze. Zelick, who was a bit further ahead, motioned for the boys to slowly move away from the snake by moving up the mountain. The Snow Cobra continued to digest the Rablope but kept its eyes fixed on James. James didn't flinch and stared back. He tried to lock his mind on that of the snake. The snake, however, resisted and would not succumb to James' mind control power. James and the snake continued to stare at each other without moving. Just when James thought the snake was under his control, it made a surprise lunge at Indra. James leapt in the air performing a triple somersault and screamed, "NO!"

Upon hearing James scream, the snake sharply swung its head towards him again. James had his Swun firmly in hand. When the snake's head and long body came close enough, James again leapt high into the air, holding the Swun over his head with both hands, arms extended upward. As he came down, he swung the Swun with a crushing laser beam blow, severing the snake's head from the rest of its body.

"Run, Indra! Get away from it!" James screamed.

Indra was spellbound by what he had witnessed but upon hearing James' voice, finally snapped out of his trance and scampered up the mountain to where Zelick was standing. Although the snake was dead, its body continued to writhe. James grabbed the hovering bobsled gliders with their supplies and headed for safety near Zelick and Indra. Gasping for breath, Indra addressed James.

"Thank you, James. You saved my life!"

Zelick felt embarrassed that James, though much younger than himself, had totally outdone him in confronting and killing the Snow Cobra. After regrouping, James, Indra and Zelick continued up the steep, winding mountain path. The air grew thinner and colder. Indra and James could see their breath as they talked. The snow got deeper. Late in the afternoon, slightly before dusk, the wind picked up and it began to snow.

"Let's go," urged Zelick. "We have to get to the midway camp before dark and before the snow gets too heavy."

Tired as they were, James and Indra redoubled their efforts, fighting the wind, leaning into the mountain and pushing their sore legs to continue as they persisted in their difficult climb. After about 45 minutes, Zelick delivered some encouraging news, "We are almost there, about ten more minutes."

Sure enough, after a bit more climbing, Zelick pointed to a flattened, semi-circular area of the mountain, which overlooked the City of Pearl in the far distance. Nestled into the mountain was a small cave opening. Although the vegetation had gotten sparser and sparser as they ascended the mountain, there were a few hardy trees and bushes, which seemed to thrive around the camping area giving it some protection from the winds. Upon arriving at the camping grounds, Indra and James set their bobsleds down near the cave opening. Zelick looked out and admired the view.

"Hey guys, take a look. There's been a break in the snow and the skies have cleared just a bit. The sun is about to set. Now you can surely see why this is called The Crimson Planet."

Indra and James ran over for a look. The sun appeared very large as it sunk beyond the horizon. A combination of yellow, orange, but mostly crimson light covered the planet, shining through a sprinkling of snowflakes still floating downward from the heavens. Something in The Crimson Planet's atmosphere and the surrounding rocks picked up and reflected the colors, making them look even more dramatic. The effect was to cover the whole planet, as far as the boys could see, in a deep crimson glow. After admiring the view for about fifteen minutes, Zelick turned to James and Indra and observed, "Nightfall will be here shortly. Let's set up camp and start a fire."

Everyone then turned and gravitated back toward the cave. Zelick gathered some stones and placed them in a circle just outside of the cave opening. James and Indra gathered armloads of brush and branches for starting the fire and placed them in the center of the stone circle. Once the fire had started, the boys gathered around it to warm up. They had a simple dinner of soup, bread and antelope, which they cooked over the fire. For dessert they roasted a clear, jelly-like fruit, which Indra referred to as a "rangefluff" which tasted very much like orange-flavored, roasted marshmallows.

After dinner, the boys sat on some rocks and talked. Zelick finally pulled out a miniature instrument that looked like a ukulele but sounded like a cross between a full body guitar and a harp. Zelick played some native tunes popular on The Crimson Planet. The music, with a rocking beat and soaring melodies alternating between guitar and harp, was incredible. Indra and James enthusiastically joined in, banging on some rocks to add a solid drumbeat. As the music continued for an hour or two, the snow picked up again and intensified greatly.

"Why don't we tell some stories?" asked Indra.

"That's a great idea," agreed Zelick.

James, Indra and Zelick gathered in a circle near the campfire.

"Indra, why don't you start?" urged Zelick.

"No, how about James going first. I'd love to hear a story from Earth," answered Indra.

"I'm not sure I can remember any bedtime stories from Earth," worried James as the feeling that he could not remember something important gnawed at him.

"Come on, James. I'm sure you can come up with something."

In the distance, there was a low rumble. That sound was followed suddenly by the flash of a lightning bolt, which lit up the night sky. Within seconds, a crushing thunderclap exploded.

"This combination of snow, thunder and lightning is very rare," observed Zelick.

James was quiet and he appeared lost in thought. Suddenly, a smile appeared on his face. Quietly, he addressed Indra and Zelick.

"I think I have one. I can't quite remember where I heard it, but now I recall it's called *The Little Seal*."

"That's great, James. Why don't you start," urged Indra.

And so, after a few moments of recalling the details, James began and retold the story of *The Little Seal* as best as he could.

"That was great," Indra exclaimed as the story came to an end.

"Thank you. Now it's your turn, Indra," James said with a smile.

Indra and Zelick each took turns telling their own stories. After a few more hours, the wind and snow had picked up significantly. The boys felt very tired after their long trek up the mountain.

"I think it's best that we turn in. We have another long day tomorrow to get to the summit. Once we're up there, of course, we begin the toboggan run descent. That should take less than three hours if it's done correctly," said Zelick.

"I agree. We should get some rest," Indra added.

The boys pulled out sleeping bags and arranged them in a semi-circle just inside the cave where they planned to sleep for protection. The campfire struggled to burn in the onslaught of snow. Zelick threw some more wood on it just before going to bed to keep it going for as long as possible. The boys settled in for the night and snuggled into their sleeping bags, dead tired after the long climb. Within minutes, their eyes grew heavy and they fell into a deep sleep. Only the boys' snores broke the silence in the cave.

After about five hours of deep sleep, James stirred. He felt the ground tremble. He turned over and tried to pull one side of the sleeping bag over his head and fall back to sleep but then he felt it again. *What the heck is that?* he wondered. James got up and peered out the cave entrance through the snow. He could not believe his eyes. Entering the midway camp were two giant creatures that looked like a cross between a white polar bear and a dinosaur. They stood about 18 feet high, more than double the height of a basketball hoop. The upper body was that of a bear while the lower body and haunches were large and muscled, looking like the back portion of a small T-Rex dinosaur. It gave the creature the ability to climb and leap great distances. A large tail provided balance. The two looked like they were foraging for food. The campfire kept them away from the mouth of the cave. On the other hand, the formerly bright burning twigs and logs were dying down to smoldering embers. As the fire subsided, the beasts got bolder, sniffing in the direction of the cave. Suddenly, through the snow they saw James at its mouth. James softly called to Indra and Zelick, "Hey, guys. Take a look! What the heck are those?"

Indra and Zelick were still fast asleep and didn't move. James finally flicked a small pebble at each of them. They stirred and awoke groggily. Again he asked them what the beasts were called. Zelick finally got up and took a look.

"Oh my gosh! Those are Bearasaurs. They're very fast and vicious. They have large, sharp teeth and nails. They can leap high into the air. Make sure everything we're carrying is safely stored in the cave. The cave opening is too small for them to get in through, but they could certainly poke in a paw."

The Bearasaurs sniffed the air and ambled closer to the cave. James certainly had drawn their attention. They paced back and forth, eying the opening.

"We've got to get them away from here," cautioned Zelick.

"But how?" asked Indra.

James and Zelick continued to watch the Bearasaurs until the fire finally died. Within seconds of it going out, the Bearasaurs were emboldened and headed directly for the cave. While en route, one of the Bearasaurs suddenly jumped high into the air and let out a mighty roar as it lunged for the cave. Horrified, James, Zelick and Indra all stepped back in unison and huddled inside for protection. The beasts continued to roar as they tried to reach the boys. Thankfully, the cave opening proved too small for them to actually enter. They did, however, reach their long arms into the cave in an attempt to grab one of the boys. James and Indra drew their Swuns.

"Set your Swun to stun," screamed out Indra. "We don't want to kill them if we don't have to."

"It sure seems like they are trying to kill us!" shouted back James.

One of the Bearasaurs again thrust its paw into the cave. This time James and Indra were ready. They unleashed stun laser blasts from their Swuns. The beast roared in pain and fell backward. As big and ferocious as it was, it was no match for the power unleashed by the Swuns. James and Indra ran to the mouth of the cave and zapped the beast again. It finally lay quiet, stunned and immobilized, but not dead. This took care of one of the beasts, but enraged the other, who fled the Swuns, running to the side of the camp near a high cliff. The boys headed out of the cave in pursuit of the remaining Bearasaur. James led the charge. As they got closer to the Bearasaur, Indra slipped and his Swun went flying. At the same time, James leapt high into the air with a triple somersault intending to distract and stun the Bearasaur.

Unfortunately, the Bearasaur hurled a branch at James that hit him on the hand, which held the Swun. James landed safely, but he too lost his Swun. The beast then made a charge for James. James ran as fast as he could seeking to get out of its way. As he was running, he spotted a tall, willowy tree on the side of the cliff. He ran over to it, jumped as high as he could and grabbed onto a branch. The Bearasaur followed in hot pursuit. James scrambled as far as he could onto an outer branch of the tree. The branch drooped over the cliff. When the Bearasaur reached the tree, it leapt and grabbed onto the tree, scratching the bark as it tried to follow James. The tree swayed dangerously as the beast worked its way up the trunk to the overhanging branch where James had found fleeting sanctuary. When James saw the Bearasaur coming closer, he inched further out toward the end of the branch. The Bearasaur roared as it reached the level of the branch, which James was on. Indra and Zelick motioned for James to remain quiet when the Bearasaur paused at the branch. James quickly thought over his precarious situation and grew quiet for a second. The Bearasaur paused. All of a sudden, James started screaming loudly.

"Come on, you coward. Come and get me!"

"Are you crazy, James? What are you doing?"

"Come on! I'm not afraid of you."

"What are you doing James? You don't even have your Swun!" Zelick shouted.

The Bearasaur became enraged and suddenly lunged for James. And that's when James knew that he had him. When James saw the Bearasaur climb onto the branch, he catapulted off the tree and landed on the ground just as the Bearasaur tried to grab him. Sure enough, due to the weight of the beast, the branch broke and the Bearasaur went tumbling, falling 50 feet off the sheer cliff to a ledge below.

"Wow, that was scary!" exclaimed James.

"James, that was amazing! How did you do that?" asked Indra shaking his head in wonder.

"Well done, James!" added Zelick. "Let's gather our things. It will be dawn soon. The snow is letting up and I think we should move on. We have to get out of here and get to the top of the mountain by 3:00 in the afternoon so we'll have enough time to make it down the Black Ice Run before dusk."

Indra and James located their Swuns and went back to the cave to pack up their sleeping bags and supplies. Zelick helped them load everything back into the toboggans, which they placed again in "hover mode." The remaining Bearasaur was still out cold and didn't look like it would stir for quite a while. Once Zelick, Indra and James had packed up, they left the camp and continued their hike up the mountain.

The early morning darkness soon gave way to the glowing embers of dawn. The snow stopped and the skies cleared. As the sun slowly came up over the horizon it bathed the mountain and its surroundings in the crimson- colored light from which Carmesí derived its name. Zelick stopped the procession for a few minutes to let Indra and James take in the beauty of the sunrise and to once again admire the view.

"It's going to be a beautiful, clear day. Since we started out earlier than expected, we should make it to the summit a bit ahead of schedule. Our path should be easier from here at least for a while, though the climb near the top of the mountain is very, very steep."

After a few minutes of admiring the view, the boys again pressed forward. They chatted amongst themselves, taking short breaks to rest and delight in their surroundings. After about seven hours of walking they entered the final phase of their ascent.

"And this is the last and steepest part of the climb I told you about. If you look to my left, you can see the beginning of the Black Ice Run. It is covered in part by a few inches of the powdered snow we had last night. The track should be very fast."

Through sheer determination and tough climbing, the boys made it to the top of the mountain by 2:00 p.m., one hour ahead of schedule. They rested after their rugged ordeal and had some lunch to celebrate.

"Well, we made it this far. It's quite an accomplishment in and of itself. This is one of the highest points on Carmesí," Zelick informed James and Indra. After lunch and a rest, James grew impatient with anticipation.

"I can't wait for the toboggan ride to begin. It's all downhill from here!" he jested.

And with that, the boys got up and arranged the hovering toboggans into a single, connected vehicle. Together, two toboggans could fit four riders. They packed the toboggans and tied down what little supplies and equipment that remained. Indra lowered the blades of the toboggans.

"James, just so you know what we are up against, the fastest recorded run down the mountain was 2 hours and 47 minutes. There are no rules. You just have to make it down the mountain, as fast as you can, in one piece."

James sat up front, Zelick in the middle and Indra brought up the rear. Zelick looked at his watch.

"It's exactly 3:07. At 3:10 we'll start. James, strap yourself in. This is going to be the ride of a lifetime. Indra and I will push to give us a running start and we'll jump in. You steer and control the ride. Indra will help out with braking."

Once James was seated and strapped in, Zelick and Indra got alongside the toboggan. Zelick glanced at his watch and counted down "10, 9, 8, 7, 6, 5, 4, 3, 2, 1 go!" Then he and Indra pushed with all their might and the toboggan headed down the winding run. Indra and Zelick jumped in at the last possible moment with a whoop.

"We're on our way!" shouted James as he lowered his goggles.

The toboggan started a little slowly but quickly picked up speed as it twisted and turned, hurtling down the mountain.

"Lean into the turn," screamed James as they came to their first sharp turn. The toboggan continued circling the mountain as its sharp blades hugged the ice on its downward path. About ten minutes into the run, the path straightened for a bit and the toboggan picked up speed. Zelick knew what was coming and yelled.

"Hold on for this one, guys!"

With that, the toboggan reached its highest speed and zoomed up a path, which rolled into a complete circle. The toboggan followed the circular path and the boys hung upside down as it did a complete loop. The toboggan continued its mad run down the mountain moving even faster. Suddenly, there was a large gap in the track with a steep drop below.

"Hold on!" yelled James again.

The toboggan sailed into the air and barely made it across the sharp drop. It landed with a hard thud, which rattled the toboggan and shook James, Indra and Zelick violently. The daunting ride continued with James as the pilot. He rarely applied the brakes and told Indra to hold off applying them as well. The ride was crazy, filled with thrilling twists and turns, shuddering shaking and giant loops. Everything went well until the boys were about midway down the mountain.

"So far we are making record time," announced Zelick as he glanced at his watch.

James concentrated on the path directly ahead of him. Suddenly, the clear blue sky grew darker and a large shadow appeared, covering the entire toboggan. James looked up and couldn't believe his eyes. Directly overhead was a flying dragon the size of a small jet, covered with emerald and crimson scales. Its mouth was filled with large white teeth and its tongue drooped off the side of its mouth. It flapped its enormous wings as it followed the toboggan down its treacherous path. Its feet had large, sharp claws, which the dragon opened and closed as it flew above the trio. For a while, the dragon just looked down and mirrored the toboggan's path. Then without warning, it dove, claws open, straight for it.

"James, it's coming straight at us!" screamed Indra.

"Shoot at it with the Swun full force!" replied James.

Indra pulled out his Swun and hurled some laser thrust shots at full power at the dragon. Unfortunately, the dragon evaded them artfully and continued on its path. James had little time to think. *I wish we had some means of protection.* The dragon would not veer from its path. Suddenly, it hurled out a large flame from its mouth.

"I can't believe you have fire breathing dragons on Carmesí," James shouted.

It was clear that the dragon had no intention of being shaken off its course and that there was a good possibility that James, Indra and Zelick would become his next meal if he was not stopped. The toboggan continued hurtling down the mountain as the dragon grew closer and closer. James felt his adrenaline rushing as the situation grew graver and graver. Then something changed. James felt empowered. He imagined protecting the toboggan from the dragon. Then, just as the dragon made a final lunge for the boys, James concentrated all of his attention on the toboggan. Suddenly, a glowing sapphire force field surrounded them. As the dragon tried to sweep down on the boys, it crashed into the field and was repelled. It fell ten feet in the air until it finally caught itself and began flying toward James, Indra and Zelick in the toboggan again. This time both James and Indra were prepared with their Swuns. As the dragon swooped in for the second time, James and Indra blasted it. Finally, the dragon faltered and fell from the sky. The toboggan continued down the mountain at full speed, twirling and twisting. As it neared the finish line at the bottom of the mountain, it went fully around one last loop turning the boys upside down again and shortly thereafter, James, Indra and Zelick hurtled across the finish line.

"James, we set a new record for the run! A record two hours and seven minutes!" screamed Zelick.

"Wow! That was incredible!" shouted James. "Indra, you never told me that Carmesí had fire breathing dragons for Pete's sake!"

"Congratulations, James. You have accomplished your first task in record time! I am sure Thor will be very pleased."

After celebrating with Zelick, James and Indra went to retrieve their Equiphins. The beasts seemed happy and relieved to be reunited with their masters. James and Indra thanked Zelick, mounted their Equiphins and headed back to the Palace of Dreams.

38

THE LAUNCH

George, Jenifer and Julia sat around the conference table in Sheldon Silver's office at the SPACETECK corporate campus on a Saturday afternoon. It was late fall and the weather had turned much colder. Sheldon pushed a button on a remote control he cupped in his hand and an ultra-thin monitor slid down from the ceiling. The picture flickered on and revealed a huge rocket with plumes of smoke at its base almost ready to launch.

"Wow!" exclaimed Julia, "What's going on?"

Sheldon smiled and spoke, "I've invited you here today to witness a very special event. I asked your father to keep this very quiet since it's top-secret. Manned space flights through galaxies, space vortexes and time are still years away. This launch, however, will put our most advanced and sophisticated space probe into space. It is equipped with the latest cameras, sensors and microphones so that we can achieve an almost virtual presence wherever it travels. Everything it 'sees' or senses can be sent back to us. The most incredible thing about it though is not what pictures or information it can send back to us, though that, of course, is very important - but to where and how fast it can travel. This probe can travel many times the speed of light through space and through wormhole space vortexes. It's our best hope of finding out what happened to James! I have thrown the full weight of SPACETECK'S most advanced resources into this. We have programmed it to follow the path of the light beams we have identified on the night that James disappeared!"

"Wow, thank you so much! Do you really think we'll be able to find James?" exclaimed Julia.

"Yes, thank you Sheldon," chimed in George and Jenifer almost in unison.

"I fully understand how difficult James' disappearance has been on your family. We are doing everything we can to help. I know from your father, Julia, that you've formed a space club with some friends at school to study space and see if you can discover anything about James. I will make arrangements for you to be able to login through a secure Internet site so that you and your club members can view the video and pictures beamed back by the James' probe as it moves through the universe."

"That would be amazing!" enthused Julia.

"Let's take a look at the launch," suggested Sheldon.

"10, 9, 8, 7, 6, 5, 4, 3, 2, 1 - liftoff!" came the voice of an on location announcer through the screen.

"Look at that. What a beautiful launch!" cried out Julia.

The four watched as James' probe lifted into outer space. Within minutes, the spacecraft disappeared into the stratosphere and the view of a camera mounted in the probe filled the screen. The pictures were amazingly sharp.

"This is the quality of picture we will have throughout the probe's journey."

The Wyatts stayed for almost two hours watching the liftoff, profusely thanking Mr. Silver and discussing what it meant in terms of aiding in the search for James.

At about 5:00 p.m., the Wyatts finally left. They continued to talk about the launch enthusiastically on the way home. One thing continued to bother Julia, though she did not discuss it with her parents. In her heart she felt James was all right, but she could not understand why she had not received a mind message from him. *Has he forgotten about us?* she pondered in silence.

39

RIDDLES

James and Indra entered the room where James had first met with Thor. Verne and some of Thor's attendants and assistants were waiting. Once James and Indra were seated, there was loud trumpet revelry to introduce Thor. He and Alisha subsequently descended together on the floating palette to meet with and congratulate James and Indra.

"Excellent job, James! Your toboggan run set a new record. I was extremely impressed with the way I heard you handled the Snow Cobra, the Bearasaurs and the fire breathing dragon."

"Thank you, Your Majesty," beamed James.

"I knew you had incredible abilities," continued Thor.

Alisha smiled as she listened to her father commend James on completing his first task.

"Now, James, I have a riddle for you. You may know it, it's pretty well known on Earth, I understand."

"I'm not that familiar with riddles," protested James.

"This one is kind of fun. I'm sure you've heard it. It's quite simple really. What do you throw away when you need it and take back when you don't need it?"

"I'll have to think about that one," stalled James as he leaned back in his chair and put his arms behind his head to think.

Alisha looked toward James as he wracked his brain for the answer. She caught his eye and he smiled back. James was frustrated as nothing came to him immediately. Just when he was ready to give up, he spotted a beautiful model of an ancient pirate ship situated atop a wooden display case. It was intricately constructed with great attention to detail to such things as sails, round cabin windows, an anchor and lifeboats. Suddenly, the answer came to him. James stood up and said excitedly. "Your Majesty, I think I've got it. I think I know the answer."

Thor turned toward James with great interest.

"Yes, James. What is your answer?"

"Well, Your Majesty, it must be an anchor! When you need it, you throw it overboard. When you don't need it, you take it back."

"Amazing. Dead on!" said Thor. "Well, James, you have two more tasks to accomplish and two more riddles to answer. You are well on your way to passing the tests I set up for you."

James, Indra and Alisha gathered and talked for a while. Alisha asked James about the Black Ice Toboggan Run. As they wrapped up the meeting, Indra looked at James.

"Tomorrow we start the second task. That Hydrashark must go. How are you going to handle that, James?"

"I'm not certain yet. I'll have to think about it. I'm sure I'll sleep soundly tonight and worry about it in the morning."

With that, the boys wrapped up their conversation with Alisha and headed back to their rooms. James feared that the next task would prove to be even more challenging.

40

TWO HEADS ARE BETTER
THAN ONE

James and Indra met for breakfast the next morning to plan the day's events.

"How did that Hydrashark get into Lake Lerna in the first place?" asked James.

"We are not sure. It may have swum up river to the lake here when it was much smaller and then it grew to the size it is now," answered Indra.

"Why hasn't it been removed before?"

"As you can see, the lake is very vast. The Hydrashark is rarely seen and it's difficult to track. First you must find it and then figure out how to kill or dispose of it. It was only discovered recently. Remember this, if you cut off a head, it quickly grows another one right back. Look, I am sure if Thor had ordered it killed or removed from the lake, it would be gone. I think he kept it a little while longer to use it as a test for you."

"Okay. This won't be as fun as the toboggan run but we have to take care of it."

"Who said 'we?'" laughed Indra. "These are your tasks!"

"I know, but you are coming along to guide me."

After breakfast Indra and James headed over to the palace stables to get their Equiphins. Icarus let off an affectionate whinny as James approached. James and Indra fed and then groomed them. Finally, they saddled and mounted them. Thereafter, they headed down the path leading to Lake Lerna. They approached the lake more slowly this time and James noted there were beautiful trees that looked like weeping willows surrounding it. The branches dipped downward and were reflected in the beautiful blue waters. Again James saw the Lilysaurs, the miniature dinosaur-looking creatures, sunning themselves on the lily pads, which he had seen the first time he and Icarus had crossed the lake.

"What do Hydrasharks eat?" asked James.

"Almost anything they can get their jaws on - lobster, squid, eels, dolphins, fish of all types. Our fish and sea creatures are not separated by water type as on Earth. There are no 'fresh water' fish as opposed to 'salt water.'

"So," James continued, "in theory, they would love to eat an Equiphin, for example."

"I suppose so," answered Indra in horror, "but surely you don't plan on feeding one of our Equiphins to the Hydrashark?"

"No, but they could serve as bait or a trap," answered James calmly. "First we have to draw it out."

With that, James dug in his knees and clicked his heels, prodding Icarus to charge at full speed directly to the Lake. After a few minutes, the two breached the shoreline and sailed ten feet into the air above the water. James guided Icarus to make a straight line from one end of the lake to the other. Indra watched from the shoreline. James listened acutely. He knew if he could sense vibrations from the lake he might be able to locate where the creature was hiding.

James clung close to Icarus as they soared above the lake's surface. Icarus seemed to sense that something was about to happen. James and Icarus made it from one end of the lake to the other without incident. James played daredevil on the way back. He prodded Icarus to skim the water's surface in the hope of drawing the infamous Hydrashark out of hiding. Again James and Icarus made it across the lake without seeing anything.

"Looks like that Hydrashark is playing hard to get today!" commented Indra. "But be careful, James. Don't underestimate it."

"I know. I think I have a plan. I need a wire basket. What are those creatures on the lilies?"

"They are Lilysaurs," answered Indra. "But please don't use them. They are cute, harmless creatures. How about using eels?"

"How can we capture enough of them?" asked James.

"There's a cove off the middle of the lake where they gather. If we get a wire basket and a prodding stick we can push them into the basket. A basket full of eels should serve as bait for the Hydrashark."

"It's worth a shot," answered James.

Indra rode back to the palace and picked up some large wire baskets and some fish to serve as bait for the eels. Then James and Indra made their way to the cove and sure enough, as Indra had predicted, it was teeming with eels. Indra put some bait into the center of the large wire basket and in turn placed the basket in the middle of the cove. The eels slithered around the basket and then through the large opening at the top trying to get to the fish placed inside. Soon the basket was jammed as the eels attacked the fish. When there were enough in the basket, James pushed the cover to the opening shut with a stick and trapped the eels inside.

"Alright, I think we have enough," shouted James. "Let's go."

James and Indra pulled up the wire basket with the help of Icarus and Tendra. The four of them then sailed over the lake with a giant basket of slithering eels being pulled behind them.

"Where should we drop them, James?"

"Let's try the center of the lake. We haven't seen the Hydrashark anywhere. It stands to reason it's down very deep. When I say 'now,' unhook the line from Tendra, pull off the top and let it drop and I'll do the same."

James came to the center of the lake and shouted "NOW!"

The basket went tumbling and plunged deep into the lake. Most of the eels were trapped in the basket but some of them started leaving as soon as it plunged beneath the surface. All of a sudden, James fell silent and held his breath. He felt a large tremor and saw the water churn white.

"Get out of here, Indra, fast! It's coming. Sail upward. Just do it."

With that, the Hydrashark crashed through the water surface of the lake with both its heads, one snapping at James and the other at Indra, ignoring the eels altogether for the time being. James drew his Swun instinctively. He circled around the Hydrashark's head and, as it snapped at him and Icarus, James cut off its head in self-defense. Within in a few minutes it regenerated another head.

"No, James! I warned you, cutting off a head is not the solution. It simply grows another one."

"I can see that but it was an emergency!" yelped James.

"Well, what's your plan, James?" screamed Indra. "The wire basket filled with eels didn't work too well."

"Yes it did!" protested James, "at least we found it!"

The Hydrashark sunk back in the water and prepared to make another lunge upward for the boys.

"Alright, ride clockwise in a big circle. I'll go counter clockwise closer in."

"Are you sure about this, James?"

"Hang in there, Indra!"

Sure enough the Hydrashark made another lunge upward and tried to follow the boys. Each head followed one of the boys, each in the opposite direction. The heads were so busy following them that the beast didn't realize it was entangling its own two necks.

"Faster!" yelled James.

Indra did as James instructed. The beast's necks grew more and more entwined. Finally, when the Hydrashark realized what was happening, it tried to stop but both of the heads continued twisting closer and closer. The circular motion was making it dizzy.

"Ride straight for the center of the circle and shoot upward!" directed James.

He did the same thing. The heads of the Hydrashark tried to follow but they were entangled. As James and Indra reached the center of the imaginary circle they had created, the two heads of the Hydrashark made a desperate attempt to grab at them. Just when it seemed they had the boys in their grasp, the Equiphins shot upward, with James and Indra holding on to them tightly for dear life. The heads collided and bit into each other. The beast roared in frustration and anger, each head now trying to bite the other. James sailed upward and pointed down showing Indra what had happened.

"That was a close call."

"Set your Swun to stun," advised James. "We should knock the Hydrashark out. If we can disable it we can ship it back to the ocean on a large barge. No need to kill it. It won't be a menace in the ocean."

"Well, as long as the barge tows it far out to sea. It could be a real menace in the City of Pearl Bay if it's dropped too close."

"Yes. Wait, I have a better idea. Don't you have hover space vehicles that can pick this beast up and fly it out to sea?"

"Yes, but I think Thor wanted you to handle everything on your own."

"Well, first let's at least knock it out."

The boys both set their Swuns on stun and blasted the Hydrashark. It was soon knocked unconscious and floated on the surface of the lake.

"Look, we managed to disable it. I don't want to have to kill it needlessly. Can we check with the palace about helping us dispose of it in the ocean?"

"Okay. I'll send them a text."

Indra checked his communicator. Before he could say a word he saw a low flying hovering spacecraft come over the horizon.

"I guess the answer is yes. Look, they're sending a spacecraft to move the Hydrashark out to sea."

"Wow, that makes two tasks completed."

The spacecraft came and maneuvered two large belts with a platform in the middle underneath the Hydrashark. Then it was slowly lifted into the air. With the Hydrashark suspended underneath it, the hovering aircraft flew out towards the ocean to deposit the beast way out at sea where it would not be a menace to the City of Pearl.

After the Hydrashark was disposed of, James and Indra rewarded each of their Equiphins for their help with a tasty Wastraw to munch on. Icarus and Tendra dug in and clearly enjoyed the refreshing treat. Shortly thereafter, James and Indra were again summoned to the palace to meet with Thor. They entered the now-familiar room and again Alisha was there.

"James, I must congratulate you for the way you handled the second task. Once again, you have used your wits to overcome a difficult obstacle, yet you have shown me that you value life. That is an admirable quality," King Thor stated.

"Thank you, Your Majesty."

It was late in the day and Thor turned his back for a moment to admire the view of the City of Pearl and the vast ocean that lay beyond. The sun began to set and the crimson glow characteristic of Carmesí took hold on the horizon spreading over the rest of the planet.

"I love the colors of a sunset and sunrise." Thor commented. Then he posed the following question, "What two sisters give birth, one to the other?

"What's that, Your Majesty?" James asked.

Thor turned and looked at him. "Oh, that's the second riddle. What two sisters always give birth, one to the other?"

James was momentarily perplexed. At first he could again not think of an answer. He calmed himself and did not panic. Thor gazed out at the sunset. The room filled with a remarkable crimson color as the sun glowed brightly and then started to sink beyond the horizon. Suddenly, James realized that the answer, which Thor sought, lay right before him. He looked up at Thor and smiled.

"Your Majesty. You have given me a gift. The answer lies before me, doesn't it?" James asked knowingly.

Thor smiled for he knew that James had solved the new riddle.

"The sisters are night and day, aren't they? Day gives birth to the night and the night gives birth to the day each and every day."

"Yes, James! Yes! You are living up to the expectations and confidence I have in you. You have only one more task to perform and one more riddle to solve. If you pass those, you will enter the Starflight Academy as promised. I feel that you have it in you. You will be a great warrior and leader one day!"

Alisha looked at James and beamed. She realized that her father admired James for his abilities and approved of him. She also felt compelled to get to know him better. Indra and James talked with Alisha for a while, giving her some more details as to how they had captured the Hydrashark. Then they headed off to get some dinner together. Shortly after finishing their meals, they each returned to their respective rooms for a good night's sleep. James and Indra would confront the last task tomorrow and wanted to be well rested.

41

ELECTIONS

Julia woke up early and got ready for school. She knew it was going to be a big day since the election results would be announced. She really wanted to win and, accordingly, was excited and a bit nervous. A victory would afford her an important opportunity to represent her class and would give her some stature and prestige. The campaigning, poster making and speeches were over. The students would cast their votes today and the victor would be determined.

Once Julia arrived in her classroom, two of her friends, Jackie and Stephanie, sat down next to her and started talking before class began.

"Julia, I am so excited for you. I'm sure you're going to win!" offered Stephanie encouragingly.

"Well, I hope so, but you never know until it's over."

"When will they announce the results?" asked Jackie.

"Voting ends at eleven today. They'll tally the votes and announce the winners at three-thirty in the auditorium right after school."

"Well, we still have a long wait," commented Julia.

Julia tried to concentrate on her studies, but she was excited and her mind wandered. Throughout the day, various friends came up to her during breaks, recess and lunch and wished her good luck. Julia checked her watch frequently. Unfortunately that didn't speed things up and actually seemed to make the hours drag on longer. Finally, the end of school bell rang and everyone headed to the auditorium to get the results.

Mrs. Clark, who was the teacher monitoring the election, was introduced by the school principal, Mrs. Baker.

"Now we will hear from Mrs. Clark who has monitored the elections and tallied the results. Mrs. Clark."

"Good afternoon. I know you are all anxious to hear who won. The winners of the fifth grade election are as follows: for Secretary, Kayla Green, for Treasurer, Jordan Midlan, for Vice President, Michael Redmond and for President, Julia Wyatt! Congratulations!"

Julia let out a gasp and all her friends surrounded her and gave her a hug. At random her friends spoke out.

"Congratulations, Julia!"

"Great job!"

"You deserve it!"

Julia glowed with pride as she let the reality of victory sink in. She was proud to have set herself a goal and to have accomplished it.

"Thank you all for your support! I couldn't have won without you! Thank you so much!" said Julia as the congratulations came in.

Finally the gathering broke up and Julia headed outside to meet her mother. Julia ran to Jenifer's car with a big smile on her face.

"How did the election go?" asked her mother excitedly.

"I won, Mom! I won!"

"Wow, that's fantastic. I guess this calls for a celebration. Let me tell Dad and see if he can come home a little early. Maybe we can go to the Charcoal Grille for a big steak dinner!"

"That sounds great, Mom. Can Grandma and Grandpa come too?"

"That's a wonderful idea. I'll give them a call."

Jenifer made the calls on her way home and made a reservation. Julia was excited.

"Julia, why don't you get your homework out of the way as soon as we get home? That way you can relax and enjoy the dinner."

Misty greeted Julia with a friendly bark as she entered the house. After petting her and playing with her for a few minutes, Julia quickly made her way upstairs and changed into more comfortable clothes. Misty bounded upstairs and kept Julia company while she finished her homework.

After she was done, Julia pulled out the tablets and some of the blue and green crystals she had found in the cave. Julia studied the tablets and tried to see if she could discover any additional meaning or messages contained in the writings. After about half an hour, she heard her father arrive and put everything away. She went running downstairs to greet him.

"How is the new President of her class doing?" inquired George happily when he saw Julia approaching.

"Great, Dad!"

"Come over here! You deserve a hug. And I hear we are going out to celebrate!"

"Yes, that should be fantastic, Dad."

George, Jenifer and Julia all got ready to go to dinner. As they were leaving, Misty seemed a little sad and let out a whimper to let them know of her displeasure. Julia ran over and hugged her as Misty licked her face.

"Don't worry, girl. We'll be back soon."

The Wyatts arrived at the restaurant and joined Grandma Jean and Grandpa Jake who had already been seated at a nice round table with a pleasant view by the window.

"Congratulations, Julia!" said Grandma Jean and Grandpa Jake.

Julia gave her Grandma and Grandpa each a big kiss. As the family perused the menu, Julia updated her grandparents.

"Well, as you know, I won the election today. I also started a space club. It has eight friends in it- five of mine, three of James'. We are going to have our third meeting tomorrow night. We meet every two weeks at our house in James' room."

Everyone grew quiet at the mention of James' name.

"Dad, I miss him so much," confessed Julia with tears in her eyes.

"I know, sweetheart. We all do, but I have some great news for you. Mr. Silver finally got that website up and running, where you and your club members can view the pictures and video being sent from the probe. I'll give you the site address and password later."

"Thanks, Dad. That'll be great. Just in time for the meeting."

"Let's order," suggested George changing the subject.

The waiter came over and took everyone's order. Julia requested her favorite dish, rib eye steak with mashed potatoes. The rest of the evening went well and everyone enjoyed their meals.

"It's a school night so we should get going soon," Jenifer said as the dinner was coming to an end. Just as Julia finished her chocolate mousse, the bill arrived. George paid the check and everyone got up to leave.

Grandpa Jake and Grandma Jean headed out of the restaurant and across the parking lot to their car. The Wyatts followed closely behind. Suddenly, a fast-moving car turned into the parking lot heading straight for Grandpa Jake and Grandma Jean. The bright beams of its headlights dazzled everyone. Julia saw what was happening and screamed, "NO!"

Instinctively she used the levitation power that James had discovered to lift the planets, to lift and suspend her grandparents in the air and move them to safety. Her parents could not believe their eyes as to what Julia had done. Grandpa Jake and Grandma Jean didn't really understand what had happened. Everyone was just glad they were safe. George, Jenifer and Julia ran over to them and threw their arms around them.

"Are you guys okay?" asked Jenifer tearfully.

"Yes, we're fine. Not quite sure what happened, but we somehow we got out of harm's way."

George and Jenifer didn't say anything but looked again at Julia in silent disbelief. Julia glowed with satisfaction thankful that she had been able to protect her grandparents from harm. The carload of rowdy teenagers who had almost hit them barely took notice of what had happened. They parked and went into the restaurant laughing.

Luckily the evening ended well but the event demonstrated how close the line between safety and disaster, life and death could be. Julia was grateful that, with the help of the powers, which she had acquired from the crystals from the Sapphire Prism Cave, she had been able to avert what could have been a real disaster.

42

THE CLUB

The next day, after Julia finished her dinner she got ready to greet the members of the Space Club, who would be arriving shortly for their third meeting. The first two sessions had focused on setting up the club. This was going to be the first meeting of real substance. Each member had been assigned a planet in the solar system to research and each week they would tell the rest of the group something about the one they had investigated. This week they would focus on the size of each planet and its distance from sun.

By 7:00 p.m. all nine members of the club had arrived and crowded into James' room. Everyone took turns peering through James' telescope at the clear night sky filled with twinkling stars for a few minutes before the meeting began. Julia took out her membership list with all the names and went around the room to make sure that everyone was here.

"Katherine?"

"Here."

"Stephanie, Becky, Rose and Jackie?"

"All here."

"All right, the guys. Let's see. Robert, Steve and Mark?"

"All here."

"Tonight we are going to start with our investigation of all the planets in our solar system. We want to find out how far from the sun each planet is and how big it is. As the weeks go by we'll all learn more by researching and sharing what we discover. Also, I have some big news that I want to share with you."

Everyone looked straight at Julia, wondering what the surprise was. Katherine spoke up first.

"What is it, Julia? Come on, tell us!"

Julia smiled and looked around. It was clear that nothing was going to happen until she revealed the news. She pulled out her new MacBook Air computer and connected to the Internet. Then she paused to explain.

"You all know that my brother James disappeared from The Sapphire Prism Cave we discovered together. I miss him so much and I have to find out what happened to him. As strange as it may sound given his unusual disappearance, I know in my heart that he's okay. I'm just very sad that we can't be together and that we can't communicate. Part of the reason I formed this club was to find out as much as we can about space. But the main reason is to find out about what happened to James.

My dad works for a company called SPACETECK. They have launched a special satellite probe that is designed to explore space and send back photos and videos from its journey. It's a very advanced probe that can travel far faster and further than any other one ever launched before. The best part is that they have programed it to follow the light path trail that they think James followed after he was lifted out of The Sapphire Prism Cave. There's no guarantee that it will ever find James, but it's the best hope we have so far. The President of SPACETECK, Sheldon Silver, has been nice enough to give me a link to the site and a special access code so that we can follow the journey of the probe and see the pictures from space. Tonight we're going to log into the site and view the first pictures it has sent back. We can also check the constant video feed it's sending back to Earth in real time."

"Wow, Julia, that's so cool!" Stephanie exclaimed with excitement.

"Let's take a look at some of the still pictures sent back so far."

Julia maneuvered through the site and found some early pictures from the flight.

"Look at this beautiful picture of Saturn from early on in the probe's journey. You can tell it's Saturn by the rings circling the planet. And in this window you can see a live feed of what the probe is 'seeing' as it moves through space right now."

The club members witnessed an incredibly clear video of space with planets, stars and meteors whizzing by all lit up in incredible colors and light glows.

"So, guys, there you have it, our direct window into space. We'll be checking this site at every meeting to get an update. This site and the whole probe mission is top-secret, so I can't give you the site address and code to enter it on your own."

"Julia, that's so incredible. What a great addition to our club and way to try to track what happened to James," added Katherine.

"Alright, now that I've filled you in on the surprise, why don't we start exchanging information about the planets. Robert, why don't you go first? Tell us what you know about Mercury."

After that introduction, each club member in turn outlined their planet's size and distance from the sun. They also took turns looking through the telescope to look at and point out items in the night sky. By 9:00 it was getting late, especially for a school night, so Julia brought the meeting to a close.

"Well, this has been great. We just have to keep it going. The more information we research and bring to each meeting, the more we'll all learn together. Great job and thanks for coming," said Julia.

The meeting came to an end and everyone headed downstairs to wait for their parents to pick them up. Katherine was the last to leave and thanked Julia for a great time. Julia was happy that she had started the Space Club and hoped there would be many more meetings filled with interesting discoveries and eventually some answers as to what happened to James.

43

THE PUZZLE

James awoke early as the sun streamed through the window of his room. He lay in bed for a few minutes. Things had been moving so fast that he had had no time to sit back and reflect on all he had seen, experienced and done. As he had on other occasions, James felt happy and satisfied in many ways with all the adventures he had experienced, yet something nagged at his heart. He felt he missed certain places and people yet he could not remember what or who they were. Just when he was starting to feel a little melancholy, he heard the now-familiar knock on his door and he knew that Indra had come by to get him for breakfast.

"Just a minute, Indra," James cried knowingly as he jumped out of bed to get ready. James threw on some clothes and shoes, combed his hair and grabbed his Swun. He then opened his door.

"Hello, James. It's another beautiful day. Today you face your final challenge of the three that Thor set out for you. If you succeed, it will be a great accomplishment and you will be accepted to the Starflight Academy. It is reserved for only the best."

"I know it's a great honor. I'm happy that I've been able to accomplish the other two tasks to Thor's satisfaction."

"It's so nice out today, let's sit on the terrace while we have breakfast."

"Okay, good idea," concurred James.

"This task is a mental as well as a physical challenge. Very few who have tried have solved the labyrinth puzzle. It is extremely easy to get lost in there. The record time of those few who have solved the labyrinth, and the time that you must match or beat, is six hours and 25 minutes. The labyrinth is situated on 20 acres of land in the woods northwest of the palace grounds. A special feature of this labyrinth is that each person who tries to enter and solve it must first construct a new portion and add it onto the labyrinth so that it continues to grow and evolve. It is constructed of large blocks, which you piece together, which are very similar to what on Earth you called 'Legos.' You construct a module and it is added to the labyrinth. It makes an extensive use of mirrors, which is one of its features that makes it so challenging. At the center of the labyrinth is a very rare lilac-colored flower called a Lilarly. You must bring out a Lilarly flower to prove you made it to the center chamber of the labyrinth."

"Have you ever actually entered and solved the labyrinth yourself, Indra?" asked James.

"No. All that I am telling you I have learned from accounts I have heard."

"So there could be a lot about the labyrinth that you don't know?"

"Yes, I suppose so."

"Are you going to join me in entering and solving the labyrinth puzzle?"

"Yes, I'd be happy to."

James and Indra were hungry and had a large breakfast served to them by the Palace of Dreams kitchen staff on the terrace as they talked. They had hot chocolate, pancakes and something that tasted like bacon. James also tried, at Indra's prodding, a pungent crimson red fruit drink made of Karmerisi berries, which tasted like a passion fruit smoothie combined with raspberries. As they were finishing breakfast, the boys paused their conversation and looked out toward the City of Pearl. James broke the silence.

"What an incredible view. The city looks so beautiful. I love how it's built around the bay with the open ocean far in the distance."

"Yes, the city is incredible. You will have to explore it up close one day."

"I hope I will soon," said James.

After breakfast, James and Indra went to the palace stables and picked up Icaraus and Tendra. The four were now familiar with each other and the Equiphins seemed to enjoy their outings with James and Indra. The boys rode their Equiphins across the palace grounds and past the palace spacecraft landing strip. They started up a tree-covered mountain.

"The labyrinth is situated on a flat clearing on the side of the mountain. It has been built using natural features in the surroundings as well as the blocks and mirrors I told you about," explained Indra.

The Equiphins floated about three feet above the ground, carrying the boys up the steep mountain path. After about one hour of riding, they came to the clearing, which Indra had described. Sprawling in front of them was a giant maze much larger than anything James had imagined. It consisted of long twisting passages connected over an area larger than 20 football fields. Many of the passageways led in circles. Some led back to the beginning. Others led to exits bringing one back out. There was only one twisting path that worked, the one that would actually bring James to the center where the Lilarly flower could be found. Then, once there, how to get back? And then there were the mirrors that created endless reflections, making the search even more confusing and challenging. James looked at the pile of blocks which had been stashed there to help with building the additional portion of the labyrinth.

"Well, let's start with something I know I can handle," James said grabbing some of the blocks. He began to fashion an intricate add-on section with several passageways leading in different directions. The blocks were many colors - deep blue, red, crimson, yellow, and emerald green. To make it even more challenging, he added mirror panels in strategic places. Indra watched but could not help. James worked for two hours straight and finally finished a beautiful addition to the labyrinth.

"Well, Indra, what do you think?" asked James pointing to the new section of the labyrinth he had constructed. "Why don't you check it out inside?" he prodded.

Indra entered and looked around. He was impressed with how James had managed to create a challenging portion of the maze with only two modules. The paths within the addition were narrow and winding. The mirrors were yet another element designed to confuse.

"That's great, James. How and where are you going to attach it, to the end or beginning of the labyrinth?"

"I think I'll add it to the beginning."

"But how are you going to get it there and attach it?" wondered Indra.

James had been thinking about the same thing. Then he had a brainstorm. He lifted his hands and turned them towards the module he had just built. He concentrated very hard and called upon all his inner strength. Slowly the module began to rise. Indra looked on in wonder. James levitated it and steered it to the beginning of the labyrinth. He slowly lowered it and adjusted it so it fit snuggly over the original entrance. He knew he had successfully met the first part of the test.

Now it was time to conquer the maze itself. James and Indra loosely tied Icarus and Tendra to a tree near the entrance of the labyrinth, where a giant hour glass stood. It was designed to time up to 12 hours very precisely and was marked with various time increments. Indra and James went up to it and turned it over to start the sand draining, thus marking the start of James' labyrinth challenge. James entered and Indra followed closely. The first part was easy since he had just built it. James simply followed the path until he spilled into the main part of the labyrinth. From there things grew incredibly more difficult. The mirrors created what looked like an endless room filled with twisting turns and paths. James looked confused and Indra sensed that this task would be a challenge. James began tentatively following one path, which wound in circles and eventually led to a dead end.

"We have to mark our paths. We have to eliminate the dead end routes and, most importantly, we have to remember how to find our way back out," James exclaimed. "What can we use? We don't have any nylon line, do we?"

"No, unfortunately not," replied Indra.

"What about our Swuns? Can't we etch marks in the walls or on the ground with it?"

"That might work. After we explore a branch of the labyrinth and it ends in a dead end we'll put an 'X' in front of it. If it goes on, we'll draw arrows showing the direction. The light from our Swuns will also help light up the labyrinth pathways."

James and Indra set out to methodically try each passageway, searching for the correct route to the center of the labyrinth and the coveted Lilarly flower. The problem with the trial and error method was that it took a very long time. Each dead end path they explored wasted precious minutes being timed by the sand pouring through the hourglass.

James and Indra meticulously checked each and every avenue. James would walk down a corridor until he came to a dead end or a branching corridor. He always was sure to mark his path and had Indra place an X in paths that didn't lead anywhere. Finally James protested, "This is taking way too long! We've got to find a faster method. We'll never beat the record if we keep going like this!"

Indra was sympathetic but didn't know what to suggest. James tried not to panic as he thought about what to do.

"Indra, does the Lilarly have a particularly strong scent?" asked James.

"Yes, and it attracts a special kind of insect, which looks like a cross between a honeybee and a butterfly. It's called a Butterbee. It sucks the nectar of the Lilarly and it can carry the Lilarly's pollen for miles."

"If we let one go in here, would it be able to follow the scent of the Lilarly?" pondered James.

"I believe it would. They have an amazing ability to detect the perfume-like scent of the Lilarly. And, oh, they also glow in the dark!"

"Perfect! That's it. We let a few loose in the labyrinth and follow their lead. One problem though, how do we find and capture a Butterbee?" asked James.

"Leave that to me. There are plenty of them in and around the mountain. They also love honey and I have some in my backpack. I will have to exit the labyrinth for a moment to attract them."

"Well, we haven't gone too far in, so let's do this quickly."

Indra followed the Swun marks back outside. He placed some honey in a cup and put it on a rock. He took out a bag from his backpack. He waited for a few minutes hoping that the Butterbees would take the bait. James continued to explore the labyrinth and was able to eliminate two routes. After a few minutes he called out to Indra.

"How's it coming, Indra? We really can't waste any more time. We have to get going."

"It will only be a few more minutes. Two Butterbees are already feeding on the honey."

Once he had four Butterbees, Indra quickly covered them with a bag from his backpack and ran back into the labyrinth. He retraced his steps and caught up with James.

"Here they are," said Indra.

Indra then opened the bag. The Butterbees glowed in the dark just as Indra had promised. There was a purple one, a sapphire one and two that glowed crimson. They looked beautiful in the dark spaces of the maze. They flew up towards the ceiling of the labyrinth once released and hovered over James and Indra. They seemed disoriented but soon seemed to key in on something and formed a colorful formation. They started gliding through the air in a slow, graceful path. It was apparent that their ultra-sensitive receptors had picked up the scent of the lilac-colored Lilarly flower and they went in search of its nectar. James and Indra had been fooled by the endless passageways, mirrors and dead ends of the labyrinth. The Butterbees, on the other hand, relying on their extraordinary sense of smell, were able to detect and follow the aroma which the Lilarlies let off. James and Indra followed the Butterbees in the hope that their gamble would pay off. At one point, the boys made their way over a rope bridge which crossed a ravine with a stream running through it. Many of the chambers were constructed of the building blocks that James had used, but parts of the walls were fashioned from rocks, boulders and the sides of the mountain. In some parts the boys had to push their way through thick vegetation. James was careful to mark their path with the Swun so he was sure that he and Indra could make their way back out of the labyrinth.

"How can we be sure they know where they are going?" asked James.

"We can't, but they seem to be doing a better job than we were doing on our own. Only a few dead ends so far."

James couldn't argue. He checked his wristwatch to see how they were doing with time. They had been searching for about three hours and forty-five minutes. James knew that if he took care to properly mark the path they would be able to make a much faster exit. Even so, he wanted to get to the center as quickly as possible. The boys plowed on, following the lead of the Butterbees. The path seemed so long and arduous that at several points James wondered if the beautiful glowing creatures he was following would be able to successfully lead him to the Lilarly flower thereby resolving the labyrinth puzzle. In the darkest parts of the labyrinth, the boys relied on their Swuns to light the way. The Butterbees kept moving slowly and purposefully. They seemed almost wise. James did not blindly follow them, but certainly relied on them to lead the way. He also realized that the search was taking a long time.

"Indra, I'm starting to get worried. It's been almost four and a half hours and we still haven't found the center chamber. Don't forget we also have to get out."

Just as James was talking, the Butterbees turned a corner and increased their flying speed greatly. James and Indra followed.

"Hey, where are they going so quickly all of a sudden?"

Finally, in the background they saw a chamber with a purple glow. The Butterbees swooped into the room first and immediately alighted on a cluster of Lilarly flowers to begin sucking their nectar. James and Indra ran in behind them. Sure enough, at the center of a large chamber of the labyrinth were several clusters of Lilarly plants and flowers. The flowers were long and slender and delicately shaped, almost like a curved champagne glass. They were lilac- colored at the top and the middle of the flower but turned pinkish-white towards the base. At the center was a long, thin bulb covered with yellow pollen. Even more impressive than the look of the flower was its perfume-like aroma, which filled the chamber. As they entered, James and Indra took a long, deep breath and felt intoxicated by the smell. After admiring the flowers and celebrating the fact that he and Indra had made it to the center of the labyrinth, James remembered his purpose. He needed to take a bunch of Lilarly flowers to prove he had solved the labyrinth and make it back out in as little time as possible.

"Come on, Indra, we have to go. I'll take the flowers we need. We have to exit the labyrinth quickly. If we want to meet or beat the record, we'll have to hurry. Time is running out."

James, not wanting to disturb the Butterbees, grabbed a handful of Lilarly flowers from a vacant plant. The boys took one last look at the center chamber where the labyrinth had ended. Guided by the Butterbees, James had been able to solve the labyrinth and now wanted to make it out in record time. Both boys lit up their Swuns so they would have better light and retraced their steps following the markings they had left along their trail. James was in the lead and broke into a giddy run.

"Come on, Indra, we can do this. If we hurry, I bet we can set a new record."

Indra followed suit. After running for a while the boys became a bit winded but James spurred them on.

"We can rest when we're outside. We've been in here for six hours. We still have a chance at the record!"

The boys rounded a corner of the path and saw the rope bridge. James sprinted over it. The rope bridge was swaying when Indra approached. Seeing that James had already crossed it, Indra increased his speed in an attempt to catch up. All of a sudden his shoe hit the swaying rope bridge in an awkward manner and he twisted his ankle. He fell forward and skidded under the suspension side barriers of the bridge. He tried to grab onto the bridge's rope to try to stop his fall. Unfortunately, he hung by one arm for a split second and then lost his grasp. He fell down into the steep, rocky divide, which the bridge traversed. He screamed out loudly.

"James, help me. Help!"

James heard Indra's scream and froze. He ran back to the bridge to see what had happened. He looked down and saw Indra writhing in pain clutching at his ankle. During the fall Indra had injured his ankle and his leg had become lodged between some rocks. James looked over the terrain and saw that there were several ledges and large boulders, which he could use to launch off of. He first jumped off the bridge to a small ledge, then to another and finally to the top of a large boulder. He finally made it to the ground next to Indra. Indra was trying to be brave about the situation, but James saw that he was scared and in pain.

"James, I'll be alright here for a while. Time is running out. Why don't you complete the task and come back for me?"

"Are you kidding, Indra? I can't leave you like this."

James examined the situation and realized that he would have to move a heavy boulder to free Indra from the rocks. In the meantime, it was clear that Indra was in great pain. James went behind the rock he wanted to move and pushed with all his might. It barely budged. James stepped back and tried to think clearly. He remembered that he had powers from the crystals and brought them to bear on the situation. He raised his hand and focused on the rock that was pinning Indra down. Slowly, he was able to raise it. When Indra was finally freed, James cried out, "Indra, roll out of the way. I've got the rock up but will put it down quickly as soon as you're out of harm's way."

Indra rolled away from the rock and James plunked it down. Indra got up and limped over to sit on another rock.

"Be careful not to put too much weight on your ankle. It could be broken."

"I know, but I hope it's just twisted."

"We are going to have to get you out of here," James observed.

"James, I'm asking you. Please finish the task and come back to get me. I'll be alright. You can still break the record if you hurry."

"Indra, that's not going to happen. I will not leave you here alone. We came this far together and we will finish this task together. It may not be in record time, but we will complete it together."

James looked around and saw it would be difficult, if not impossible, for him to scale the walls while helping or carrying Indra to get out of the ravine. He would have to come up with a different way. James wracked his brain, but was at a loss as to what to do. Finally, an idea came to him. James realized he might be able to levitate Indra back up to the rope bridge. He concentrated and thrust his hand forward, focusing it on Indra, and moved it upward. Slowly, Indra began to rise. James lifted him carefully so that he would not fall and after a minute or two, James brought Indra to rest on the bridge. James quickly jumped upward from ledge to ledge to join Indra on the rope bridge.

"Thank you, James. You are truly amazing!"

"How's your ankle feeling?"

"It hurts, but not as much as before."

"Come on, let's get you out of here. Put your arm around my shoulder. If we follow the markings, we should be out in no time."

James glanced at his watch. They had already been in the maze six hours. He knew that they would never be able to match or beat the record time.

"James, you might still be able to beat the record. Go on without me and finish. I'll be alright."

"I already told you, Indra. That's not going to happen. I won't leave you by yourself."

James lifted Indra and the two made their way through the rest of the labyrinth as quickly as they could, but it was at a much slower rate than when they both could run. Indra limped, but although his leg had been badly scraped and his ankle twisted, it did not seem broken. James tried to support him so that he would place as little weight on it as possible. After following the path they had been careful to mark entering the labyrinth and finding their way to the center chamber with the help of the Butterbees, they finally made their way out.

The sun was setting as the boys emerged. Icarus and Tendra bobbed their heads up and down and whinnied signaling their happiness at seeing their masters return. James helped Indra onto Tendra and then mounted Icarus. James looked at the giant hourglass. It showed that seven hours and 42 minutes had elapsed since the boys' investigation of the labyrinth had begun. They had finished the third task, but clearly not in record time. James briefly felt a tinge of regret, knowing he could have set a new record if Indra had not fallen, but quickly put it out of his mind. The boys descended the mountain and returned to the palace before stowing the Equiphins so that Indra could have his leg and ankle tended to. James then brought the Equiphins to the stables and returned to the palace to check on Indra, grab some dinner and then some sleep. He knew that he and Indra would be meeting with Thor the next morning.

44

HANDLING CHALLENGES

After breakfast, James and Indra walked quickly towards the now-familiar room where they would meet Thor. Indra's ankle had been tightly bandaged to give it support. He used a crutch so that he could keep his weight off it and walk faster. The palace doctor had confirmed that it had been badly twisted, but thankfully it was not broken. James was satisfied that he had succeeded in meeting the challenges which Thor had placed in his path, though he realized he had not met or bested the record time on the labyrinth challenge. James and Indra arrived in the room and sat on a comfortable emerald, red and sapphire blue puffed sofa awaiting Thor's arrival.

Predictably, Thor arrived with Alisha on a pallet descending from the ceiling. This time there appeared to be many more advisors with him. Verne, who had apparently returned to The Galaxy Cruiser for a few days, was back. Devlin, Thor's advisor was also present. There were two boys who James had never seen before. There was someone who looked like a spaceship commander and many others. Devlin quieted everyone down and Thor took charge of the gathering.

"Ladies and gentlemen, I have brought you together to join with me in congratulating James on completing the three tasks I set out for him. As I have stated publically before, I believe that James has unique abilities, intelligence, characteristics and qualities that suit him well to be a leader of some kind one day. I want him to be trained and educated by the best and, accordingly, I have made arrangements for James to enter The Starflight Academy."

Thor paused briefly and then turned and spoke directly to James.

"Now, James, you might rightly wonder why you have been put to these tests, why I asked you to perform these tasks. Life consists of a journey filled with many tests, challenges, opportunities, conquests, victories as well as disappointments. It is only when one is faced with them that one can demonstrate what one is truly made of. What is a person's true worth? It is easy to pilot a ship through still waters. If you are a true leader and a captain, you must be able to lead a crew and pilot a ship through a storm and come out alive on the other side of its fury. There is nothing better to bring out one's true inner self than challenges and adversity. You must possess skill, conviction, determination and demonstrate bravery to confront them and prevail. You must use your wits, but never forget or surrender your heart and intuition, for they'll guide and tell you what to do when all else fails."

Thor looked at James and fell silent for a moment. Then he continued, "And there is one more thing. When you look for purpose or meaning in life, you will find it in love. Without love, you are hollow and empty, devoid of purpose. Love of a friend, a soul mate and of your children. You will find it in the glimmers of light during a sunset, in an emotion called music and in touching, helping others in need and sharing the lives of others along your way. And you will find it in doing something you truly love. You will never achieve anything truly great unless you love what you are doing. And if you have done your best and given something your all, well, no one can ask for anything more."

The room remained silent as Thor stopped speaking for a moment and let his words sink in. Then he continued.

"Yesterday you solved the labyrinth puzzle using your wits as well as your abilities and certain powers. You did a great job."

"Thank you, Your Majesty. I know though that I failed to meet or achieve the record time for solving the puzzle and entering and leaving the labyrinth," James said modestly.

"Quite true. You did not set a new time record, yet you demonstrated something even more important. From my briefings, I learned that you rescued and stood by Indra when he tripped and was injured. This showed me that though you are ambitious and capable, you have heart and loyalty, that you would stop and help someone even if it would have an adverse impact on your personal achievement. From what I understand, you could have bested the record time if you had chosen to leave Indra and come back for him. Yet you didn't. You thought more of his safety than your own personal gain, and for that I applaud and admire you, James."

James thanked Thor for his kind words and then he remembered something he had meant to do. He stuck his hand into a leather satchel he had slung over one shoulder. With some flourish, he pulled out the Lilarly flowers, which he had taken from the labyrinth. He then stepped up onto the elevated palette and handed them to Alisha. Everyone applauded upon seeing the proof that James had indeed successfully entered, solved and returned from the labyrinth.

James remembered that after each task Thor had posed a riddle for him to answer. He expected no less this time. And in a minute the question came.

"James, you are in room with three goddesses who can grant you a wish. The first one offers you wealth and power. The second offers you victory in all battles, glory and wisdom. The third offers you true love. Which do you choose?"

James thought for only a minute. A pain went through his heart as he continued to feel that certain emptiness he felt due to the loss of his memory. He knew he missed certain people he loved but he could still not remember them. In a soft voice he answered.

"Love," he said simply, "because without love, the others don't have much meaning."

Thor was silent and stunned. James had shown that he not only had the abilities and powers that Thor admired, but that he had also acquired some wisdom, even at his young age.

"That question was not only posed as a riddle. Your answer to it reveals another admirable aspect of your character. So, James, you have performed all your tasks and answered the riddles I have posed. From those accomplishments and everything else that I know about you, you have earned a place at The Starflight Academy. You will start in a matter of weeks.

"Today I would like you to meet two students about your age who are already enrolled at the Academy.

"Constantine and Alexander, please come over here. Constantine, who I told you about before, is my brother's son. Alexander is the son of my trusted advisor, Devlin."

James extended his hand to both Constantine and Alexander.

"Glad to meet you."

"Same here," answered Constantine warmly with a smile.

"Greetings," Alexander mumbled distantly as he shook James' hand.

Constantine had bright blue eyes and blond shoulder-length hair and a slender, but strong build. His demeanor and laugh were friendly. Alexander, on the other hand, didn't laugh or smile much. He had brown hair and brown eyes. He effused a certain aloof, almost hostile, toughness. Although James said nothing, he immediately noticed the difference in character. Thor continued.

"James, I have two surprises for you. First, I have arranged for you to go on a tour of the City of Pearl tomorrow in the late afternoon, starting at about 5:30. Alisha will accompany you. A week from this Saturday evening, we will be hosting a giant intergalactic ball at the palace. Heads of various planets in our and other galaxies will arrive and spend a week here. There will be many meetings, dinners and other celebrations during the week. The gathering culminates with the intergalactic ball next Saturday. You will attend as my guest. This will be a fitting way to transition you into the Starflight Academy. Once again congratulations! You have performed admirably. Take the rest of the day to relax and enjoy the palace facilities and grounds. Tomorrow will also be a big day when you will tour the city for the first time."

Indra, James, Constantine and Alisha congregated and made plans to meet for a swim in the palace pool. Alexander was invited to come but declined. About half an hour after the meeting with Thor ended, the four rendezvoused at the pool. It had sliding glass panels on the sides and the roof, which could be opened in good weather. If the weather was cold or rainy, they could all be shut. The pool had beautiful tropical plants, trees and flowers growing in the greenhouse-like structure that covered it. There were many palm trees with coconuts, red flowers and orchids of blue, purple and white. The pool was shaped like a large lagoon with ample swimming sections as well as some twisting passageways lined with small bays. Five separate waterfalls were built in and around the pool, providing a beautiful backdrop of cascading water falling in sheer sheets, each emitting the calming, rushing sound of water tumbling over rocks into the pool below. Jets of water shot upward in certain sections of the pool. At one side of the pool was a giant, twisting water slide. Underneath one of the waterfalls was a swim-up bar which served tropical drinks and various snacks. James arrived wearing a bright red and blue bathing suit ready to jump right into the pool. When he saw the giant water slide, he couldn't resist.

"Wow, look at the size of the water slide! I've got to try it!"

With that, James dove into the comfortably heated water. He swam to the slide and climbed up the stairs to the top. Without hesitation he bounced down and began his thrilling ride.

"YES!" he shouted with glee as he shot downwards, gaining speed with every twist and turn.

Indra, Constantine and Alisha saw James and followed suit. For a solid two hours the four ran up the stairs and slid down the slide, laughing and shouting on their way down. After the slide ride, the four swam together through the lagoon portions of the pool. James and Indra dove under the water and held their breath as long as they could before surfacing. Alisha found a float and sat atop it as Constantine and James pushed her through the lagoon until they mischievously turned it over, making her fall with a splash into the pool. They went behind the waterfalls and looked out at the palace grounds through the sheer back of the waterfall and the glass walls surrounding the pool. James could sense that he and Constantine would become good friends.

After four hours of horsing around, the four dried off and headed to the adjoining arcade room. James challenged Constantine to a laser blast game of dueling spaceships. Within minutes into the first game, James had blasted Constantine's spaceship out of the sky.

"Next victim! Come on, Indra," cried James.

Indra stepped up to the arcade game. He put up the best fight he could, but he too fell to James' incredibly fast reflexes and dexterity.

"Come on, Alisha!" James challenged.

Without hesitation, Alisha stepped up to the challenge.

The game started quickly. Surprisingly, at least to James, Alisha held her own and the two dueled back and forth, shooting laser beams at the other's spaceship. Each player evaded the blasts of the other or managed to block the shot with a defensive shield of their own. *Wow this is going to be harder than I thought,* James reflected, realizing that he had underestimated Alisha's abilities. In a split second, while James was thinking about his opponent's surprisingly strong fight, Alisha shot two quick laser blasts at James' spacecraft and blew it out of the sky.

"Game over! I won!" gloated Alisha.

"I want a rematch," protested James.

"No, I beat you fair and square!" Alisha laughed.

"Come on. Just one more game," pleaded James.

"Okay. One more game - that's it," Alisha answered.

This time, James was much more cautious and concentrated harder. After a long-fought battle, James called on all his skills and managed to blast Alisha's spaceship out of the skies.

"Yes," he shouted. "One more game, Alisha?" James asked.

"No. Now we're even. Let's leave it at that."

"Okay," conceded James.

After a few more hours of fun in the arcade and pool, the four reluctantly agreed that they had had enough for the day. They decided to get changed and meet to for a walk through the palace grounds before dinner.

45

COMET

One Saturday after breakfast, Julia was up in her room think-ing about James. *I miss him so much.* She looked through some pictures of him on her iPod. She also checked the video feed of the probe on her laptop computer. That only made it worse. George sat in the living room drinking a cup of coffee reading the morning paper on his iPad. Jenifer was on the phone while clean-ing up in the kitchen. Suddenly, Misty started barking. Seconds later the doorbell rang. George got up to open the door. Before him stood Mrs. McKenzie.

"Come in, Mary Ellen, come in."

"Thank you, George."

As she stepped into the house, George noticed a very small, cute puppy on a thin leash. It was a rich reddish brown with a small white patch over one eye and on its chin.

"Jenifer, Julia, come on down. Mrs. McKenzie is here for a visit."

Julia heard her father's call and bounded down the stairs. Jenifer wrapped up her telephone call and came in.

"Hello, Mary Ellen. Please sit down. Can I offer you some tea?" asked Jenifer.

"Thank you very much. I'd love some."

Julia came down and immediately spotted the little puppy.

"Wow, that puppy has grown so much since I last saw the newborn litter. It's so cute."

"Yes, it has. That's what I've come to talk to you and your parents about. The puppies are getting bigger and I have too many. You might recall this is Comet."

"I remember. It's the runt that was James' favorite and we named it together."

"Exactly, Julia. What I want to know is, if it's okay with your parents, of course, whether you would like to keep Comet? That way he'd still be close by and could come over for visits and I'd know he was in safe, loving hands."

"Wow, I'd love to keep him. Mom, Dad, is it okay? Please?" pleaded Julia enthusiastically.

Misty first looked at the cute puppy with a tinge of jealousy. Gradually, after she saw how excited Julia was, she came to accept it and seemed to realize that it would be fun to have a playmate. She finally went over and playfully licked Comet, giving him her seal of approval.

George and Jenifer looked at each other. After seeing how excited Julia was, George shrugged his shoulders and said "Why not? It's okay with me."

"I agree, as long as you promise to take care of him, Julia. She will be *your* responsibility not Dad's or mine. Agreed?" asked Jenifer knowing full well that she and George would likely have to pitch in if Julia didn't fully keep her end of the bargain.

"Yes, Mom, I promise!"

"Well, Mary Ellen, I guess the answer is yes. We'd be happy to adopt him," Jenifer answered.

Jenifer then went to the kitchen and brought the tea out to the living room. George, Jenifer and Mrs. McKenzie chatted while Julia and Misty played with Comet. Julia threw a ball and Comet went charging after it, letting out high-pitched puppy barks as he hunted it down and brought it back to Julia to throw again. Misty jumped in one time and grabbed the ball while it was in midair. Comet gave his yipping bark and nipped at Misty's heels in protest.

"I think it would be best if I brought Comet over a few times to play so he can get used to your house before I leave him. That way the separation will be gradual and not such a shock."

"That will be fine. I'll explain it to Julia."

"One more thing, and I hate to bring it up because I know how hard it must be for you - have you learned anything more about James' disappearance or his whereabouts?"

George and Jenifer were silent. George put up a brave front.

"Nothing concrete yet but we are working on a few leads. We won't give up until we understand what happened and we get him back."

Mrs. McKenzie just nodded and said, "That's good. My prayers are with you."

The Wyatts chatted with Mrs. McKenzie for a while longer and then she got up to leave.

"Come on, Comet'" she called out. "You'll be back."

Comet was so involved with Julia and Misty that she ignored Mrs. McKenzie's call for a good five minutes. Finally, Mrs. McKenzie bent down and put a leash on him. Comet was having so much fun that Mrs. McKenzie almost had to drag him out.

"I can see he loves it here already. I guess the transition period will be shorter than I thought."

"Thank you, Mary Ellen. I know Comet will be happy with us. You've made Julia very happy with your thoughtful generosity."

46

A GLITTERING NIGHT

The late afternoon sun started to sink beyond the horizon as James dressed with care and combed his hair for the third time. He knew that in a few minutes he was to meet Alisha in the central palace courtyard for the special tour of the City of Pearl which Thor had arranged and he wanted to look his best. Finally, when he had his hair, clothes and shoes just right, he ventured out of his room and headed to the palace courtyard.

When he arrived, he observed a large transport vehicle hovering above the ground with a glass dome covering it. There was a driver in the front and a lady who sat next to him. James approached the craft and peered inside. He did not see Alisha, but the lady noticed him and got up to welcome him.

"You must be James. Please, step in. Alisha will be here in a few minutes. My name is Luna. I will be your chaperone and guide tonight."

James mounted the stairs leading to the hovering vehicle. The seats were covered with soft leather and swiveled slightly so that he could change his view, almost like a swiveling lounge chair.

There was a bar stocked with interesting drinks colored red, orange, lavender and pink and tasty-looking snacks.

"Welcome to the royal limo hovercraft. We'll be serving soft drinks tonight, of course, and the snacks you see at the bar. If you're thirsty or hungry, please help yourself, James."

As she was talking, Alisha arrived wearing a beautiful pleated, long, blue dress. Her raven black hair was braided behind her and almost reached her waist. She wore a gold crown with a crimson red gem in the front center. Alisha was accompanied by Esmeralda, one of her favorite handmaidens. James jumped over to the entrance and helped Alisha and Esmerelda open the door and get seated.

"Hi, Alisha. Good to see you tonight. You look really great. I'm excited to finally get the opportunity to get to know the City of Pearl."

"Hi, James. Yes, it should be a lot of fun. I've also asked my cousin, Constantine, to accompany us. He always runs a little late, but he'll be here in a couple of minutes. I want you to meet my handmaiden, Esmerelda."

"Hello, Esmerelda. Pleased to meet you," James replied.

James, Alisha and Esmerelda sat and talked together waiting for Constantine. After greeting Alisha and Esmerelda, Luna talked with Cervian, the pilot of the hovercraft limo. Esmerelda was quiet and reserved but had a shy, winning smile. She was very beautiful with long, golden hair and green eyes that sparkled with mystery. Finally, Constantine arrived and the tour began.

To James, the limo hovercraft felt almost like a flying carpet covered with a glass dome. Cervian opened the glass covering slightly at the top so that fresh air could circulate. The hovercraft limo glided smoothly out of the palace courtyard and followed a long road leading to the heavily guarded main gate. Once outside the palace compound, the limo hovercraft accelerated onto a large highway, which wound its way down from the plateau on which the palace was situated to the City of Pearl below. The highway provided an incredible view of the city as well as of the ocean coastline. An amazing reddish-purple Carmesí sunset began just when the hovercraft limo was about a quarter way down the mountain en route to the city.

"As you can see, James," Luna began, "the City of Pearl is built wrapped around the beach. Near the center of the city is the Fire, Wind and Thunder Stadium. Not far away is the Heroes' Arch. The city is laid out in concentric circles surrounding the enormous Shooting Star Park in the center. That large structure near the beach and boat piers is the aquarium. It contains many exotic sea creatures, some of which are completely different from those you would find in an aquarium on Earth. For example, it contains stingrays which can actually fly for short distances above the water. There are also some smaller versions of the Hydrashark. Aside from those sea creatures, there are dolphins, swordfish and baby whales in giant tanks. There is also a special creature called a Swidron, which looks like a green, yellow, blue and black sea serpent. First, we will drive through the city streets and visit some of the landmarks I have pointed out to you. Then we will circle back to the aquarium for a tour and dinner before returning to the palace. I think you will enjoy it."

"Wow, that sounds incredible," agreed James.

James sat next to Alisha and Esmeralda sat next to Constantine. The four talked, laughed and giggled amongst themselves as they watched the city sites unfold from the comfort of the limo hovercraft.

Once they arrived in the City of Pearl, Cervian followed the coast. James took note of how beautiful the beaches were. The sand was silver and gold colored and had an eerie glow in the dark. The ocean's vastness stretched on for as far as the eye could see.

"Wow, look at that!" James cried out. "The sand here is silver and gold and it glows!"

Alisha, Constantine and Esmeralda looked on with amusement and took heart at how enthusiastic James was about things which they took for granted. As the tour continued, Luna carried on.

"On your left is the Fire, Wind and Thunder Stadium I pointed out to you earlier. This is where tournaments, jousts, games and concerts are held. The stadium can hold over 100,000 spectators. James, you should definitely come and see a tournament one day!"

"I would love to when I get the chance," answered James.

One by one they passed by the various sites that Luna had pointed out earlier, along with many others. She explained and commented on each in greater detail. After about one and half hours, the group seemed to get restless and hungry for dinner. Noticing their impatience, Luna made an announcement.

"Now we'll head back to the coast and the aquarium for dinner."

"Yeah!" everyone cried.

When the limo hovercraft pulled up to the aquarium, the captain lowered the craft so that it rested on the ground, making it easier to disembark. Luna escorted the party into the aquarium.

The tanks were huge, the size of an eighth of a football field. As promised, there were many incredible species of exotic-looking fish and other incredible sea creatures. They were multicolored and came in all shapes and sizes. James especially enjoyed a tank filled with rainbow-colored electric eels. He also liked the seals, dolphins and seal lions. The largest tanks were reserved for a whale shark, the Swidron and the dolphins. After the tour of the aquarium itself, the four headed up to an elevated revolving restaurant situated in a tower on the roof of the aquarium.

The party took a table for six right next to the window. The city lights twinkled in the background as darkness settled in. Looking out toward the water, James could see dark waves lapping at the shore of the beautiful gold and silver colored beaches. The restaurant revolved slowly, taking a full hour to complete an entire turn.

Alisha and James looked at a menu together until James briefly glanced up and into Alisha's eyes. He had never seen a girl look at him in quite that way. Slightly embarrassed he quickly refocused on the menu. When everyone was ready, a waitress named Kaitlyn came over to take dinner requests. James ordered a broccoli cheddar soup and steak. Alisha ordered a special dish known on Carmesí as "sunrluke," which consisted of seafood and mushrooms mixed with pasta. Soft music played overhead. James and Alisha talked until their dinners came. About midway through dinner, a special announcement was made on the restaurant loudspeaker system.

"Ladies and gentlemen, please turn your attention to the bay in front of you. The nightly show will begin in five minutes."

James looked mystified. "What show?" he asked.

"It's a surprise. Just watch down there," said Alisha, pointing to the waters in front of the aquarium.

Bright lights were turned on around the bay in front of the aquarium. After a few minutes there was a large swirling of the waters and the Swidron's large head and body shot out. It rose and dove several times.

"Wow, that's cool. Is it dangerous?" asked James.

"It's constrained by electric fields surrounding the bay. Also, this Swidron has been in captivity for so long that it is used to human beings. It is essentially harmless," Alisha answered.

A few minutes later two large dolphins and a large whale appeared. They took several laps around the bay and leapt high into the air twisting and turning and splashing down into the water. Next the serpent bent its long body creating three U-shaped openings. The dolphins and the killer whale went to one edge of the bay and swam quickly towards the Swidron. At the last possible second, they shot upward out of the water and did a flip in the air, passing perfectly through the U shapes created by the Swidron's body. All the onlookers from the restaurant clapped as the dolphins and killer whale completed their jumps. The show continued for about half an hour more with the dolphins jumping high into the air and doing a backward flip. Not to be outdone, the killer whale went to the center of the pavilion and dove very deep. Within seconds it shot straight upward and came crashing down in a spiral creating a huge splash.

"Looks a little like the gymnastics show you gave," Alisha joked.

James smiled and gave her a playful nudge in return.

Dinner was delicious. James, Alisha, Esmeralda and Constantine all polished off their meals. They each ordered a large piece of chocolate cake for dessert. As the dinner came to an end, Constantine and James spent some time discussing the Starflight Academy. James had a lot of questions and Constantine was happy to try and answer them. James' initial feeling that he would become a good friend was reinforced the more the two spoke.

Alisha and Esmeralda talked and laughed, whispering amongst themselves and giggling. Finally, James looked over at Alisha.

"Hey, what are you guys laughing at?" he asked.

"Oh nothing," Alisha replied.

James shook his head and rolled his eyes in exasperation. Then he finished up his conversation with Constantine. Everyone was getting a bit tired. Finally, Luna announced it was time to go.

"We still have a bit of a ride to the palace. We'd better get going."

Everyone took one last look at the bay and the city from the revolving tower restaurant and then made their way back to the Limo Hovercraft. James slid into a seat right next to Alisha. He felt that he wanted to talk to her and get to know her better. Constantine sat next to Esmeralda. They seemed to hit it off. Once everyone was seated, the Limo Hovercraft commenced its return to the palace.

Cervian once again chose a route that stayed close to the beautiful City of Pearl beaches. Finally, he branched off to the road, which wound up the mountain to the plateau on which the palace stood. As they rode higher and higher, the city lights became glittering, yellowish-white specks, emitting a peaceful glow. It had been a great evening. James loved the City of Pearl tour and especially the aquarium show. He felt closer to Alisha and Constantine and was glad to see he was making some dear friends.

The limo hovercraft finally arrived back at the palace and stopped at the security gate. The gate seemed familiar to James, but he could not place from where. Once back at the palace square, the four tour guests, now quite tired, thanked Luna and Cervian for the incredible evening. They said goodnight and headed back to their respective rooms to get a good night's rest. Just before they closed their eyes, James and Alisha thought back on the day and of each other and then drifted off into a sound sleep.

47

BLINDED

Julia's heart filled with excitement as she waited for the Space Club members to arrive for the final meeting before the winter holiday break. At tonight's meeting, each club member was going to point out a significant feature about the planet they had chosen to report on and reveal if it was named after a Roman or Greek god or goddess.

By 7:35 everyone had arrived and Julia began the meeting. The club members gathered in James' room and sat in a semi-circle. Robert horsed around with James' telescope until Julia asked him nicely to sit down and pay attention.

"Katherine, why don't you go first? Which planet are you covering again?"

"Mars."

"Okay, let's listen to what Katherine has to say about Mars this week."

"Mars has two moons named Deimos and Phobos," Katherine began. "It's reddish in color and was named after the god of war of the ancient Romans."

"That's very interesting, Katherine, anything else you can tell us?"

"Well, I also found out it has two polar ice caps."

"Great. Now how about you, Robert?"

"My planet is Mercury," began Robert. "It was named after a Roman god. Mercury has a very oval-shaped or elliptical orbit. At the closest point, which is called the perihelion, it's about 28.58 million miles from the Sun. At the farthest point in its orbit, which is called the aphelion, it's about 48 million miles from the Sun."

"Very cool. We are really learning a lot by sharing information like this. Let's hear from Stephanie about Venus before we take a break to check on James' space probe."

"Venus is named after the Roman goddess of love and beauty. Venus is known as Earth's 'twin sister' because it is relatively close to Earth and is about the same size. It is covered in clouds filled with sulfuric acid."

"Great, Stephanie. Now let's take a short break and check on the pictures and live feed being sent back to Earth from the probe."

Everyone looked forward to this point in the meeting. The pictures from space were always spectacular and the live video feed was amazing. It was something they were unable to experience anywhere except at the meeting. Julia logged on through her laptop and beamed the picture to a large screen TV, which her father had brought into James' room for that purpose. The Space Club members looked on excitedly. The screen flickered to life. Everyone admired the still pictures, which included planets, a swirled galaxy, stars and comets.

"And now for the coolest part!" announced Julia, switching to the live video feed.

Everyone craned his or her neck to get a closer look. The stars and planets sailed by in real time. There was even a way to zoom the camera lens. The club members watched for a good ten minutes. Julia was getting ready to turn it off and move on with the meeting, but just as she was about to do so, there was a loud explosion and a fiery reddish-orange flame, which filled the screen. After a few seconds, the video feed went completely dark.

"Hey, what happened? That looked pretty scary!" called out Katherine nervously.

Julia tried to refresh the screen and then closed down the browser and tried to restart and re-enter the site to look at the live video feed again. Again the screen was black. Now Julia was really concerned.

"This doesn't look good. I've got to find out what happened. I'm going to get my dad."

Julia went charging down the stairs. Breathlessly, she approached her father in the living room, where he was watching some TV.

"Dad, come quickly. There seems to be something wrong with the video feed from the probe. It's blank. Completely black."

"Don't worry. It's probably just a technical glitch. I'll come up and see what I can do."

"Come on, Dad. Please hurry. Everyone's waiting."

George climbed up the stairs two at a time. He followed Julia into the room and greeted everyone briefly. He took control of her laptop and shut down the web browser and restarted it. Everything came up fine and George logged onto the probe site. As Julia had before, George first saw the still photos, which came up beautifully. George stopped a minute to admire them. Then he moved on to the live video feed area of the site and tried to make it come up. It remained black and there was no picture. He pulled out his iPhone and made a call to SPACETECK.

"Hello, it's George Wyatt. Please patch me through to Jimmy in operations monitoring."

George waited a few seconds and Jimmy answered the call.

"Hello, Jimmy, its George Wyatt. I tried to log onto the live video feed site from James' probe but it's coming up blank. Do you guys know what' s going on?"

"We are aware of the problem. In fact, we called Mr. Silver to tell him about it. George, I have to level with you, things don't look good. We are not one hundred percent sure as to what happened, but we do know there was a large flash and an explosion just before the video feed went dead. This is only speculation on my part at this point, but I feel that I must tell you - it is likely that that the probe exploded. There is a small possibility that it is intact and the picture just needs to be reactivated by sending some signals to the probe. We are just not sure yet and we are trying to get the signal back."

"Thank you, Jimmy. I guess we'll have to wait and pray," said George.

George tried to remain composed as he hung up the phone.

"I know this is going to be hard to accept, but SPACETECK has informed me that there is a possibility that the probe has blown up in space after colliding with something. There is a slight possibility that transmission of a signal from here on Earth can be sent that would reactivate the probe camera, but that is very doubtful."

Tears welled up in Julia's eyes. Her last possible avenue to find or contact James seemed to have evaporated right in front of her. She did not take the news well.

"I am sorry - I have to call an early end to this meeting. This is really terrible news. Our last possible connection to James seems to be lost," said Julia, bravely fighting back tears.

All the Space Club members came over to Julia, and one by one gave her a hug. They then chatted quietly about the situation as they waited for their parents to pick them up. Julia became withdrawn, sad and silent as she thought of the potential ramifications of the loss of the video feed. It had been her and her family's one last hope to find out what had happened to James and now it had vanished.

48

BEWARE!

Just as Thor had described to James, starting a week ahead of
the Intergalactic Ball, droves of visitors arrived from many planets throughout the universe at the City of Pearl Spaceport, a super
modern landing strip for spacecraft. Some were shuttled to the finest hotels in the city. The very special guests were escorted directly
to the palace and given a room of their own. Thor played the con-
summate host, greeting each and every visitor to the palace. There
were parties, meetings, and dinners where everyone talked about
various problems confronting the galaxies.

One evening, while Thor was having dinner with some
guests, he was interrupted by one of his advisors, who hurriedly
whispered something into his ear. Thor got up and excused
himself. He asked Verne, who was at a nearby table, to come
with him. They headed back to Thor's private living quarters in
the palace, which also contained a large media and control room
filled with screens, tablets and the latest computer equipment.
He flipped on a special monitor and was instantly connected to
Captain Jahl, the Captain of The Galaxy Cruiser.

"Good evening, Your Majesty. There has been an incident I want you to be aware of, especially in light of the upcoming Intergalactic Ball."

"Yes, Jahl, I'm all ears. What's the problem?"

"As you know, the Sytheons have attacked various supply spacecraft from numerous planets in order to steal the supplies and resources on board for their own use. Things have gotten particularly bad lately - they are attacking with more frequency and success. They use a special force field that disables the targeted vessel so that it can't move or defend itself. Then they board and take the supplies and thereafter destroy the spaceship. It seems that there are shortages of supplies both on their home planet of Sytheus and for use in powering and supplying Sytheon spacecraft."

"Go on," prodded Thor.

"To counter their operations we put together a multi-planet strike force of skilled space fighter pilots. Yesterday, when a Sytheon spacecraft tried to take the supplies from a transport craft, the strike force in stealth mode swept down on it and successfully destroyed it. Later we learned that the Sytheon spacecraft was commanded by Pluto, who was the youngest son of Vlexor, the ruthless ruler of Sytheus. Vlexor is said to be grief-stricken and outraged at the loss of his youngest son and has vowed to seek revenge. He specifically mentioned you and The Crimson Planet as potential targets."

"Thank you, Jahl, for the warning. We'll certainly have to be vigilant. We'll redouble our security efforts around the City of Pearl and here at the palace. You and your men will have to secure Carmisi's airspace. Vlexor is ruthless and powerful, but I am confident our forces can defeat him in a head to head battle."

"I agree, Your Majesty, but when he acts irrationally and unexpectedly, Vlexor can be very dangerous."

"Keep me posted, Jahl, and thank you again for all your efforts."

Thor contacted Devlin and ordered him to advise the palace guard, the fighter space pilots charged with protecting the city's airspace, and other officials in the City of Pearl to be vigilant and to heighten security. Thereafter, Thor and Verne returned to the dinner and apologized for their absence. They then continued with the banquet as if nothing had happened, so as not to upset their guests.

The week flew by with numerous events scheduled, all leading up to the Intergalactic Ball. James had heard so many accolades and rumors about it, that, by Friday, he was very excited.

"One more night until the Intergalactic Ball. I can't wait," James exclaimed.

"It's something you have to see to believe. The food, the music, the entertainment - the sheer magnitude of everything will be something you will never forget."

49

THE INTERGALACTIC BALL

At 7:00 p.m. on Saturday night, the line of limo hovercafts stretched for two miles beyond the palace gate. After passing through the gate, the limos continued along the palace roads until they got to the special circular drive entrance to the Crystal Ballroom. After guests were dropped off at the entrance, the heads of each of the invited planets and their assistants, family and associates made their way up a crimson carpet leading them to the amazing Intergalactic Ball.

The Crystal Ballroom was enormous, easily the size of two huge Earth-sized cruise ship ocean liners placed side by side. It could hold over three thousand people. There were sparkling crystal chandeliers hanging throughout the room. In the center of the ballroom was a high, glass-covered ceiling dome, which allowed sunlight to enter during the day and bright moonbeams to filter in during the night. There were smaller stages and platforms, featuring dancers and gymnasts performing for the guests, scattered throughout the facility.

Jugglers and mimes walked around the ballroom, providing further entertainment. Large, circular dinner tables were set up for the representatives from each planet. The tables were elegantly adorned with golden goblets, delicate fluted champagne glasses, beautifully patterned china and amazing sapphire, crimson, yellow and purple orchids as centerpieces. The tables surrounded a giant dance floor in the center of the ballroom, which featured tiles which looked like elegant white marble squares but whose color could be changed from below to create whole pictures or pulse in sympathy with the music. Aside from human-looking visitors, there were many other intelligent life forms from planets throughout the galaxies, varying in size, shape and color. Some looked like upright walking antelopes with the head of a ram with horns, others like giant snails with human-like heads and antennae. There were numerous other variations.

In the middle of the ballroom, against one wall, was a stage featuring an intergalactic band with musicians from various planets who performed music and songs. Some of it was soft and melodic, moving the guest to tears, some rhythmic with a strong drum beat, some sounded much like classical music on Earth and some rock, and as the evening wore on, more and more dance music. Near the stage, on an elevated platform, was a special semi-circular table reserved for Thor, his closest advisors, the leaders of some of Carmesí's greatest allies, Alisha, Verne, Constantine, Devlin and James. Acrobats leapt, spun and swung from special swings hanging from the ceiling. Food stations serving all kinds of incredible foods and drinks were scattered through out the Crystal Ballroom. Waiters dressed in elegant tuxedoes circulated, passing out hot and cold appetizers to the guests. Video monitors showed changing pictures and videos from different planets, space explorations and the visiting dignitaries. The guests continued to filter in. By about 8:00 it looked like most of the guests had arrived. At that point, the music quieted and the bandleader made an announcement.

"Ladies and gentlemen, our host Thor, will be arriving momentarily. Everyone please take your seats."

This time James had been invited to gather with Thor, Devlin, Alisha, Verne, Constantine, Indra and others in Thor's inner circle so that they could all enter together. Because James entered with the royal party, he was allowed to bring his beautifully decorated Swun. The doors at the far end of the Crystal Ballroom adjoining the palace were thrown open and Thor, accompanied by his party, entered to loud applause and great fanfare. Thor climbed onto the platform where his table was located and waved to the visitors as they cheered him. He mouthed the words, "Thank you! Thank you! Please sit down." After a few minutes of applause, the room quieted down and dinner was served. James looked around in amazement, taking in the entire scene and looking at all the visiting dignitaries. He leaned over to Alisha and exclaimed, "This really is amazing. I can't believe the size of the ballroom and all the food, entertainment and visitors."

"Yes, things just get better from here. After dinner the dancing begins!" hinted Alisha.

The waiters brought out some appetizers, steaming onion soup, a colorful fruit salad of mixed berries, Wastraws, mangos, papaya, bananas, a mixed salad, exotic barbequed meats, rice and pastas. Everyone talked, drank and ate large quantities of food.

Once the guests had mostly polished off their dinners, 20 pairs of accomplished dancers dressed in red and blue leotards took to the dance floor. The bandleader signaled for the lights to be dimmed. Suddenly, a single piercing beam of light shot down straight from the ceiling and lit up a portion of the dance floor. The muffled sound of beating drums got louder and louder until finally there was a giant flash of light and a sudden explosion. At that point, a loud band cut in and revolving strobe lights started flashing, lighting up the room and dance floor. The band then exploded with a fast paced-rock song, which was a hit on Sadrune, a planet just beyond Zerros. The dancers started things off performing incredible dance moves. Gradually they coaxed the visitors out onto the dance floor until it was nearly full.

Alisha glanced at James several times as he took in the scene. Finally, he couldn't sit still anymore.

"Come on, Alisha, let's dance!" James shouted above the music.

Without waiting for a reply, James reached over and grabbed Alisha's hand. Alisha had been waiting for this moment, so she gladly jumped up and followed James to the dance floor.

The bandleader saw James and Alisha go to the dance floor. Thor noticed also and motioned for the band to come to his table for a few words.

"Bruno, that boy, James, who is dancing with my daughter is a very special visitor from the planet Earth. Do you think you could surprise him with some hit songs from the United States from Earth? I'm not sure he will recognize them since he has had some memory loss, but hopefully it may jog his memory and he'll appreciate them."

Bruno gave Thor a wink signifying that he would certainly accommodate Thor's wishes and headed back to let the band know. Luckily, they did in fact know some very old hits, which had been blockbusters on Earth many years ago. After finishing up the song that was playing, Bruno interrupted the music with a brief announcement.

"We have a special visitor from Earth here tonight. It is his first Intergalactic Ball. We'd like to play a special medley of old hit songs from Earth in his honor."

James and Alisha were on the dance floor and they danced up a storm. Alisha met him move for move, except when James started combining his dancing with some of his gymnastics moves. The band started with a wild version of "Ain't Nothin But a Hound Dog," moved into "I Saw Her Standing There," then let loose with "Jumping Jack Flash", "Brown Sugar" and "Beat It." Many of the visitors clapped along. The music, lights and dancing whipped James and Alisha into a feverish pitch. The crowd was astounded when James actually jumped up and grabbed one of the overhead acrobatic swings and did a triple flip in the air returning to the dance floor. The visitors signaled their approval with loud applause. After a few more songs and wild dancing, James and Alisha decided that they wanted to take a rest.

"James, this is great but why don't we take a break and have some dessert. You are truly an amazing dancer!"

"Thank you, Alisha, I can tell that you too are an incredible dancer. You're extraordinary!"

"Thank you!" responded Alisha blushing slightly. "I can't get over your flips. How in the world can you do them? How did you get to those bars?" asked Alisha in disbelief.

James escorted Alisha back to the table then he excused himself. He explained he was thirsty and wanted a fruit drink from a special station he had seen on the other end of the dance floor. The drinks looked pretty special, sort of like smoothies that glowed red and orange in the dark with curled transparent straws. He, of course, offered to get Alisha one and she accepted. As James left to get the drinks, Thor got up to give a short toast.

"Friends, I want to welcome you to the twentieth Intergalactic Ball and thank you all for coming. It is a time to celebrate, meet with old friends and make new ones. It is a time to make sure our galaxy and the universe is on the right path. We must learn to live in peace and accept others who are from different planets. Unfortunately, there are also evil forces in the galaxy and evil rulers who seek to hurt peace-loving people. We must be vigilant and unite to stand against them. We must fight the forces of evil and make our planets safe for future generations. Tonight I want to toast you and thank you all for coming. Let us work together to build a safer universe for our children, for they represent the future."

As he finished, Thor raised a glass filled with champagne as a toast to his guests and the room erupted with whistles and applause.

Suddenly, without warning, all the lights in the ballroom went out. There was a whistling sound as ten masked individuals swung through the air and landed on the platform where the royal table was situated. The guests tried to peer through the darkness to see what was happening. Suddenly a spotlight shot through the commotion and focused on the stage. It became clear that the masked men had surrounded the royal table and were holding laser rifles, threatening Thor and everyone at the table. One of the men raised his laser and shouted.

"Justice for the Sytheons! Long live Sytheus! We are here to avenge the death of our leader's valiant son, Pluto!"

The guests at the ball were stunned and frightened. The band had stopped playing and everyone froze. A feeling of panic permeated the room. A few men scattered throughout the ballroom slunk into the darkness trying to avoid drawing the attention of the Sytheons. They however kept their eyes glued to the stage. Each one of them had a small earpiece in his ears. One of the men looked around and, once he felt everyone was in position, he sent an inaudible signal to the others. They quickly took out laser guns and blasted them at the Sytheons on the stage. Luckily, the men were specially trained undercover security forces put in place to mingle with the guests by the palace to prevent or intercept just such an attack. They were expert marksmen and managed to kill most of the Sytheons in one swift strike. Unfortunately, there was one Sytheon who was behind the others, standing directly in back of the chair where Princess Alisha was sitting. He had avoided getting hit. When he saw that his comrades had been wounded or killed, he grabbed the Princess from behind and put a laser sword to her throat.

"Everybody stop and back away or the Princess dies!"

"No!" screamed Thor. "No, take me!" he implored.

"No. Stay back or she dies. Everyone back!"

Suddenly there was silhouetted figure cutting through the spotlight. It swung from one of the ceiling swings used by the acrobats causing many to think it was actually one of the gymnastic performers. The figure sailed through the air performing three mid-air somersaults just before crashing down on the platform directly next to the Sytheon holding Princess Alisha.

"RELEASE THE PRINCESS! Release her NOW!" James snarled as he thrust his Swun against the Sytheon's throat. The Sytheon pushed Alisha away and concentrated on James. James, spurred on by his desire to protect Alisha, was on fire. He moved at lightning speed and brought all his force to bear with his Swun blows. The Sytheon was larger and stronger, but James was faster and much more agile. He danced circles around him and finally knocked his laser sword from his hand. Once James had disarmed him and Alisha was out of harm's way, the security forces opened fire. They were about to finish him off when Thor shouted wait.

"Keep him alive. We need to get some information from him. I want to know how they got to Carmesí and how they entered the ball."

The security forces stunned him and took him away for questioning. Most of the other attackers had been killed, aside from two who were badly injured but still alive. The security forces took them to get medical attention before taking them to a holding cell for questioning.

"I am sorry for this terrible incident. Thank goodness no one here was injured. I think it's best we end the ball at this point so that we can clean up and make sure there are no other security breaches. I just can't understand it. I specifically told Devlin to heighten security. Thanks to our topnotch security guards. And to James, our very special visitor, I can only thank you from the bottom of my heart. You saved my daughter's life tonight. There are no words that can express my gratitude for that act, for your courage and amazing abilities. You have once again demonstrated to me, this time in an actual situation, your abilities, courage and loyalty. Thank you, James. Thank you."

With that, Thor grabbed James and gave him a heartfelt bear hug. Tears welled up in his eyes as he reflected on how close he had come to losing Alisha and how thankful he was that James was here and saved her. Still trembling, Alisha looked on and then approached James. She too gave him a warm hug and thanked him. Then she sought comfort in her father's arms for a few moments.

As the ball broke up and the visitors left, Alisha went to James and asked him to come with her. The two disappeared together arm in arm and returned to the palace. Alisha took James to the private area where only the royal family lived. She brought him down a corridor until she came to a special spot.

"I have something to show and tell you. Come on, James."

With that, she opened a secret passage in the wall using the method she had previously shown him. She led him up a flight of stairs and then through a heavy, hand-carved wooden door, which led to the roof. The stars were out and the three moons of Carmisí glowed brightly. The lights of the City of Pearl glimmered below. It seemed that finally, at least for now, all was quiet and at peace in the galaxy. James and Alisha were silent letting the beautiful setting and images sink in.

Then Alisha turned to James and looked straight into his blue eyes. It was almost like she was looking through him to his very soul. The wind played with Alisha's raven hair and her eyes sparkled in the moonlight. Her heart pounded.

"Thank you, James. Thank you for saving my life."

"Alisha, there's no need to thank me again. I did what I had to."

"Ssshh," she said, placing her finger over James' mouth for a second.

She then placed her arms around James' neck. He looked deep into her eyes and felt uneasy but happy. Then, without warning, she gave him a long, soft kiss right on his lips. James was in shock. The kiss seemed to go on forever and he felt as if he was floating. He had never been kissed by a girl before - certainly not like that. He decided it was amazing and kissed her back. Finally, their lips parted. Alisha smiled and coyly said, "Thank you again, James."

"Thank you!" replied James smiling.

The two held hands looking at the moons and didn't speak. They felt more than they could say. They stayed that way for a good quarter of an hour. Not moving, but just holding hands and letting everything sink in. Finally, Alisha broke the silence.

"Well, it *is* getting late. My father will worry. I think we should go."

James didn't want the moment to end but he knew that Alisha was right and sensed that many days of shared moments lay ahead. The two made their way down to the ground level of the palace. They said goodnight and Alisha gave James another small kiss on the cheek. *Definitely not the same* thought James smiling. The two parted ways. Alisha headed to the royal residence area and James to his room. He was tired after the evening's events, but still extremely excited. He wanted to sleep, but was not sure he could. He entered his room and prepared for bed.

50

MOONBEAMS

Julia lay in her bed gazing longingly out of her window at the bright moon, whose light beams delicately painted her room with pale brush strokes of illumination. It looked so close, yet so far away at the same time. Julia's heart was heavy with pain as she thought about James. Her mind raced with thoughts about her brother, his whereabouts and his safety and so she couldn't sleep. The holiday season was supposed to bring joy and cheer, but Julia couldn't enjoy it. The possibility that the SPACETECK probe had exploded dampened her long-standing optimism and replaced it with a sense of helplessness.

"James, James I really miss you. I wish I could see you. I wish we could talk and play ...," Julia mouthed the words softly. The night was quiet. A light breeze gently rattled the windowpane.

Julia turned on her side, closed her eyes and tried to sleep but she couldn't. All she could think about was James.

✳ ✳ ✳

James stood on his balcony and looked out at the glittering lights of the City of Pearl. He closed his eyes and reflected on the incredible events that had transpired. He remembered his amazing journey through the galaxies to arrive at The Crimson Planet. He remembered how he first met Thor and Alisha. How he completed the tasks, which Thor had challenged him with. He was thankful that he had been able to rescue and save Alisha from the horrible Sytheon plot at the Intergalactic Ball. He closed his eyes and savored his first kiss, that first amazing kiss and embrace he had received from Alisha in gratitude for saving her life. And finally, the deep heartfelt thanks he had received from Thor for his courage in rescuing his daughter.

James had begun to discover a simple, but great, truth. Namely, that the most valuable thing in life was true love, whether of family, friends, a soul mate or a combination of those. He started to realize it was not something you understood with your brain; instead it was something you felt and knew with your heart. It was not something everyone could find, but if you wanted it badly enough, it would find you and when it did, you would know it. James thought about all he had seen and experienced, yet in his heart he knew something precious was still missing. Something was still holding him back, something he longed for, yet he did not know quite what it was.

James threw himself on his bed and continued to think. He played over and over in his mind rescuing Princess Alisha. Something about it seemed so familiar. James could not put his finger on it and his mind continued to race. *What is it? What am I missing?* Round and round went his thoughts as he tried to remember every detail of his life. Frustrated and tired, he turned on his side and tried to sleep. He could see the moons of Carmisí and their beautiful glow calmed him. His eyes fluttered and he thought he heard a soft voice.

"James. James I miss you so much."

At first he couldn't believe the voice he thought he heard. He looked around, but there was no one visible. The room was empty and quiet. Suddenly, he realized what was happening.

Julia?

James? Came the unspoken reply.

He was mind messaging with Julia!

James, you're alive! I knew it.

James' mind suddenly cleared. In a revealing flash, he abruptly remembered what he was missing and had been searching for in his soul. His memory of his life on Earth, his love of his family, his discovery and exploration of The Sapphire Prism Cave, all came rushing back to him. He shed some tears as he finally remembered with joy and some sadness all that he had left behind to embark on his journey. At least now he remembered, and Julia knew he was alive.

James, where are you? Are you safe? We all miss you so much! Come home!

I miss you and Mom and Dad, too. When I was pulled from the cave I hit my head and suffered some memory loss. It's a long story, Julia, and I will tell you all about it over time. For now, you, Mom and Dad should know that I am safe and in good hands. As far as coming home, I will one day, but it's going to be hard and it will take awhile. I'm billions of miles away. I have traveled to another galaxy to a planet known as The Crimson Planet or Carmesí. I don't yet know how or when, but I'll return to Earth one day!

James, after all this time, we can finally mind message again. I have to let Mom and Dad know that you're all right.

We'll be in touch.

I love you, James.

I love you, Julia.

With that last thought, Julia jumped out of bed, ran through the corridor and burst into her parents' room, without warning, where they lay fast asleep.

"Mom! Dad! James is alive! He's okay!"

George and Jenifer were startled awake and felt confused to say the least. George mumbled groggily.

"Julia, what are you talking about? How do you know?"

"I finally got a mind message! A mind message from James! He's okay!

"A mind message?" asked George skeptically, half awake. "Where is he, Julia?"

"He told, I mean, mind messaged me that he's billions of miles away on a planet in a very distant galaxy known as The Crimson Planet or Carmesí. I don't know all the details yet, but we're in touch and I know he's okay!" shouted Julia with glee.

George and Jenifer looked at each other. They wanted to believe Julia, but there was no other proof or sign other than her claim to have communicated with James by "mind messaging." Having observed some of Julia's other extraordinary abilities and powers, her parents, although skeptical, decided to place their faith in her newfound hope and optimism.

James had finally remembered his past and his family, who he missed and loved, despite living the adventure of his life. Now it was time to embrace the present and forge his future. He couldn't let memories and longings of the past hold him back. He was now ready and looking forward to entering the Starflight Academy. After all, what boy wouldn't want to fall in love with a beautiful Princess, learn how to pilot a spaceship, explore space and battle for justice against the forces of evil? James had completed one leg of a long journey, but new adventures and challenges loomed ahead and he was anxious to meet them!

The End of Book 1
of
A Journey Through The Space Vortex

Peter M. Leschner has been a practicing real estate and corporate attorney in New York City and New Jersey for over 30 years. He has been a Partner and Of Counsel at several major New York law firms. He is a graduate of Colby College (BA), New England School of Law (JD) and New York University (LLM). Startling Connections was his first novel. The Sapphire Prism Cave (Book 1 of A Journey Through the Space Vortex trilogy) is his second novel. He wrote it for and with his daughter Katherine. Peter lives in Tenafly, New Jersey with his wife and two children.

www.ingramcontent.com/pod-product-compliance
Lightning Source LLC
Chambersburg PA
CBHW070834250626
47159CB00003B/782